I0583042

It's not just a good thing...

IT'S A GOD THING

BY DANUELLE ROBERTS

ForKeeps

IT'S NOT JUST A GOOD THING,
IT'S A GOD THING

Copyright © 2018 by Danuelle Roberts
All rights reserved.

Published by:
ForKeeps Publishing Company
Carrollton, TX
contact@ForKeepsPublishing@Gmail

All rights reserved. No part of this book may be used or reproduced by any means, graphic, electronic, or mechanical, including photocopying, recording, taping or by any information storage retrieval system without the written permission of the publisher. Copying this book is both illegal and unethical.

ISBN print: 978-0-6928719-7-3
Library of Congress Control Catalog-in-Data Number: in process

Categories:
1. FICTION / 2. Christian Fiction 3. Romance

Printed in the United States of America on acid free paper

Acknowledgement

I would like to thank the Lord for encouraging me to embrace the one thing I love to do, and that is to write! Thank you Lord for allowing me to hear the powerful words of Philippians 4:13, "I can do all things through Christ who strengthens me!"

I want to thank India, Tyrek and Ajarri, my kids, who have been so supportive and so loving during the process of writing this novel. I could not have done this without them. My mother has been by my side since the beginning. She played a major role in supporting my dreams and she reminded me that God was with me along the way. Thanks big brother, Koronta Roberts, for always encouraging me to do big things for God! He has always spoken positively to me, even when he was not in the best place in his own life. He believed that God had a purpose in my writing. He was right!

Sometimes, pursuing the very thing that you love to do can also be a challenge. During the season of writing this novel and going step by step in the publishing process, there were times that I experienced personal attacks. I kept going and trusted that God would get the glory out of this book!

Thank you, family and friends, for your prayers and love. I pray that each person who will read this love story will be blessed, inspired to love God's way, and will wait on God to bring His best! We all fall short, but God loves us and He will show up at the right time!

Thank you to everyone who has worked on this book; editors, and my book cover designer. I also want to thank you Michelle Cameron on your wonderful coaching and sharing your feedback during the process of editing this book. I am humbled and grateful that you were touched by the message in this book. You have been a wonderful editor/coach! I pray for everyone who has left their mark in the process of publishing this book that God will bless your hands and lives abundantly, and that He will take your businesses and books to higher ground! I pray that He will enlarge your territory!

God bless you all!

Table of Contents

Chapter 1

LOOKING FOR MR. RIGHT

Let me introduce myself. My name is London Kia Kennedy. I am a thirty-year-old single black female. I graduated from Spelman College with honors. I was in beauty pageants since I was a baby until middle school. How could this be? How could I still be single at the age of thirty? Maybe I am too beautiful for my own good? I don't want to sound conceited, but I don't have problems catching a man; it's keeping him that's the problem. It is Friday morning, and I am ready to find my husband today. I slipped on a short, red, tight dress for the office lunch party. Very important prospects will be there. NFL players will be there, and actors! Oh, I can't leave out this attractive youth minister Brandon; there is nothing like a man who loves the Lord! I was raised in the church, and yes I am saved! I am still growing, but at least I am not where I used to be. I pulled up in the parking lot in my black Mercedes that I worked hard for and guess who I saw? Mr. Brandon.

I jumped out of my car, picking up my red Coach purse that matched my red dress and red stilettos.

"Hey, Brandon, I was just thinking about your new project that you are working on," I said.

"Oh, how are you, Ms. Kennedy?" Brandon replied while walking toward me. Brandon is handsome. He is about six feet tall, light caramel skin like mine, with light brown eyes, and an athletic body.

"Brandon, I am really happy that you are setting up a project to sponsor low-income families to help their children enroll in performing arts schools." Brandon and I both began walking towards the office elevator.

"Well, Ms. Kennedy, I put God first, and faith will take you to that dream or goal." Brandon and I walked in the office together, just talking office talk, nothing major. I knew one day he would be giving me those digits.

I walked to my desk and saw that I had twenty missed calls.

"Ms. Kennedy," Sherry said.

Sherry, my secretary, was standing at my desk calling for me. She was wearing the cutest Gucci outfit.

"Hey, Sherry, love your outfit," I said while I was standing by my desk looking at a bunch of files piled up.

"Oh thanks, Ms. Kennedy. Mr. Jack Crosby said he could not meet you at ten o'clock this morning. But I called him back, and he said that he can meet you at twelve at lunch time," Sherry said.

"Oh no!" I said, shaking my head. "Call Mr. Crosby and tell him that we have to change it to Monday."

I was not about to miss my office party. Mr. Crosby could wait, but my biological clock was ticking, and I needed to make sure I was around single, successful men.

I sat down at my desk to listen to my messages while Sherry went back to her cubicle. Sherry was a good worker. She was a lot younger than I am. She was about twenty-three years old. I knew that she would be a good team player; that's why I hired her. Sherry was very cute; she loved to shop, and she had a sugar Daddy to pay for all her expenses. Sherry lived in a penthouse in the downtown area of Dallas. I knew that she could not afford all of that on her salary. I made three times her salary, and I could not afford what she had established.

I had to give it to the girl; she found her a man who would give her almost everything but the world. I guess I will find my true love one day. Listening to all those messages were getting on my nerves until I heard a familiar voice. I could not believe it. I had a message from an old friend from my old neighborhood. It was Jason. Jason and I dated, when we were just young teenagers. I was eighteen and he was seventeen. I love that boy; we only dated for two months and then we just became friends for all these years.

I would call him every six months or he would call me just to check up on me. I rushed and called him. Jason picked up after the first ring.

"Hello, cupcake," Jason said while sounding very attractive.

Jason has called me cupcake since we were teens.

"Hi, handsome! What are you up to?"

It felt great talking to Jason. Could he be my Mr. Someone? Had he waited all these years to tell me he was now ready to start a relationship with me? My thoughts were running through my mind.

"Actually, cupcake, I have been teaching sociology at UCLA for about three years now."

Jason had always been smart; that is why I liked him so much, but since something happened back in the day when Jason and I was dating, he could never forgive me. Jason never believed me; he thought I was cheating on him. No matter how I explained to him that the guy was drunk and randomly choose me to kiss, Jason laughed and never wanted to talk about it again.

I think that was the reason that Jason broke up with me, only to come back in my life later as my friend. I spent years trying to tell Jason that I was not that type of girl.

"How did you know it was me?" I said, amazed that he just called out my nickname before I could say anything.

"Girl, you are still clueless… You know everybody in the world has caller ID on everything now, ha!"

Jason was about five ten, not very tall but very handsome; he was buff not buffed up, but boy… the last time I saw him he was fine — muscles everywhere and yes, a six-pack that would drive women crazy. I guess Jason and I were friends, and I knew he made me melt like butter, but he was special to me. Back in the day we would talk forever during the summer time when we were just teens. I did not look at him as some guy. I looked at him as someone I could not have because he stood for everything I wanted for a lifetime—friend, lover, and husband. He was too good to be true.

I pushed that thought out of my mind because Jason did not see me in that way. If Jason and I dated and some crazy horrible thing happened like Jason breaking up with me, I would be crushed. I just would not want to be hurt by Jason. I had my heart broken many times but to have Jason break my heart would devastate me and ruin our friendship.

"So, cupcake, what's up with working for the biggest promotional company in Texas!"

I slumped down in my chair while Mr. King Wallace walked by, giving me that disgusting smile. It was the type of smile that said, "I want to grab you and love you down." Mr. King Wallace was a short and stubby, bald-headed Caucasian man, and he always stared at my breasts while I was talking to him.

I quickly answered Jason.

"Jason, I love working here. You know me. I am not afraid of hard work."

Jason paused, and I could tell something was wrong.

"Well, I was calling to tell you that I am getting married."

I could not breathe. Did I hear Jason correctly? He was calling to tell me that he was getting married?

I finally spoke.

"Jason wow....uhm... that's good. I am happy for you."

Jason was going on and on about his wife-to-be, but my mind had drifted off to when we were together. I could remember when Jason and I would sit on the swings at the park and talk about how he cared for me.

"Jason, I hate to cut you off, but I've got to go to my company's lunch party." Listening to Jason made me want to at least take some action in my non-existing dating life. Jason spoke quickly.

"Therefore, I am coming down there on business in two weeks."

Jason kept talking.

"I was hoping we could spend a little time together, you know just hang out."

He sounded very urgent.

"Jason, I would love to see you, but what about Karen?" I paused.

"Cupcake, look, I told her that you're like a sister to me. I have not seen you in three years, so it's time for that visit."

I had all these emotions going on inside of me. I could not explain why I felt so hurt like I wanted to cry. I mean, what Jason and I had was a long time ago; we were just teenagers. But I wanted to have something with him, and it was Jason who kept bringing up that kiss and how it hurt him to see that and how it was just best for us to be friends. So I did my part years ago; he knew I had always wanted more. Everyone used to say, you guys are going to fall in love with each other one day. The sad thing about wanting to fall in love with Jason was that I had already fallen in love with a man who did not want to date me. I was just Jason's friend.

"Okay, Jason, call me and let me know when you are coming this way."

"Will do," he replied and then hung up the phone. My secretary buzzed in my office. "Ms. Kennedy, Mr. Crosby said that Monday morning at ten o'clock would be fine for the meeting."

"Great, well look I am on my way to the lunch party on the third floor, so go ahead and take your lunch," I said.

I went in the ladies' room to freshen up my makeup, and Lady Tina was standing in her black conservative business suit looking at me with her nose in the air. Tina and I had a few words with each other on many occasions in the past, and they were not nice words.

"Hello, London, have you been to London yet?" Tina said while brushing her blonde hair. Tina was a beautiful Caucasian woman; she had a nice light gold tint complexion, ocean blue eyes, and an athletic body. I liked Tina until her boyfriend, Shun Mark, started working here two years ago. Shun just was too handsome for his own good. Shun was a tall, dark chocolate brother; he was an accountant for our company. Shun and I went out a couple of times, and I found out that he was playing both Tina and me. Shun told her he was sorry and he loved her and well, she kept the sorry Negro, and that's the end of that story.

Tina never got over the fact that he wanted to date me—a black woman—but that was two years ago. She need to put that drama in the past where it needed to be, but the last thing I heard about Shun and Tina was that they got married. Tina was so proud, but the black women in the office were upset, saying, "See that's where all the fine black men are going: to white women or gay men!" I did not care about things like that, but maybe there was truth in what they were saying.

I believe we should worry about our own lives and relationships.

{So what} is my motto. Get over it and let God find you your husband. I should take my own advice.

"Tina no! I have not been to London yet, but soon I will," I said, while fixing my red dress. "Maybe I will after I make this deal on the Crosby account."

Tina looked shocked because she knew that the Crosby deal was big. I couldn't believe I stuck my foot in my mouth. I had not sealed this deal all the way yet, and anything could happen between Friday and Monday.

Tina left the ladies' room. I still had Jason on my mind; my best friend was getting married. I looked in the mirror at myself; I was about five seven with caramel light skin complexion, and very slender. I knew I was cute, but I wanted people to see me from the inside out. My problem was that most of the men looked at me from the outside, not caring to find out the real me.

The last relationship I was in, the guy did not care about me nor did he want to find out about me. I guess I was just good for one thing and that was sex. I tried to date without having sex, but it was too hard. The last guy was sexy and successful, and I love successful men.

I am now looking for love, not just sex. I decided that I am worth the wait. But what am I doing wrong? I have been finding love in all the wrong places. I told myself that maybe love would come around and find me. I was very excited to know that the men at this lunch party were professionals.

The room was decorated in blue, gray, and white in honor of the Dallas Cowboys. Our company helped promote all of their players. Platinum Opportunities Promotional Company (POPC) specialized in taking our product and exposing them through commercials and magazines and making them household names. We also worked with big companies, and we created programs to help with certain needs in the community, cities, and throughout the states.

I stood there holding my glass asking for punch; the waiter was very polite. The food smelled good. The caterers did a wonderful job at making everything look good. I grabbed a plate and began to fill it with green salad and baked beans, baked chicken, and potato salad. I was in food heaven.

"Hey, Ms. Kennedy, how is the food?"

I was not expecting to hear such a deep, attractive voice so I jumped a little.

"The food tastes great!" I said, looking up to a six-five-foot gentleman who was very handsome. He had a Spanish accent; I never dated anyone outside my race, but I love to do things outside the box.

"How do you know my name?"

"I can't believe you don't remember me," he said.

I had to take a second to look at him and then it came to me. "Oh! You are Aalen Caribou! I worked with you on getting you the commercial for Footlocker shoes," I said.

"Yes that's me, Aalen Caribou the actor. How are you these days, Ms. Kennedy?"

"I am still working hard trying to stay in the game of life," I said.

"So you feel like life is a game?" Aalen replied.

"Yes," I said, while sucking my teeth to make sure food was not playing hide-and-seek.

"You are very attractive lady, and you seem very mature, so for you to think that life is a game, well, I am a little taken back by that," he said, while smiling and giving me this weird look.

I did not know if I should feel offended or just stand there and say nothing.

He said, "I feel that life is a gift and life is far too precious to be mistaken as a game. Because in real life you only get one chance before you die, so take life and make sure you think very carefully about the choices you make before rolling the dice."

He smiled and walked away.

Wow, what was that all about? I thought to myself. The advice was good, but he made me feel stupid. I was ready to go back to my office before some other person targeted me and make me feel weird again. I spoke too soon… there goes bald-headed Mr. King Wallace.

"Hey, Ms. Kennedy, you sure look nice in your red dress."

I did not say a thing to him. I just shook my head while I walked through the crowd of people to get to the other side of the room. I did see a lot of fine young men. The men in the room that I passed by were not paying me any attention. I stood out in my red dress, but everyone was just focusing on their business partners.

I felt so invisible. I saw Brandon talking to some football players. This was my chance to feed my emotions with some good old-fashioned attention! I heard a small voice inside of me say, "Why do you search for the attention in men when I am right hear waiting for you to see me?"

I pushed that voice back down and allowed my heart to beat faster at the idea of a potential life partner. How could I leave this office party without making myself seen?

"Brandon, it is so nice to see you again."

Brandon was surprised to see me. He said, "Hey, Ms. Kennedy this is Mike and James. They play for the Raiders. I helped promote their non-profit children's foundation."

I nodded my head while the gentleman who was wearing a designer suit greeted me with a smile. This was more like it; they could not take their eyes off me. I could hear that small voice again saying, "You will never be satisfied with searching and needing the affirmation of men. Seek me and you will have love, joy, and life more abundantly."

Lord, I know. I have you in my life. I just need someone I can talk to in the flesh,

I thought to myself while this handsome guy stared at me.

"Hi, my name is Mike," he said while holding out his hand. I gave him my hand, and he kissed it. Mike was tall, about six feet; he was not really my type, but he was smooth and he had a nice smile.

"Mike, nice to meet you."

"Likewise, Ms. Kennedy. I would love to take you out for dinner," he said while showing those nice white pearls.

"Mike, wow that sounds nice. Just make sure to give my secretary your information. I will get back to you," I said while walking to the other side of Brandon.

"Brandon, I really need to speak with you," I nodded, while walking with him away from the young football players.

"Ms. Kennedy, what's wrong?" Brandon asked while looking very suspicious of the idea that I was taking him away from the crowd.

I stood there, nervous to ask Brandon this question for some reason. "I just need to talk to you about something private," I said, acting a little shy. "Brandon, you are a man of God, right?" I asked while we both stood in the midst of a corporate party and we could barely hear each other. "When a woman wants to be married and tired of being single, should she seek out a man for marriage?" I said, almost yelling over the music and the chatter.

"That's a good question, but I just don't want to tell you no without explaining why you should not seek to find a man for marriage," Brandon said while trying to talk loud but keeping his voice at a medium level.

"Look, it is kind of hard to talk!"

"Is it okay for us to meet and have coffee on Saturday morning?"

Oh my gosh, I thought. If I would have known that asking Brandon that question would get me a date with him, I would have asked him a long time ago.

"That sounds great. Just call me and let me know," I said, and Brandon walked back to the football players. He smiled and gave me a wink.

The lunch party was coming to a close. I had to make my way through the crowded room to go back to my office. Once I made it to my desk, I was ready to work on the Crosby account. I had so many creative ideas that were going on in my head. I started quickly doing some research on this project for the Crosby account. The day went by so fast it was now six pm and I was ready to go home. My secretary Sherry had already left.

"Ms. Kennedy, don't forget to call me."

I looked up from my computer to see the tall, dark gentleman that I met at the lunch party call out to me.

"Hey, Mike, that's your name right?" I said, smiling from ear to ear.

"Yes, and don't you forget my name," he said flashing those nice, white teeth.

"I won't. Trust me."

Mike began to smile again while leaving. I grabbed all my things to head for the elevator. I hated getting on the elevator by myself. Elevators made me feel closed in, but I was saved by the bell. Brandon was getting on with me. I turned and gave Brandon a big smile. He looked at me like he was not in the mood for small talk. "Brandon is everything okay?" I asked ,while getting off the elevator. He got off as well. Brandon finally looked up at me, and I could tell that something major was wrong.

"Brandon, is everything okay?" I yelled.

"I will be fine, Kennedy, I just need to go home and get some rest," Brandon said. He sounded so weak and drained. I knew he had come down with something.

"You don't look well, Brandon," I said, very scared. I had never seen Brandon look so pale. He had a light complexion as a black man, but he was sweaty and pale.

"Thanks, Kennedy, but I will be okay," he said while getting in his car. "Kennedy, I will see you tomorrow at Dan's Bros. Coffee shop off the tollway," he yelled out while driving off in his new luxury car.

I shouted out okay while I jumped in my car. When I walked into my three-bedroom, two-story townhome, I could not wait to jump in the shower. I turned the shower on while I reached to check my answering machine. My father left messages saying that Mom was really sorry for what she said at dinner last week. I loved my father very much. My father, Robert Kennedy, he is a peacemaker. I guess that's why he wanted the family to get along. I thought that would be impossible.

I had two younger sisters. Terry was twenty and married with a baby on the way; Lisa was twenty-three and married with no kids. I was the oldest, unmarried, and I disliked my mother for making me feel like there was something wrong with me for not being married. My father is not my real Dad, but he loved me like I was his. My mother married Robert Kennedy when I was just a year old. I was told that my real Dad was very abusive to my Mom, and she left him after a bad fight with him. I learned early on to never ask about my biological Dad.

When I was ten years old, I had overheard my mother talking to her sister about whether she should tell me about my real Dad. I ran to my mother crying, asking her if Robert was my Daddy. My mother in tears cried out, "No!" But he loved me like I was his daughter, and I was very mad at my Mom for not letting me in on her secret.

I tried to ask more questions about my real Dad, but she yelled at me and said, "Don't ever mention that man again; he is not your Dad. Robert is your Dad and you should be grateful he took us and loved us both."

I was so hurt because of my mother's secret about my Dad. Don't get me wrong, I loved Robert, but there were so many things I just wanted to know for myself. I kept my anger from my Mom. I disliked her for being so selfish.

Last week at dinner, I had told her I was going to look for my real Dad. I am a thirty-year-old woman, and I knew that it was time to meet the man who gave me life. My mother who goes to church every Sunday stood up at the table and cussed me out. I could not believe her; she had said, "London Kia Kennedy, you have shamed me in a way that's so hard to forgive you! How can you disregard all the things I told you not to do! If you go and look for him, don't you ever come back to my house, you blank-blank!"

She had never cursed around me. I guess I made my mother Linda mad. I am always making "Linda" mad; my mother and I bumped heads all the time about everything. I called my Dad. Speak of the devil… My mother answered the phone. "Hello, may I speak with Daddy," I said, trying not to start anything with her.

"London, you could have at least asked me how my day was," my Mom said. "I am still your mother."

My mother was just so hard to get along with. I wished we could have had a mother-and-daughter relationship.

"Mom, how was your day?" I asked.

"Look, London, I am sorry for being upset with you." The tone of my Mom's voice sounded very apologetic. She spoke again before I could reply.

"London, baby, I was so hurt and abused by this man… I was scared for you. I didn't want you to have anything to do with him. I was so wrong for all these years to keep you from the man who gave you life."

Was this my Mom talking here? I could not believe my Mom was saying sorry. "Mom, this means the world to me. Just the fact that you are giving me a chance to make my own decisions is something I need," I said, while walking in my closet trying to find my favorite nightgown before I jumped in the shower. This was one of the best conversations that I had with my Mom in a long time.

"I love you, Mom, even when we don't agree," I said, feeling a weight lifted from my heart. Mom sometimes appeared to be tough, but I knew under that anger she was a sweetheart.

"I want you to promise me that you will be careful with that man and don't tell him where I live. I still don't trust him!" Mom said.

"Okay, Mom, I won't tell him anything about you. Don't worry," I said.

"I won't worry," Mom said. "I just want you to know that I thought I was protecting you."

My mother really wanted to make things right with me.

"Mom, one day you should tell someone about the things my real Daddy did to you. It will help you heal," I said, hoping that my mother would tell me what happened to her. What made her run so far away from my father and his family? My voice dropped, and I could hear her inhale to only exhale as if the memories were too painful to think about, let alone talk about. My Mom wanted to make sure I knew she was all right when I knew she had masked her pain for years. She had managed to cover up her pain with cosmetics and the soft, blue-cushioned church pews. So many of us run to church to hide from things we dare not talk about. I was always left feeling confused because I thought church was the place for hurting people, not people pretending to be alright and perfect.

"I am just fine as long as I don't see that man," my mother said. My Mom was very stubborn to admit that she needed help.

"Okay, Mom, I will make sure that my real Dad won't know anything about your life," I said, trying to get her off the phone. I wanted to talk to my Dad.

"Well take care, London. I hope you will find all the pieces that are missing in your life."

It felt crazy. In one minute, I was so mad at my mother, but in an instant she made me feel so happy. I could not believe that she was okay with me finding my biological Dad. I was so happy to hear my Daddy Robert, who raised me, on the phone. "Sweetheart, how is life treating you?" Daddy said.

"Daddy, I have so much to tell you."

"I got the Crosby account, well not yet… but I do have a meeting with Mr. Crosby.

"Well that's my girl! I knew you could do it. You have been telling me about the Crosby account for months now!" Daddy said, while sounding so proud of me!! My Daddy always made me feel like I could do anything. "London I am so proud of you." Daddy said while coughing.

"Daddy is everything okay?" I asked while turning the shower off. I had spent thirty minutes talking on the phone and neglected my shower. "Daddy, that cough does not sound good. You should go to the doctor."

"Well, London, your mother already set me up with an appointment for tomorrow," Daddy said. "I will call you and tell you what the doctor's report is."

I needed to tell Dad about Jason; he almost slipped my mind. "Oh yeah, Jason called me, Daddy. He will be visiting soon," I replied while Daddy was coughing, sounding bad.

"That's good, London... I always liked that guy. Hope you and Jason can make something work," Daddy said while clearing his throat.

"Well….hate to say this, but Jason is spoken for, Daddy. He is getting married soon."

There was an awkward silence. "Jason said he just wanted to spend some time with me before he gets married," I said. I was trying to update my Dad on Jason.

My Daddy was confused. "I don't understand. I know I am old-fashioned but you and Jason used to date when you guys where younger," he said.

"So why would he want to spend all this time with his ex-girlfriend before he gets married?" Daddy was right. Why would Jason want to hang out with me?

"Well, Daddy, he could probably just want to spend time with me. I guess for support." I said. I was feeling unsure of Jason's plans too. Why would Jason want to spend time with me? I thought to myself.

"You know we are just friends, Daddy." I said. I don't think that my Dad was buying that story.

"London, when a man becomes friends with his ex-girlfriend, it changes the game. That young man will always trust in his friend which is you and care a great deal for you."

Dad kept talking. "Don't get me wrong. I am not saying that a man can't be just friends with a woman. I am just saying that in most cases dealing with women for best friends, especially the ones they dated before, could be taboo."

This is why I loved my father; he always will make sure to give me a man's point of view.

"So, Dad, you think men and women who are friends can get caught up with emotions and feelings if they are not careful?" I asked.

"Yes, it is too dangerous to be in a committed relationship with anyone other than your spouse. The man with a wife and a friend who is a girl is asking for super trouble."

"I truly believe that."

"Jason has gone out his way to make sure he sees you before he gets married." My Daddy was getting real. "I personally think he wants to make sure there's nothing between you and him."

Now, my father just did not know that I was feeling the same way. I thought to myself. "See, he will commit to this other woman," Daddy replied while coughing again. I was taking all of this in because even though my Daddy was old-school, he was still a man.

"Okay, Daddy, maybe that's true, but I still look at Jason as a friend."

"You are fooling yourself. I know for sure you have more feelings for him than you are leading me to believe. London, things are going to change if Jason gets married. I know that one of you ladies will get more attention than the other." My father was right, but Jason was not really up for discussion because he was not even my man. I was getting frustrated.

"Daddy…look, I know things will change once he marries."

"London, when a man marries a lady, he becomes one and everyone else would be second or last in his life," Daddy said, trying to make sure that I knew that Jason's and my friendship would change dramatically.

Now I understood what my father was trying to say. " Daddy, I hate to cut this conversation off, but I got to go," I said while yawning.

"Goodnight, suga, love ya," Daddy said, while hanging up the phone. I had been waiting to just relax. I did not mean to rush my father off the phone, but the conversation about Jason was going on and on.

I turned the handles on the shower and jumped in. The warm water ran down my back, washing all my pain and my worries away. *God, I thank you for working out all my problems.* Brandon popped in my head. I was going to meet him tomorrow morning. I was happy that I was going on a date with the man who loved the Lord. *I have never dated a Christian man,* I thought to myself. This would be very interesting. I got out of my shower, slipped on my nightgown, and looked outside my window and stared out at the stars before I fell asleep.

Ring, Ring, Ring! My cell phone ringing at one o'clock in the morning startled me. "Hello?"

A deep male voice began to speak. "Hey, sexy, this is Mike from the lunch party." I was surprised that he was calling me. "Look, Mike, it is really late."

"I am sorry, but I just couldn't sleep. I was thinking about your beautiful face," Mike said with his sexy, deep voice. "I was wondering what you're doing tomorrow night."

"Well, I have to meet Brandon in the morning, but I am free later," I replied. "London, will you meet me at this cool jazz spot at Edelman at seven pm.?"

I was thrilled that this sexy football player wanted to take me out on the town. "That sounds great, but please don't ever call me this late!" I demanded some respect.

"I just got in from a late photo shoot," he said. "I won't do that again."

"Okay, see you then," I said while hanging up the phone.

I couldn't believe that my prayers were being answered. I was finally meeting all the right men to choose from. I really wanted to see Jason. Jason was the only man that I loved. How could this happen? Why was he marrying some woman who would never be me? What did she have that I didn't have? I drifted off to dream land.

My alarm clock went off, sending me into a frantic mess. I jumped out of bed and grabbed the loud beeping black and white clock that had nine o'clock am flashing. I was supposed to meet Brandon on this Saturday, but he did not tell me what time.

I called Brandon and was surprised to hear a soft woman's voice answer the phone.

"Yes, this is Ms. Kennedy, and I was calling for a Brandon," I said.

The young lady told me that Brandon had to go to Trinity Medical Center.

I got dressed and rushed out to the hospital to see what was going on with Brandon. I could not stop thinking about how he looked last night. I knew something was wrong with him, and I was just hoping he was okay. I pulled my brownish, shoulder-length hair back from my face while I began to ask the lady who was behind the desk of the medical center questions.

"Look, ma'am, we cannot give out that kind of information." The small-framed, beautiful Spanish lady said while looking through folders and files.

"Well, since you can't tell me what's wrong with him, can you tell me his room number?" I said, looking around at the dull colors on the walls and the fake plants that sat up on the clerk's desk.

"Yes, we sure can. His room is 205 straight down that hall and take a right." I walked in Brandon's room, and he was lying down.

"Hey, I told you that something was wrong," I blurted out.

"Hey, Ms. Kennedy, I cannot believe you. How did you find me?"

"I called you, and your wife answered the phone and told me you had to go to the hospital."

"Well, that was not my wife. That was my friend. Mandy and I have been friends since college," he said while smiling. "Anyhow, London, I did not want to tell you, but I have diabetes," Brandon said as he reached for the TV remote.

"I am just puzzled that you would have something like that. I just think you are too young to have that." Brandon smiled while the nurse came along his bedside to check his IV and fluids.

"Ms. Kennedy, it is not based on age. Even some kids have it," Brandon said.

I was shocked. "Wow, so do you have to take medicine for it?"

Brandon's other nurse buzzed in to make sure he didn't need anything. I sat down in the empty chair while noticing that Brandon didn't go anywhere without his Bible.

"Yes, London, I have to take insulin and eat right. If I don't do both, I will find myself here in this stupid hospital," he said, while we both laughed. Just then, a dark brown, beautiful woman and a little boy came into the room.

"Brandon… I told you that you were doing too much." The beautiful woman walked around his bed to grab his hand as if she were his mother. But clearly she could not be his mother; she was too young for that.

"Brandon, I am so upset with you not eating right and not taking your medicine," the young lady said while kissing him on the forehead.

"Oh, I am sorry. My name is Mandy, and this is my son, Raymond," the young lady said when she noticed that I was in the room. I looked right at Mandy. I noticed her shoes; they were simple black flat shoes. Based on Mandy's entire outfit. I could tell she was a low maintenance type of woman. Her skin looked smooth and soft. This woman looked just like a famous actress, especially her smile, I thought to myself.

I noticed I was gazing too long at her.

"Forgive me, but you look so much like a famous actress," I said while giving her my hand to shake. "My name is London Kia Kennedy, but you can call me London."

"Well, it is a pleasure to meet you," she said in her southern accent. Brandon was looking awkward, so I felt like that was my cue to leave.

"Well, Brandon, I hope you feel better and I hope you will take off Monday," I said. I like Brandon, but I really did not know him well enough to be in love with him like I was with Jason.

"I will make sure he will get his rest," Mandy said, while waving goodbye.

I waved while Brandon nodded his head as I walked out the door. Miss Southern Belle was making sure I had it very clear that Brandon belonged to her. I guess nowadays you have to make sure that the men that you love won't get away - even though I am not in love with him. On the other hand, I wanted to know more about him. I did not care if Mandy had something for him. Brandon said it himself; she was just a friend. It all made me think back on what my father said. Just because a man is just friends with a young lady does not mean he does not have a love for her; he just needs time to find a place for her in his world.

I wondered if Mandy was someone Brandon might see as more than a friend. Who cared? Brandon was single, and I was going to give Miss Southern Belle a run for her money because Brandon is everything I need. I got a phone call, and it was my beloved sister Lisa.

Lisa was my baby sister who had a heart of gold. Lisa is so pretty, five-nine with light skin and a small, slender figure; she writes for her own magazine, *Black G Mag*.

"Lisa, what are you up to?" I asked, while parking outside of Macy's department store.

"London, I saw Jason out here in Los Angeles with some new model."

I could not believe Lisa was calling me to tell me about Jason and the possibility that this could be the woman that he was going to marry. "Yeah, Lisa, he told me about her already."

Lisa blew her breath in the phone. "Oh, so he told you that he was marrying a model," Lisa said while laughing.

"Look, Lisa, what is the big deal? Jason is a grown man! He supposed to find someone to make him happy, and if he found happiness in Karen the model, then it is okay with me!"

Lisa was quiet for a second. "I am so sorry. I did not mean to make you upset, London, I just thought that you and Jason have been friends all this time, I thought that maybe you and Jason both would grow up and stop playing games and hook up."

Lisa was the type to tell how she felt. I was the one to hold my feelings in until I exploded. "Lisa, look, I have always felt that maybe one day that would happen, but Jason never really tried to hook up with me on that level," I said, looking at the sale prices on the Coach purses.

"May I help you?" the young black girl asked while I was holding my cell to my ear with one hand and a bright tan leopard and gold purse in the other hand.

"No, that's okay."

Lisa was just going on and on telling me what was going on with her life and her family. "London, you will never believe this. London, look out, you are going to be an aunt to the baby in my tummy!" My sister shouted so loud that the lady who was standing next to me while looking at boots heard her.

"Wow, congratulations!" the lady said.

"Lisa, this lady said congratulations."

"What lady? The lady in Macy's?"

Lisa started laughing again. I said, "Yes, Lisa, you were so loud that the lady that was shopping right next to me heard you through the phone. I am so happy for you, Lisa! How many months are you?"

"I am four months. I found out about two months ago. But Tony and I decided to wait before telling everyone."

I was numb. My baby sister was now becoming a mother. I wanted so badly to have that special someone and a family.

Did I do something so bad that God would skip over me and forget about my prayer? I could not help but feel this way. I was the oldest out of all my sisters, and they both were married. I would say this prayer as a little girl: *Please, Lord, let me have a great big family. I want to be a wife to a man who loves you, Lord.*

Maybe, when I became a teen, my evil twin took over my body and changed me to think that it was not just about waiting on God but it was about getting what you want and making things happen!

"I don't know what to say," I said while leaving Macy's with a black silk dress that was knee-high short. I had to buy it; this dress was beautiful. I got in my car and drove off. I was headed home.

I was still talking with my sister, changing the topic to something I could relate to. I asked her what was going on with *Black G Mag* and when she would come out to Dallas to visit.

"London, you still never told me how you felt about me being a Mom," my sister said.

I really was happy for her; it was just so many people were moving on in their lives but me. I had been single for too long, and I was tired of it. My career was all I had going good for me. I could say I was happy with my career because I put so much of myself in it. "Sis, I am sorry. I am so happy for you and Tony. I just have a lot on my mind lately," I replied.

Lisa could tell that maybe all this talk about family and babies was making me feel pressure.

"London, you need a break. You should take a break and come out here to L.A."

"I should take a visit to LA?" I said while imagining the palm trees, the beach and the social scene.

"Maybe after Jason leaves from his visit from Dallas, I will come out to see you and Tony."

Lisa got really quiet. "What do you mean… from the visit? From Dallas? Who does Jason know in Dallas besides you?" I could tell that she did not like that idea at all.

"Well, Lisa, since you're asking all these questions, he said that he wanted to hang out with me," I said with a smirk on my face.

"Oh my God, London, what if he falls in love with you again? You remember he was head over heels for you until you broke his heart," I could not believe that Lisa was bringing that up, I thought to myself.

"Yea, you know what I am talking about, Jason saw you kissing somebody else!" Lisa blurted out.

I was so sick and tired of hearing the same story. However, Jason and Lisa wanted to keep reminding me of this party.

I mean, this happened when we were teenagers. I have told them over and over the guy walked up and just kissed me. I did not understand why they insisted that I cheated on Jason with a kiss. "Yea, But I told Jason that the guy kissed me." I said. "Lisa, we were at a party, the guy came up to me and said ooh you have nice lips and to my surprise he just kissed me out of the blue. "We all were college students back then, and Jason never got over it." I said, hoping that my sister would finally see things my way.

"So is that the reason why he has kept you in the friend zone for years now?" Lisa asked.

"Yes, that is the reason why!" I said. The traffic was not that bad on this beautiful Saturday.

Lisa realized I was telling the truth; Jason just could not trust me. "So I guess all things work for the good of them who love the Lord," Lisa said.

"I really do believe that we were just meant to be friends," I said, feeling sad about that being the truth.

"London, I think there is a season for everything. Maybe back then you and Jason was just meant to be friends while God was working on your garden getting you both prepared for each other now."

"Well, Lisa, remember Jason is getting married, so that means it is over for me and him."

That would be a blessing if that was not the reality for me, I thought. "Look, Lisa, I've got to catch up on some things. I will be calling you soon. Love ya!"

"London, remember what I said. God will lead you to all your blessings. Wait on the Lord."

I pulled up to the front of my home. The bright sunlight danced across the blue sky. Everyone was outside with his or her significant other. I smiled, at the couples. This moment only reminded me of what I desired.

I entered in the front door. When I walked into my large living room; the aroma of vanilla air freshener filled the room. I kicked off my heels and allowed my feet to sink into the nice plush carpeted stairs.

I walked in my bedroom and threw myself on my bed. I realized that it was four o'clock pm and time was passing fast. I had not eaten at all.

I called my assistant Joel. "Darling, I need you right now."

"Yes, Ms. Kennedy, what do you need?" Joel sounded bothered. I knew I could be a big pain in the you-know-what. But hey, I was paying this guy a thousand dollars every two weeks to be on call for me.

"I need you to pick up some Chinese food. I want the peppered chicken and iced tea."

"I am coming from this modeling shoot, so I will be there in about twenty minutes," Joel said while hanging up the phone. I knew that Joel was going to make a good man to some woman one day. Joel was honest and very handsome; he was on his paper chase. He didn't mind me yelling at him when he would forget something or if I was just having a bad day. Joel is not a soft man, but he is far into black history and not degrading women in any fashion or form.

My phone began to ring. I ran to answer my home phone, and it was my Mom. I talked to her for a while; she told me that the doctors said that Dad was fine. My Mom told me that Lisa finally told her about the baby. It was nice talking to my mother without arguing. There was a knock at the door. I got off the phone and went downstairs to get the door; it was Joel with my food. "Joel, don't you look handsome."

"Thank you, Ms. Kennedy," Joel said while standing in my doorway.

"You may come in," I said, motioning for Joel to come in while I sat my food at the kitchen table.

"Ms. Kennedy is that all? I have to attend a black tie event with my girlfriend."

I was astonished that he said girlfriend. I never thought he had a girlfriend at all.

"I am going to need you to call and set up a car for me on Monday at seven am to pick up Mr. Crosby and myself to meet at the restaurant in downtown Dallas called the Madison."

"No, problem. I will do that first thing in the morning," Joel said while walking away.

"Wait, Joel, who is this girlfriend?"

"Her, name is Tiffany and she is going to be more than a girlfriend… I am going to ask her to marry me tonight at the dinner," Joel said, while his brown complexion lit up from blushing. "I really love this girl. She is sweet, and when I need her she is always there for me; she is my best friend."

I gave Joel a big hug before he walked out the door. I hoped for the best for those two young people. I thought to myself how it would feel nice to have someone to laugh with, to love, and even to disagree with.

Chapter 2

CHASING LOVE

I lived in a three-bedroom townhouse, and sometimes I felt so alone. I did not hear any sounds of children playing or the voice of another. I only heard my own voice. My house was silent and cold. I really felt like the single life was not for me at all; I wanted so badly to have someone to share my life with. I was just thinking about Mike and whether I should go out with him tonight. Why not? It was good that I occupied my mind with someone else even if I didn't really care for him. But the thought of hanging around someone that I knew upfront that I didn't really care about was a bit dishonest.

Well, there is nothing wrong with pure fun! At least that is what I told myself. The small voice whispered, "London love yourself more. Choose to have a night alone and be filled with joy overflowing in your soul. Let a man named Jesus touch you in places that no earthly man could touch or heal. Places like your heart, your secret places in your soul that's been wounded. Only God can fix you!"

I looked around my room to only feel goosebumps on my skin. *Lord, I want that, but I am not broken. Lord I am ready for love in the flesh. Bring me my husband. But until then I will go out and have some fun for now!*

I called Mike to confirm our date for tonight. He said to meet him at Edelman at seven o'clock. It was now six; I needed to get ready. I was so glad I ate before I had left just in case the food was crummy. I made to Edelman about a half hour late. I paid the valet parking and headed in. Edelman was a jazz spot that was very popular in Dallas. People were everywhere! Black high-society doctors and lawyers surrounded me.

I was wearing a Vera Wang black cocktail dress and some silver and black pumps to set it off. My diamond tennis bracelet was the complete package. I knew that I was diva luscious. I was escorted to the table where Mike was sitting. I sat down while Mike's eyes where glued on me. "Hello, you finally made it!" He said, while taking a sip out of his apple martini.

"I am so sorry that I was late. I had to see Brandon earlier, and I lost track of time," I said while the waiter asked me what I would like to drink. I replied, telling the waiter the same as Mike.

"That's ok, Ms. Kennedy. You are looking good," he said while grabbing my hand across the table then kissing it.

"You can call me London," I said while pulling my hand back from his soft kiss; there was a loud buzzing coming from my cell. I reached in my purse for my cell phone. It was Jason. I wondered what he wanted.

"Jason, how are you?" Jason was talking about his family, asking about me and wanting to know if I was coming to the wedding. I did not want to be rude, but I had to get off the phone because I was on a date. "Jason, look I am not trying to be rude, but I have to go. I am on a date." Jason got really quiet and then he said, "Oh

I am sorry. I did not mean to talk your ear off; I just miss you a lot. I will be down there on Friday. I will call you when I am settled in my hotel room."

"Okay, so talk to you then," I said, while hanging up.

"So that must be your boyfriend," Mike said while taking another sip.

"No, he is just an old friend who will always have a special place in my heart. He is getting married soon." I could not believe that I was saying that about Jason. I guess somewhere in the back of my mind I thought that Jason would be marrying me instead of her.

"On the other hand, that is good to know that this guy is only a friend. That gives me a chance to get to know you," Mike said, reaching for my hand as he pulled me up from the table to meet some people who were standing by the bar.

Mike rushed through the crowd and had a tight grip on my hand, making sure I would not get lost in the crowd.

"Mike, how has it been?" The man said while reaching for my hand to shake.

"Hi, my name is Edelman." My eyes stood out because I was flattered that I was meeting the Owner of Edelman; he was a very attractive man.

"Hello, my name is London, and I just love your place… the Poets and the live jazz band are really cool."

"Thank you. I really appreciate that coming from such a beautiful woman like yourself."

Mike looked at me as if he did not like the attention that the owner was giving me. "Well, Edelman, I have been fine; it's been a while since I've seen you."

Edelman replied, telling Mike how he traveled to New York City for a while and he was setting up more jazz clubs all around the states. Mike said hi to a beautiful olive-toned young lady with the blonde hair who barely said a word;

she didn't speak to him. I could tell there had been a bad connection between them.

"It would be nice if you would introduce yourself to the young lady," Edelman said while placing a firm grip around her arm.

"Hello, my name is Brenda," she said in a very sarcastic way.

"Yea, well my name is London," I said; ready to walk away from Edelman and whoever she was. "Mike, can we go back to our table?" He took my hand and led away. I sat down, and my drink was sitting at the table. I took a sip; man,they had the best apple martini ever.

"Mike, this is a great drink."

"Well, I am sorry we had to run into my ex-wife and an old friend," he replied.

That made sense on why that young lady was rude, but it did not explain why she would be mad when she had a very handsome man who seemed very successful.

"I am not trying to disrespect you, but why would she be so mad at you if she is with Edelman? He seems very successful plus he could have any woman in this place."

"True, so… true maybe that's her problem, competition. Well, my ex-wife did not know that Edelman was one of my close buddies. She regrets that because she is always bumping into me at his parties or at one of Edelman's clubs. Edelman is not a one-woman type of guy, so she has to share him, and

I guess it is embarrassing to her for me to know that she has not found her Mr. Right," Mike said while waving his hand for the waiter.

"Waiter, another apple martini please for me and the lady," Mike said. I was having a good time. Mike and I were really getting to know each other; we talked a lot about our family. "I really was not planning on having this much fun," I said to Mike. He gazed in my eyes as if he were hoping for a fat kiss on my soft lips. I gave him the look like don't even try it. Mike laughed out loud and gave me the sweetest kiss on my forehead. "Look… Mike even though I am having a good time, I need to go home. I've got church in the morning," I said. I was hoping that he would let me in on if he had church in the morning too, but Mike just nodded his head. I guess we did not have that in common.

"That's fine. I had a good time too; you better keep in touch," he said while we both stood up to go get our cars from valet parking. Mike's masculine frame hovered over me as we walked outside the club. I was holding myself because of the cool breeze. I knew that soon we would get a major downpour.

I wanted to make it home before the storm. Mike noticed that I was cold because he cuddled up with me while we both where waiting for our cars. I saw my car pull up and gave Mike a big hug. "Mike, I will call you soon," I said before getting in my car. When I arrived home, I took a nice, warm bath and put on my silk tan nightgown that Lisa bought for me last Christmas. I got in my bed and lay down to the sound of thunder and rain. It did not take me long to fall asleep.

Chapter 3

DISCOVERING THE DESIRES OF THE HEART

I had just come back from my meeting with Mr. Crosby, and I was so happy that I could not hold my joy in. I had to tell somebody. Sherry would be the first person I told on this Monday morning.

"Sherry, you know your boss got it going on right about now!" I said in a very loud voice.

"Oh my gosh! You did it! You go, girl!" Sherry said while rushing to her desk to catch the phone. I could not believe that I had the Crosby account, but I had to give God all the glory. Sherry came rushing back to my desk. "Ms. Kennedy,

I am so happy for you!" She was holding her cell in her hand frowning at it.

"Sherry, are you okay? What is wrong?"

"Ms. Kennedy, umm….he is leaving me for someone else." I did not know what to say. I stood and embraced her while she began to cry.

"Sherry… look, you can take the day off to get yourself together," I said. I knew Sherry didn't have anything of her own only her clothes and that two thousand and seven red Bentley she drove. The penthouse and her other cars belonged to her boyfriend.

"He told me that he found somebody who loved him past his pain. I don't know what the hell he is talking about past his pain." Sherry was frantic and upset. "I am the one who has been there for him through all the bull crap." Sherry went on and on. "I took a lot of mess from that dud. He would do all kinds of illegal activities, and I never said a word." She was going on and on about how she thought they were going to get married. I was even fooled. I thought they were going to get married as well.

"Sherry, look, at least you won't spend a lifetime reaching for something and end up with nothing," I said while she slowly wiped her tears from her face.

"Ms. Kennedy, what do you mean reaching for something? I don't understand."

"I am talking about spending all your time trying to reach and touch love that does not exist in that person. It is good that you found out now that he was a jerk than much later. I am happy that you won't be like some women who stay with a man for twenty years and then find out he was a cheater all that time."

Sherry had a blank stare on her face. I could tell she was hurt.

"Sherry, you make sure you call me and tell me what is going on okay?" I said while Sherry got her things and left the office.

I did not see Brandon all day. I guess he was working from home today. I sat back in my chair and thought about the sermon on Sunday. I was full of the good gospel on Sunday. Pastor Jeff Ramon preached about the true meaning of a Christian. It really made me think a lot about my own life. Pastor Jeff said that most people think that coming to church is the key to being a Christian. Being a Christian is giving up your will to follow God's purpose for our life. I wondered if I was truly giving up my life to give to God because He gave his life up for me? Jesus covered my sins with his blood. I had been stuck on relationships and focusing on what I didn't have than focusing on what I do have.

I really felt like God was sending me Brandon. Brandon made sense to me. He was handsome, and he loved God. I didn't know how he felt about me, but Brandon and I could really make a good couple. The soft voice again began to say, *What about me? How can you love a man right when you have not loved me right? How can you be faithful to your future husband when you have not been faithful to me?*

But, Lord, I said. I have been doing well for a while now—no sex, no wild nights. Lord, I am ready!

There I go again. I guess I can't help but think about relationship and marriage. I really wanted to be married so badly, but I will do what my Pastor said and that is to wait on the Lord and embrace the family and friends that are in my life. I had a lot on my mind, and I could tell because I was feeling down. I had been working too much; I knew that I needed some days off, but I knew I could not take off. I had the new account with Mr. Crosby, and Sherry would probably be off her game since her and that ex broke up. I needed to be here to make sure everything would go smoothly.

The day went by so slowly, but thank goodness for the end of my day. It was six o'clock and time for me to make my way out of there. I was walking to my car when I saw Brandon. Yes, I was smiling from ear to ear, but I had to play this cool. I don't want him to notice me noticing him.

"Brandon, you look great," I said. I closed my car door, and Brandon was standing right there on my side of the car wearing an Armani suit that made him look very intelligent and fine as hell! Please God excuse my language even though I didn't say it out loud. Lord, help me grow more in you Lord. I thought to myself.

"Hey, London, I did not thank you for coming out to the hospital," Brandon said, while looking at me with the perfect smile.

"That's fine, Brandon, I just wanted to make sure that you were okay," I said while blinking my eyes and smiling to make sure he could tell I was very interested in him. I don't think Ruth flirted with Boaz? Lord you really need to help a girl out, all these rules! Flirting was not a Christian thing to do, the answer just popped in my head. Thank you Lord. I thought to myself.

"London, I want to make it up to you by inviting you to dinner at my favorite restaurant tonight at Houston's around seven," Brandon said while looking in my brown eyes. I felt like he could tell that I was blushing. I could not believe that he was asking me out again.

"Brandon, that sounds great. I would love to!"

I drove fast as I could just so I could make it to my house to get ready. I wanted to be so classy and sexy. Miss Southern Belle was cute, but she better watch out because I was leaving my house looking like Dallas' Top Model. I was wearing my black designer jeans and a black see through top with a black tank underneath with my pink high heel boots. I made it to Houston's restaurant; the men were turning their heads like they had never seen a pretty woman before. My sleek curves and my dashing looks had already captivated this young Caucasian man who was coming up to me asking me, "do I model?" Brandon saw me before I could call him on my cell.

"London, over here," he said while waving his hands, motioning me to come to the table. I walked past the gentlemen and headed to the table, but to my surprise we had company. Guess who was sitting at the table? It was Miss. Southern Belle and two guys that I had not met before. I could tell they were not my type at all. I thought to myself, *What is going on? But why does Brandon have them here? What kind of date is this?*

I sat down at the table looking so fashionable, and I could not believe that everyone was dressed so simply. I could tell that Miss Southern Bell was not too happy to see me either.

"Hello, everyone," I said while taking my seat.

"Hey, London, this is Jake and Tim; fellas, this is London," Brandon said while pointing to them.

"You have already met Mandy," Brandon said.

"Yeah, Brandon, I met her when you were in the hospital," Mandy said, while holding Brandon's arm. I was sitting across from them, but Miss Southern Belle was sitting right next to Brandon. Mandy made sure she was getting VIP treatment.

"I wanted you to hang out with my friends, London. I thought that you would have some good fun."

Before I could speak, my cell phone rang. It was Jason. Jason never would call me like this unless he was in town. I answered my phone.

"Where have you been?" he said.

"I've just been busy, Jason," I said.

"Cupcake, look I need to talk to you," he said, sounding so depressed or something like that. "Where are you? It is loud and I can hear a lot of people talking," Jason said.

"Jason, I am hanging out with some of my friends on my job. Can I call you back?"

"Look, cupcake, I really want you to call me back if you can."

I told him I would, but I really wanted to avoid him. I hung up the phone because Jason was getting on my nerves. He kept calling me cupcake; it was cute to me, but now that he was getting married I wanted him to just stop. Brandon and all his friends were laughing and joking with each other. I was bored out of my mind. I was going to leave before dinner. I did not like the fact that Brandon had his friends at the table with us. I guess I wanted to get to know Brandon, not his friends. But Brandon's friends seemed like good guys, real cool and honest people.

It must be true that you are whom you hang out with. I say that because Brandon's friends seemed honest, even Miss Southern Belle.

"What's wrong, London? You seem really bored."

Brandon was right. I was bored. I guess because I thought that Brandon was taking me out alone, not hanging out with his friends. I wanted all of his attention. I thought about what Pastor Jeff preached about how the Lord could be trying to bless you, but if you are thinking that God should only bless you one way, you could be cheating yourself out of a true blessing if you are expecting your blessing to come in a different way. This time the small voice began to tell me to have patience and let truth work in me. But the word patience made me more anxious.

"I am so sorry, I am just so tired tonight. I had a long weekend and oh yeah, Brandon… I got that Crosby account," I said playfully while Brandon reached out and grabbed my hands from across the table.

Brandon's face lit up. "Oh my gosh! You get out of here! That is a good thing. That's why you should stay here and celebrate."

"No, I am calling it a night. I hope all of you have a good night." I stood up and walked away. So many feelings were going on inside of me. I headed back to the parking area without looking back.

I was waiting for my car to pull up, and I noticed Brandon walking toward me. "Hey, London, look what's wrong? I am sorry. I did not know that Mandy, Tim, and Jake were going to be there," he said. Brandon's facial expression was priceless, so apologetic. "They were there before I arrived, so I told them to join me."

"Look, Brandon, you don't owe me nothing. I just thought maybe you were inviting me on a date," I said while Brandon came up close to me.

"I was, London, I want to get to know you better." I looked up at Brandon, and I could not believe that a man like Brandon really truly wanted to get to know me for me, not my body. I was very delighted that Brandon came outside just to tell me that he wanted to get to know me. Brandon was handsome, but he had this strong persona. "Brandon, so maybe you can start off by calling me sometimes." Brandon smiled while we both looked at my car pulling up.

"Yeah, I will give you a call. Maybe you will give me another chance to take you out again," he quickly said.

"That sounds like a plan," I said while getting in my car and driving off.

I brushed my hair back and put it up in a ponytail. The sun was beaming in my living room. Two weeks had passed and no Jason. I guessed since I kept blowing him off, he decided not to come down to visit.

I didn't blame him. It was Saturday morning, and Brandon and I were meeting up at my house for tea and lunch. Brandon and I had been talking since the night at the restaurant. I had learned a lot about Brandon; he was not only handsome, but he loved God with all his heart and he loved family. I have been so blessed to have someone who is truly a good friend. Yeah, we have not started dating yet, but I am hoping that will happen soon. Something was happening to my heart. I was changing.

I saw love very differently now. It was not about having just anyone, but it was about having God's best. Then the question fell right back to me: was I the right one for him? Brandon knew his Word; he seemed like he had it together. Brandon was a youth minister at his church back home in Chicago at the church he grew up in. When he moved to Texas from college, he had been visiting different churches. Brandon fell in love with my Pastor, and he has been attending my church faithfully since we have been talking. God was moving in both of our lives. I had a small feeling that maybe we were moving too fast, but in the natural we were only friends. I could feel that God was doing something deeper in the spirit between Brandon and me.

I was learning from Brandon—how he viewed life and love. Brandon and I would laugh and have great discussions over the phone. When I saw him, I saw God in him.

I rushed to my front door as the doorbell rang. "Hi, handsome what's going on?" I gave him a sweet kiss on his cheek while Brandon walked in. "I am doing fine," he said. I could not take my eyes off of Brandon. He looked so handsome in his light blue eagle t-shirt and his light blue slightly baggy jeans.

I love it when Brandon wore that shirt because it showed off his muscles.

"You look great, London, and what smells so good, girl?"

"Well I fixed smoked turkey legs, mashed potatoes, and made us both a green salad; I added sliced strawberries to the salad."

Brandon grabbed my hand and pulled me close to him, and he kissed me right on my mouth!

I had on a nice white summer dress with spaghetti straps; the dress stopped a little over my knees, and my boots were light tan leather cowboy boots. I loved dressing up like a Cowgirl. Brandon was looking at me as if he never seen any woman that was as cute as me.

"Look, London, I am sorry if I made you feel uncomfortable. But I will only be fooling myself if I did not tell you that I really like you, and I want us to start dating." Brandon was looking at me right in my eyes. I wanted this, but why did I feel so numb inside? Maybe we were rushing it. I wondered if I had really let go of my feelings for a soon-to-be married man. Jason was out of sight and out of mind.

"Wow, I am shocked, but I like you too and yes let's start dating," I said, not really knowing what this really could lead to. I had been out of a relationship for about three years now. Could I really date this young man of God? Could I date him God's way?

I had tried to date the right way but failed at it time and time again. I was not worried about Brandon but I was worried about myself.

I was worried about sex. Sex was my biggest downfall with all the men that I dated. I did consider myself a Christian, but I always struggled in that area. I know that's a shame; how could I say I loved Jesus and at the same time when it was time to stand up for what I believe in I just gave in to my flesh! I didn't want to mess this up, and if he tried to mess this up with sex, I would have to love God more by giving Brandon up!

I had made up in my mind that I would let the Lord show me how to be a woman of God in all areas of my life, including the bedroom. I was tired of letting my flesh lead me down a sinful path. I wanted to be free to love Brandon God's way. I would have to stand up and let the Lord lead me.

"Okay, well, London, we should take everything slow and make sure God is first in this relationship. Is that okay with you, baby girl?" I stood there while Brandon was holding my hands and just was amazed. I knew this was the type of relationship that I prayed for.

"Brandon, I am ready to put God first in this relationship. I have so much to learn about dating God's way, Brandon, this is the first time for me."

"I know. I remember when you asked how a woman was supposed to find a husband."

I smiled because I had learned a lot since then. I read the story of Ruth, and it taught me how both women, Ruth and Naomi, were strong women; they stood by each other even in the time of hopelessness. Naomi and Ruth looked to the Lord to bring them out of hopelessness. God did bring them both out. I was reading more of my Word, and the Word showed me that I did not have to look for love. God was love and still is, and He will always be love. "Yeah, Brandon, I have learned that women do not have to look for love; we just need to look to love the Lord, and He will add everything to our lives in due season."

Brandon looked at me while we both sat down to eat. "This is really good, London," Brandon said while he was eating a smoked turkey leg.

"I am glad you are enjoying it!" I said while stuffing my face with a spoonful of my creamy mashed potatoes.

"London, you have really changed in these few weeks," Brandon said.

"Have I changed for the better?" I said while taking a sip of my tea.

"Yeah, baby, you have changed for the good. I mean, it seemed to me that you have put down this wall you had up."

"I have known you for about three years, and I could tell you were friendly, but there was a wall up."

"It just takes me a while before I let someone in my heart," I said while getting up to answer the phone.

"Hey, cupcake, I am here in Dallas. Sorry I have not had a chance to talk to you; it has been crazy on my end. I am staying at the Hilton."

I could not move my mouth. I was looking right at Brandon, so I blurted out, "Oh good that will be great! I will call you later okay? I will let you get settled in your room, call you later."

"Baby who was that?" Brandon said. I was trying my best to tell him the truth, but how could I when all of these feelings were surfacing to the top of my heart? Just two weeks ago, I thought Brandon did not want anything more, yet because of how slow Brandon was moving, just now right in this moment Brandon finally showed me he wanted more!

I really liked Brandon and felt this natural pull to want to know him better. The fact that Jason had called me over and over told me he wanted to tell me something. Could it be the very thing that I had waited for? Jason wanting to start a relationship with me. Could he really be the one?

Brandon still giving me that look like he was picking up that something had changed.

"Well, it;s just a guy that's down here… He is like family; he is here on business," I said, but I could not look Brandon in the eye.

"Oh that's great. How long will he be staying in Dallas?" Brandon asked.

"I don't really know, but anyway look I have a lot of work I need to do this weekend. The Crosby account has me so busy. I need to go over these contracts and plus I need to catch up on some rest." Brandon leaned his head back as if he were thinking to himself, trying to figure out what was going on. "Why do I feel like you are getting rid of me," Brandon said while laughing.

"No, Bran, I just need to get started on some of this work. You know Sherry is still not coming in to work like she should, and she's making it hard for me," I said as I took Brandon and my dishes to the dishwasher.

"I like it when you call me Bran," he said while hugging me. "You should make Sherry get it together. Just because her and that guy broke up does not mean she should give up on her job," he said while whispering in my ear. Brandon then leaned in and gave me a kiss on my forehead.

"Well, Brandon, I will see you at church tomorrow," I said while I walked him to the front door.

"Yeah I can't wait. I like your Pastor Ramon, but next Sunday you should come visit my church that I visit from time to time," Brandon said while heading out the front door.

"I will. Take care, Brandon; call me tonight," I said while blowing him a kiss.

I cleaned up the kitchen and jumped on my couch and then called Jason. "Jason, I am sorry that I rushed you off the phone, but I had company."

"So you have a boyfriend now?" Jason asked.

"Yeah, his name is Brandon; he works at my company."

"Oh really? He must be getting paid."

"Well yeah," I replied. I could tell Jason was here in Dallas for more than just hanging out.

"So you must really like this dude?" Jason said. "Yeah, you are right I do. I am just blessed to have someone like Brandon," I said. Talking about Brandon only reassured me that I really did like Brandon for all the right reasons.

"Well look, cupcake, I want to come see you tonight," Jason said.

I was a little nervous about seeing Jason, but I really wanted to see him. My feelings were kind of all over the place.

I did not know how I felt for Jason, but I did know I felt something pulling. With Brandon it was different, innocent. "That would be great because I want to see you," I said. Those words just jumped out of my mouth. I was supposed to say no! But I did not.

"I think seven would be a good time because I have a lot of work to do," I said, not really giving Jason time to speak.

Jason laughed. "Cupcake, look that's cool. I won't stay too long. I don't want your boyfriend to be upset."

I was feeling guilty already because everything was happening so fast. I had not told Brandon the truth about Jason. "I have not told my boyfriend about you, Jason," I replied.

"Well, should I even come over?" Jason's voice had a lot of uncertainness in it.

"No, I want you to come over. You're like a brother to me, and I will tell my boyfriend everything okay?"

"That sounds great. Well, tell me your address and I will be over there in a few."

I told Jason how to get to my house, and I could tell we both were feeling something more for each other. I got off the phone and flat-ironed my hair and put a little lip-gloss on. I even changed into my designer jeans and my baby blue silk shirt.

When I heard the doorbell, I knew it was Jason. I stood by the door, and all of my feelings started to rush through my body. I open the door there he was standing in his black blazer and Malcolm X glasses. He was not only handsome, but he looked strong and intelligent. I stood just gazing at him. I finally came back to myself. "Oh my gosh, it is so good to see you!" I said. I ran right into his arms.

Jason's embrace was warm and loving. The scent of his strong cologne danced in the air.

"You look so good, cupcake. Dang girl, you don't look thirty." Jason sat on my couch, and I took his coat.

"Would you like some tea?" I asked while placing his blazer jacket in the closet.

"No thank you, just come and sit down, cupcake," he said as he motioned me to sit next to him on the couch.

"So you are getting married," I said.

"Well, we decided to push the wedding back for a while."

"What do you mean you guys are going to wait?"

"I told her we needed space apart before we got married."

He went on explaining why they were taking a break from each other before the wedding.

"Jason, tell me, why is it so important for you to see me?" I asked.

Jason was looking at me so serious. "London, I wanted to see you face-to-face to make sure that I didn't have feelings for you. I guess now I know," he said while moving in close to me so close that I could see his heartbeat.

"Look, Jason, I don't know what you are trying to say, but whatever it is you need to say it now!"

Jason leaned in and kissed me right on my cheek then my lips. I began to kiss him back. I was now wrapped up in his arms; his hands began to move all over my body. I didn't want this to end. I could not believe that he was back in my life at this moment. I pulled back and asked Jason to tell me what he was going to say. Jason caught his breath. "I was going to say that I know that I still have feelings for you," he said softly. "I just can't get you out of my head lately."

I had been waiting for him to say that to me for a very long time. I liked Brandon, but I had loved Jason from afar. Jason leaned back in and started to unbutton my top while he kissed me softly on the neck. Jason and I had known each other for years now, but we had never had sex. Back when we were young, we kissed and touched, but I never would let him go all the way. I was now ready to give into this passion for the man I had always loved.

My mind was only thinking of him and how he was going to give me what my body needed. I let him caress me with his tongue down my neck while I was giving him a sweet kiss on his neck. Neither of us said a word.

I was in a daze. I could not believe the man I longed for all these years was right here with me tonight. He picked me up and started down the hall to my bedroom. I pointed to my bedroom door, still not saying one word. We both knew that we had waited for this moment.

But I had pictured us married. Just that thought alone made me feel like I needed to stop this madness. *What about God!* I yelled in my mind. *What about Brandon!* I slightly screamed, stop, but he could not hear me. If only I could walk away from this. I felt my body fall on the bed and felt my pants come off. Jason was kissing my tummy, and the chills were all over my body. It was too late. I grabbed Jason, pulling his shirt off while he took his pants off. Jason and I were already deep in this act of passion, and it was too late to stop this explosion of my desires. Jason lay on top of me while our bodies became one; he was sending waves of emotions to every curve of my body.

My body had yearned for this; his touch gave me chills down my spine. I could not believe that we both finally made this love connection happen. While he kissed me all over, the feelings were so pleasurable, and my body was running over with sensation and satisfaction. Jason and I went on and on with this dance of passion. Jason lay beside me when the dance was over. I felt so stupid. How could I have done this? Jason was not my boyfriend, and plus I just cheated on someone who was very special to me. I wanted to just pack my things and run away from Jason, Brandon, and even myself.

I just lay there confused. Not only did I cheat on Brandon, but I cheated on my Lord with the sin of lust that always got the best of me every time. Jason turned to me and noticed tears running down my face.

"Cupcake, what is wrong?"

"Jason, I just cheated on somebody that I really care about, and on top of it I was saving myself for marriage," I said through tears, my voice trembling.

"You mean to tell me that you are a virgin?" Jason replied while he began to reach for his clothes. "Look, you just scared me… London, you made me feel like I raped you or something. I have never seen a grown woman cry after sex." He was standing in my bedroom fully dressed.

I was upset by Jason's comment. I did not think he understood what I stood for. "Look, cupcake… what we did will stay between me and you. Your boyfriend will never know." Jason seemed so calm, like what we had just done was nothing. "Jason, I am going to tell him so he will know about us, and honesty is the best way to go even if it means losing someone you love."

Jason gave me the strangest stare. "I would have married you. I just wanted to close the door on you and me before I moved on with my life," he said.

I rolled my eyes.

"I did not plan to sleep with you!" Jason said in a very stern voice. "Look, I did not mean to lead you on… but I never told you that I was not getting married!" He yelled while looking at me in hopes that I would understand. I stood there wishing that Jason would have never come. I did not understand why could I just for once love myself enough to not fall for this sex act. The question was, what did I really want from the Lord? I kept asking God to forgive me and help me to start over, to only end up in some guy's arms. The big question was what was in my heart? I have allowed men to become my priority.

I needed to learn how to stand up for what I believe in! I started thinking to myself again.

I should have said no! Jason, it is too late to come by or maybe yes, Jason come over and meet my boyfriend. I wondered why it was so hard for me to do the right thing. I just had to do the wrong thing. How could I call myself a Christian?

"I understand that you never told me that you wanted something with me, but why would you allow yourself to sleep with me knowing that you did not want anything from me, and that you say you love your wife? No, Jason, I have had sex plenty of times, it is just… I gave myself to God, and I am now walking a God-fearing life style by not having sex before marriage."

I could tell Jason did not really understand why I was so upset over a night of passion.

"Look, cupcake, I know you loved this guy, and I am not trying to stand in the way. I still love my fiance," Jason said with a very calm tone. Jason had no intentions of being with me!

"I am not asking you to walk away from your whole life you have here in Texas with that guy," Jason said while looking so sure he wanted nothing with me. I stood up, holding the sheets from my bed over my naked body.

I shouted out with anger, "What you mean you did not want to start something with me, Jason? Why would you want to come to Texas to only visit me for a fling?!" I was so mad. I always thought that Jason was a fairly good guy, but he was not a godly guy… big difference. He did not care about being celibate or the things of God. And from the looks of things, I did not care either.

I grabbed my clothes and put them on; Jason was looking furiously at me. "I came here to see an old friend, the woman that I would have married! I just wanted to close the door on you and me before I moved on with my life."

I rolled my eyes again. "I did not plan to sleep with you!" Jason said again in a very stern voice. "London, I really did not mean to lead you on, but I never told you that I was not getting married."

Jason did not know what to say, but he wanted me to act as if nothing bad happened. Like we both wanted to have a fling. But he knew that was clearly a lie; I had always wanted more from him.

"London, you trying to make me out to be the bad guy!" he yelled. "But I did not force you to sleep with me, plus you have a boyfriend. Why would I leave my soon-to-be wife for a woman who will cheat!"

Jason was right; I did cheat on Brandon only because I thought that maybe Jason was the one. But at any cost I was willing to run after love or at least, what I thought was love.

"I am not a cheater. I just started something with Brandon, but I thought we had something much more, but I was wrong trying to follow my heart," I said.

Jason just shook his head. "Yeah right. Just like you cheated on me back in the day."

I could not believe that this Negro would go way back when we were in college. "I am so sick of you bringing that up!" I shouted while I threw a pillow at Jason's head. "You, know good well, I DID NOT KISS that guy! I am so tired of you using that as an excuse to kiss me and feel me up and then turn around and take another girl out and do whatever you want with them. Oh, it was okay because we were just friends! You know that guy kissed me!" Jason grinned a little.

"Okay, maybe I used that to my advantage to keep you on a string while I played the field." Jason admitted it.

"Wow." The truth was finally coming out Jason! I said, "So, Jason, you can allow yourself to sleep with me knowing that you did not want anything from me?" I asked.

Jason's cell phone rang; he looked at it and ignored it. "Look, London, I thought that maybe we both were on the same page. We never hooked up with each other, and I have always wanted to touch you in that way and, baby, you are so awesome in bed." Jason grinned a little bit.

This was the first time I wanted to slap that smirk off his face. I had feared this very moment. I never wanted Jason to hurt me in this way; how could he just want sex just like the other men who had walked in my life to only try and sex me down and sex me up.

I felt so hurt. I could not control the tears from rolling down my face. Jason stopped smiling and realized I was crying again. "What, London? I am not saying that was all I wanted from you. It is just that we never did it, and plus I did not know that you really cared so much about me. You always seemed like one man was not good enough for you." I gazed at Jason while he went on and on.

"London, look baby girl, I never came at you serious because you always made me believe that you were not a one-man girl. I am not trying to be rude, but I thought of you as being too sexy for your own good, someone that every man would just want to have an affair with."

Jason thought he was saying something good; he had no clue that he had just insulted me. "Jason, you know what? All these years I thought we were friends because you cared about the real me. I was wrong. You only cared about yourself, and if you loved the woman you're going to marry, you should have never come to see me. But I know why you came to see me. You wanted to make that fantasy of us making love come true and vanish off to your happy ending with your soon-to-be wife. Get out of my house, Jason. Go please!" I said while starting to cry.

Jason walked out of my room. He said good night and went home. I knew that I needed to tell Brandon about this. I needed time so God could tell me how. The scary thing was, I thought I was ready for a relationship, but what had just taken place was clearly a sign I needed to be healed, and if healing meant being alone, then I was ready.

I let the warm shower hit my skin, wishing that the steam and the water could wash my shame away. I knew I needed to give this to Jesus because my pain came from a deeper place. The next morning, I was all ready for church. I really felt bad like somebody had died. I could not control my tears, and my eyes were red from crying so much. I wanted so badly to tell Brandon, but I needed to seek God first.

Brandon was knocking at the door. "Hold on. Here I come." I opened the door, and there he was handsome as ever. I was blessed to have a man of God like Brandon. But I guess the big question was, was I ready for a godly man? I knew that the time to tell Brandon would be soon.

"Hey, baby, did you get your work done?"

When Brandon said that, he reminded me of last night with Jason. I just could not go through this. I wanted to tell Brandon, but I knew I could not do it.

This was not the time; my emotions were a wreck. I looked up at Brandon and smiled. At least I tried to cover my pain up with a smile. "Brandon, I can't go to church. I just can't do this." I started to cry. I fell to my living room floor. Brandon was so confused, but he knew that something was wrong. Brandon picked me up and looked right in my eyes and said, "Tell me what is wrong!"

I wanted to tell him so I could feel released from this guilty evil spirit that rested on me, but I could not. I looked at Brandon and lied. "Brandon, I am just over worked. I even think I am stressed out."

"Look, baby, you have to slow down. I knew something was wrong with you when you opened your front door. Look, just go and lie down and rest. Play some worship music and relax. I will call you later." Brandon was so smooth; he knew what I needed. That's why I liked him.

"Okay, Bran, thank you so much. I am going to miss you."

Brandon gave me a kiss right on my forehead; it made me feel safe and warm all over. "I really care for you, Ms. London Kennedy."

I lay on my couch and began to think how I could get out of this mess. I was a cheater! I needed to really get down to the bottom of what I was really feeling. I needed to know one thing and that was, "Who am I?" Who was this woman that was trapped behind this flesh? Who was the woman that couldn't get past mistakes? Why were men my downfall? Why did I choose to make the wrong decisions with men? I was on the mission to finding me!

I now know that in order to do God's will, I needed to really go into a secret place and learn from my Creator first. I needed to know all of His promises for me. I wanted Jesus to fill me up with wisdom, because if I knew my Creator, then I would know who I am; and if I know who I am, then I won't fall for anything.

Lord, my prayer is to guide me on this journey to finding myself, to finding the little girl who used to sing and play. Help me find the young lady who lost her way through sex and sin. Help the grown woman who lost her vision along her journey of life. Help, Lord…Help me find myself.

Chapter 4

MY JOURNEY TO FINDING ME

The alarm clock went off, flashing ten o'clock.

I had overslept.

I did not want to go into the office today. Monday was not my best day out of the week, but all the drama that took place over the weekend didn't make it any better.

I called into my office to see if Sherry had made it into work, but she had called in as well. I needed her. I had not missed a day of work in a long time. I wanted her to cover for me today, but she was not in. I could not believe that Sherry was still taking off days off from work; she should be over this guy by now. I dragged myself out of bed and put on my clothes. I was late, but I needed to go in. I made it in the office, and there was a vase full of roses at my desk and a card.

Brandon was so sweet. This was so special to me—roses on a day when I really needed them. I picked up my phone and called Bran to thank him. "This is Mr. Gains."

"Hello, Mr. Gains, you have just made my day!"

There was a pause. "What are you talking about?"

I thought maybe he was trying to trick me by pretending that he did not know about the roses. "Okay, Brandon, stop playing. I want to thank you for the roses that you sent me."

Brandon got quiet. He said, "Sweetheart, that must be from a client because I did not send you roses."

"Oh yeah, I didn't read the card. I just assumed you sent them," I said, trying to figure out who sent me the roses. I started to think real hard about who could have sent them. "Well, baby, you sound real good today. Don't overwork yourself. Make sure to talk with Sherry. She is getting paid to help you; she is your assistant." Brandon was right. I needed her to help me with this workload where I was starting to fall behind.

I told Brandon that I would talk to her. I got off the phone with Brandon and read the oversized card that was attached to the vase of roses:

Ms. Kennedy, I am so sorry that I destroyed such a friendship like ours. I really never could have been the real man you needed.

I was too busy being scared of you. Yeah, I said scared of you. Too insecure to pursue you for what you are worth, so I remained your friend for all these years wishing that I could be that man in your life. I thought that a beautiful woman like you would get bored with me and maybe leave me or cheat on me. I stereotyped you. I knew you were a good woman, but I felt like you were too good to be true. I kept you close to me because I wanted you in my life. I did not just want a part of you. I was wishing I could have all of you. I played it safe for all these years by being just your friend.

I knew I cheated myself by hooking up with a woman who reminded me of you in so many ways but she was lacking a lot of who you are and that was character strength. Her weakness made me feel like I was in control so I was not threatened by her at all so I asked her to marry me. I asked her to marry me for all the wrong reasons. One of the reasons was the fact that I knew I loved you. I was too blind to see that and was in too deep to get out of my relationship with her. Yeah, I am still a coward.

I can't bring myself to tell the truth to her, but I can tell the truth to you. I do love you, and that night was neither out of lust nor greed, but I loved you since we were both in our teens.

I know I might never see you again, but please forgive me if I have ruined you or your relationship. I know you love this man, and he will be a good man for you. Love you always. Take care. Love Jason.

I was shocked that Jason wrote that letter for me. I did not understand why would any man not marry for the right reason. I guess I should be thankful that he shared the real reason why he did not want to commit to me. I think being afraid to love someone who you are really supposed to love is crazy to me.

I looked up, and Sherry was standing in front of me with a bright smile and a three-carat diamond on her wedding finger. I was not happy to see her, so I could not really smile. "I know you must be real mad at me, Ms. Kennedy, but look I have been going through so much. I did not have anywhere to live for about four days now, and on top of that I am pregnant!" Sherry was begging for me to be happy for her. I could not stay mad at her for long.

I stood up and embraced her. "So what's up with the ring?" I said, hoping that her and that guy did not hook back up. Sherry smiled while she pushed back her light brown hair from her face. I knew that Sherry was going to tell me something. "Well, Ms. Kennedy, Jay-T and I are going to get married." I was astonished when she said what she said. "Well what about the other woman he was going to marry?" I asked while putting my card from the roses in my desk drawer. I did not want anyone to see the note.

"No, you got it wrong. He started dating this other girl, and he told me that he wanted to date her because he felt like he was in love with her," Sherry said. "I guess he found out that the grass is not always greener on the other side.

"I just hope that this is a blessing from God," I said, while Sherry stood there, still smiling like everything in her life that was bad had disappeared.

"Ms. Kennedy, he is a good man. Trust me," Sherry replied.

I was bothered by what Sherry said. I know she did not mean any harm in what she said. I just felt compelled to inform her about what I felt about all of this.

"Sherry, no disrespect, but I feel like so many of us women, especially black women, settle for less. We date out of need and not from a place of wholeness. I mean, just because you are now dating someone wealthy and he can afford to take you to the best restaurants, spend money on lavish trips, and shopping sprees does not make him a good man. It just makes him a wealthy man. My definition of a good man is someone who loves you no matter what, and he desires to spend time with you and only you. Now, I just don't want a good man, but I want a godly man! But so many of us women have defined a good man with wealth and status, but those same men that we claim and say they are good most of the time lack character and wisdom. But the sad thing is that these men are a shame before God!

These same men who give you what you want will cheat, beat us, lie to us, but hey we keep them and we marry them because they can take us on lavish trips, yachts, and buy us expensive gifts, but yet he secretly cheats on you with models and beats you behind closed doors! What a good man! Just because he is different from the last broke joker does not mean he is a good man!" I said. "My concern is, even if he is a good man, is that enough? Being a good man should be more than just living up to the image of a family guy or a rich guy! Maybe he is a hardworking man who knows how to love you and maybe he won't cheat, but is he a godly man! The Father leads godly men. Godly men are the head of the house, and if he is following the Father, then the woman should be following him! I wonder why we seek just a good man. Your idea of what a good man is will vary with every different woman! So it is not about having just a good man, you must seek a godly man! And trust me, a godly man is not just the ones going to church or behind a pulpit. It is his actions and his personal relationship with God, because those who claim to be Christian men can trick you too. A good man follows himself, and if he is following himself then the woman who he marries will follow him, and they both will be following themselves in the whole love walk called marriage to hell!"

I had ranted on and on about a good, godly man for at least ten minutes. Sherry was giving me a blank stare.

"I think that is dangerous to follow yourself and not follow the Creator." I looked up at Sherry and said, "You should always want to marry not just a good man but a godly man!"

Sherry face was red and flushed. I guess I lost it for a second.

"Yeah, you are right, Ms. Kennedy," Sherry said. She quickly agreed just to get me to shut up while looking up at the young man who was walking toward Sherry and me. This young man was very much breathtaking. Sherry and I both could not take our eyes off him.

"Hi, my name is Kevin Hanes, and I am applying for the assistant position that is open for a Ms. Kennedy."

I stood there with my mouth open wide. I knew I did not put out request to hire someone to replace Sherry. I liked Sherry. I really did not want to see her leave. I looked at Sherry, and Sherry looked at me.

"Okay, Ms. Kennedy, I am the one who posted an ad on the website for someone to replace me."

I did not know what to say. Sherry had been working for me for five years; I did not want her to just quit. I acted as if it did not bother me. "Okay, Kevin, may I see your resume?" I said, being very stern.

I looked over his resume and noticed that he had a master's degree in law. "Kevin, you are way too smart for this position. I mean, you have a law degree from Harvard."

"Yeah, that is right. I worked really hard for that degree, and I really would like to work for this company even if it means starting from the bottom and working my way to the top," Kevin said while placing his dark brown hands in his pocket. "Sherry, what do you think about this? Should I give him a try?"

Sherry smiled. "I really think he wants to work for you, Ms. Kennedy," she said. "This is what I am going to do. I will place you on a trial-based period while I do a background check. When that comes back, then I will call you no later than tomorrow. Because I am working on this account, and I really need some documents drawn up and notarized," I said while handing Kevin back his resume. "Yes, Ms. Kennedy, I will jump right on the job as soon as you call." Kevin walked out the office with the biggest Kool-Aid smile. I was upset with Sherry that she did not handle that in a professional way. I thought, *Today is really not my day.* I got up from my desk and paced the floor by the large office window. The sun shined and the day looked beautiful even though I felt horrible. I sat back down at my desk just trying to make sense of my life. Sherry walked toward me while I was sitting at my desk checking my emails. "I am so sorry… I can tell you're upset just by the way you just walked to your desk," she said, trying to get me to say something.

I felt like Sherry was being selfish this whole time she had been working for me, taking advantage of the fact that I was her friend and boss. "Sherry, look, you did not tell me how many days you were going to be out when your boyfriend left you," I said, hoping that the frown on my face did not give it away, but I needed to get the point across to her.

"You left me with a workload for this account. I have never had an account at POPC this big." They did not call this company platinum for nothing; we were dealing with million-dollar accounts! I was proud to have made it to the top of the top, to be the first one in this entire company to handle a billion-dollar account! I refused to let anybody mess this up!" Sherry just stood there looking at me, but she could not say anything because she knew I was right.

"Sherry, look, you really cost me to lose a lot of time, and you think going behind my back and placing an ad for someone to take your position was going to make up for it? I think not!" I yelled. "Look, just leave your badge and the company emergency credit card on my desk as you leave."

Sherry had tears in her eyes and slammed down her badge and her company credit card on my desk.

"Look, Ms. Kennedy, I am sorry; you are right." Sherry was looking for me to say that it was okay, but I keep reading my emails and pretended that she was not talking to me. I guess she got the message, because she headed for the elevator. I looked up and saw Brandon coming in with both hands full.

There was a vase full of red roses in his right hand, and he had a vase full of yellow roses in his left hand. I was so happy to see him!

I kissed him right on his cheek. "Thank you, Bran, just set them on my desk while I go to the bathroom before we go to lunch."

I did not stay too long in the bathroom. I was walking toward my desk, and Brandon was reading the card. Brandon must had saw the card while placing his card in my drawer

The card! My heart was in my stomach. I could not breathe. What should I do? I watched his smile turn inside out; he was angry for sure! Should I walk over to him and lie? No, I had to tell him the truth. So I walked slowly to my desk where Brandon was standing. Brandon was standing with both arms folded, and he had a frown on his face. I had never seen him turn this red, but I would be mad too if I found a love note from another woman.

"Brandon, can I explain. Let me tell you everything before you walk away," I said. Brandon did not even look up at me; he just stormed out of my sight. *Lord, I need you. Brandon was the only man who wanted me for me! I messed this up!*

All my life I wanted to have a godly man now that he was in my life, I ruined it. I wanted to go home, but I could not go home. I needed to finish up my work. I left the office to go to my coffee spot that I loved so much for lunch. When I walked in the coffee shop, I saw Brandon at the table alone drinking some coffee. I sat down at his table, and he looked at me as if I smelled.

"Brandon look… can we talk for just a second?" I said hoping that he would at least look at me.

"No, I just want you to leave me alone!" he said while leaving. I just wanted to at least tell him I was sorry.

My phone rang; it was my sister Lisa. "Hey, Lisa. Look, I've got to go call you later." I did not have time to talk to my sister because I was going through too much to hear my sister tell me about her cookie-cutter life. My life was a disaster. *Lord, I need you right now. Father, please forgive me.* I prayed to God to help me through this mess I caused. I walked out of that coffee shop and got in my car to go back to work.

Chapter 5

FAITH DURING THE STORM

******Three months later******

Darkness was all around me, and I could not see a thing. I stood there afraid of not being able to see. I was now running in my house trying to find a light switch, but I could not find one. *Lord! Lord, I yelled out! Help me!* I began to see the light shine in where I stood, but before I could see who, or what, was shining the light in my house, I woke up; it was just a dream.

I was sweating, so I needed a cold glass of water. I walked downstairs headed to my kitchen. I heard a noise outside. I was a little jittery from my dream, which was more like a nightmare, but the noise made me want to check out my backyard to make sure nobody was there. I only saw a cat from next door going through my bushes. I realized it was one in the morning it's been three months and no word from Brandon or anybody. I have been hiding from everyone in my family and from my friends at work. I have been avoiding seeing Brandon so I work from home now. Kevin has been handling most of my major meetings.

I did hire Kevin. I really trust him. Kevin was always on time and plus he was a very good businessman. I had lost my zeal for my job. I was lonely and hurt. Brandon was the type of husband that I wanted, the man who could love me spiritually, mentally, and physically. I was the Jezebel who lost my man because of my filthy cheating. Brandon never would let me explain; he just walked away with my heart. Brandon and I had just officially put a title on our relationship right before Jason brought up old feelings that I thought were long gone. I do believe it is best to spend time alone to clear out old feelings from old lovers so you could be more prepared to date someone new without having a question in your mind about someone else.

I went back to bed. I started to think about my dream. I was in my home walking around in the dark feeling so scared. In my dream, somebody had shined a bright light down on me, and I felt safe. I know that the dream was trying to tell me that God was going to shine a light in the darkness in my life. The sun shined really bright in my room on this Thursday morning. I could feel God's love all around me. This was going to be the day that God's light shone in my darkness.

I brushed my wet hair from my shower. While I began to blow dry my hair, my cell phone lit up. I did not want to stop because I hate to have wet hair. When I glanced at the phone, it was Brandon.

"OMG!" I said out loud. My hands were shaking because I was nervous. My phone kept ringing. I guess Brandon really wanted to talk to me. I picked up the phone with my hair half wet and curly hair and the other half straight and dry. I picked up the phone. "Hello, Bran… oh I mean, Brandon." I was acting like a teenager; my voice was even trembling.

"Yeah look, we need to talk. Can I come over?"

I was so scared. I really wanted to see him. I wanted him to tell me he loved me. I wondered if God answered my prayer. Was Brandon coming back in my life? "Brandon, I don't mind, you can come over Friday morning," I said, hoping that he would say yes.

"Look, London, I am going to come about seven am sharp is that okay?" "Brandon, I just want to see you….I really miss you."

"London, I have a lot to tell you, and I don't really want to talk to you on the phone. Take care, and I will see you on Friday morning," he said while politely getting off the phone.

Oh Lord, I prayed, *thank you for showing me that it is not about people, but it is about Jesus being the center of my life!* For these past three months, I had been working at home, but most of all my time was praying. I had been praying and worshiping God and loving every moment I spent with Jesus. I could not believe that the last time Brandon and I were together was July. We had spent that whole month getting to know each other until I had to mess things up with Jason. I knew I could not go back and change what I had done.

I had to get ready to leave for work. This was my first day back at the job officially, besides me dropping in and out for these last months. My phone was ringing and ringing while I was in at my desk. I had a good day at work and nothing was going to take my joy. I answered the phone, and it was Sherry. "Hey, girl, what's up, Sherry?" I said.

"I miss you so much, Ms. Kennedy."

"Sherry, don't call me Ms. Kennedy. You can call me London remember? You are not at work."

Sherry started to laugh. "London, I am just so used to calling you by your last name. So, London, what's been up with you and Brandon?"

I wanted to keep my personal business private. I knew Sherry shared a lot of her business to me, but it did not mean I wanted to share my personal life story with her. "Well so far, we are just cool," I said, hoping that she would be satisfied with my answer. Sherry and I began to catch up on old times, and she told me how her marriage was turning out great! Sherry and I said goodbye. It was good to know everything was working out for her. I sometimes wondered how some people who were not true Christians seemed to have everything all worked out in their favor. I guess sometimes you really never know the truth about a person's life unless you lived with them. People will hide the truth, just like how I was hiding the truth from her. I refused to tell Sherry that Brandon and I broke up over me cheating on him and messing up my relationship. Nevertheless, my first day back to work felt so good. I had been busy all day. It felt good to be back in action.

Everybody welcomed me back with open arms. Mr. King Wallace was back at his old tricks staring at my goodies when he was speaking. "Mr. Wallace, my eyes are up here, not down here," I wanted to say but did not waste my breath on trying to school this old man on manners.

I quickly dismissed him with a yeah and an okay. Less is always better when talking to Mr. Wallace. I was leaving my office, and I saw Brandon and Mandy. They were hugging. My heart elevated, my ears got warm, and my hands started to sweat. I was not feeling so well. I stepped on the elevator, and before the door closed, the lady who won my Brandon's heart was racing to get on the elevator with me.

I glanced at her for about a second, and she looked me up and down. Miss Southern Belle was not so friendly like she pretended to be. The door on the elevator closed, and we both were standing side by side: the two women who were competing for the same man.

I think she had won Brandon's heart already now that I had failed to stand up to show him that I was the right woman. But who was I kidding? Bran knew Miss Southern Belle longer than he had known me.

"Hello, I see you made it back to work," Mandy said in a dry tone. While looking at me with my faded complexion and my low-maintenance hairstyle that was pulled back in a simple ponytail, with my long, thick, curly locks that were bouncing and frizzy because I had not been to the hair salon in a while and my manicure was also long overdue.

Mandy was brave enough to say something about me. "I cannot believe you would even leave your home to come to work with non-manicured nails, and your hair used to be shinny and straight, the look of a diva… what happened to you, girl? He heeee…" she said with a chuckle. Mandy was the same old Mandy. She was pretty, but her shoes were flats, and they were cheaply made, and her dress was a light blue baby doll dress with a floral print. The dress looked to have been from the local fashion shop. I bet she paid no more than eight dollars for that outfit. "Well, Mandy, I am glad you noticed that I don't always look this way," I said, gazing in her fiery eyes. "I am just giving my diva wardrobe a rest. I mean, I am still wearing a Vera Wang blouse and skirt. I cannot leave out my two thousand-dollar pair of red bottom Christian Louboutin shoes, which I bought them on sale. Girl, you know you can't get those shoes for two thousand unless they were on sale!" I said in a bragging tone. We both were acting like two high school teenagers on the elevator. I wanted to be just as mean as she was being. I love nice things but I am not the type of person to brag. Mandy and I both stepped off the elevator to the parking lot.

Mandy was looking very frustrated. "London, you know now that I am pregnant, those labels won't do me any good, girl."

What did she mean pregnant?

"Look, Mandy, I have not done anything to you, so what is your problem?" I said. "Okay, you want to know," Mandy said as she walked up close to me, so close that our noses almost touched. "I don't like women like you! You think you can have what you want just because of your fancy clothes and your high-paying job!" Mandy's face was no longer the sweet, innocent southern girl; she was bold and mad enough to tell me how she truly felt.

"I never liked you," Mandy kept going on, telling me different reasons why she hated my guts.

"Mandy! I don't care about what you think of me. The bottom line is, you don't like me because of Brandon!"

Mandy gave me a smirk, standing, holding her knock-off version of Gucci purse in her hands and her keys. She began to walk toward her car as if she finally was tired of the shenanigans.

Mandy yelled while getting in her car, "My baby is Brandon's! And yes, you're right, I don't like you because of Brandon!"

Mandy drove off in a hurry. I could not believe this was happening. Brandon and Mandy sharing a baby together, what? Maybe that was why Brandon wanted to come over to my house on Friday to talk to me about the baby. No, this could not be. Bran was practicing celibacy. But hey, I was too and still failed to keep my Christian standards.

What is going on with us Christians? We say we love Jesus, but as soon as we are tested with that right person, we forget to whom we belong.

I got in my car and drove down the freeway listening to the sounds on the radio. I kept seeing her in my head over and over again. Mandy's true side showed up in the worst way.

I just needed to step aside and let them have their family—the family that I wanted so badly. The sun was setting, and I wanted that gusto I had that morning, but my joy was taken. I finally made it home after the long traffic jam on the busy freeway in Dallas. I saw on my home phone that my Mom had called me.

"Hey, Mom, how are you?" I said after calling her. I enjoyed hearing my mother's voice; it had been about three months since we really had a long conversation. Lately we only talked to check in on each other, and I would find any excuse to make the conversation short.

"Well, London, I have been worried about you," she said while Dan was in the background barking. My Dad and Mom love that dog so much. I think that Dan the dog thought he was human.

"Mom, you don't need to worry. I am fine, just been working," I blurted out.

"Well, I know we talked the other day, and you told me everything about your job, but what about this new guy you were dating?" Momma said.

"Well, Mom …I am just friends with him right now. We needed some space to sort out some things," I said, hoping that was good enough information.

"Well, baby, I want to know everything. What happened? I mean, did you do anything to make this young man pull back?"

She is pushing me, I thought. I wanted my mother to ask me other questions, but instead she wanted to know more about my love life. No matter how much I wanted to change the subject, I realized one reason why I was not so close to her was because I never liked to open up to her. So I tried to trust my Mom and hope she would not turn this into an argument. "Well, Mom, I did, I made this bad choice to hook up with Jason while starting a relationship with Brandon."

My Mom was quiet on the other end. "Did you pray about this?" she said in a gentle voice.

"Yes, I did and God began to heal me over issues that I thought I was over like my real father not being in my life," I said.

I was remembering the moment of finding out that my Dad was really not my Dad. I felt like a part of me was missing.

"As long as you prayed, trust me, God will send the right one in your life no matter if you think everything is all wrong." My Mom began to laugh; she knew that to be true because she was not a stranger to making mistakes and things not going right. But God turned her life around. If he could do that for my Mom, then he could do it for me. My Mom made me feel good, but the truth was she did not know the whole story.

"Mom, thanks for your advice," I said while fixing a warm bubble bath.

"Well I am going to let you go for tonight. Your father has dinner plans at Houston restaurant." My Mom's voice was smooth, and she sounded happy and not worried. "Mom, what happened? You sound so happy and refreshed."

"It is because of your advice. You told me I needed healing and to release pain and hurt from my life," she said with excitement "So I called a Christian counselor and that is my way to release everything."

"Mom, I am happy for you. Tell Daddy I will make a visit soon. I know Thanksgiving is coming up in three weeks plus Christmas is around the corner, so I will try and plan a shopping date with you. Have a good night with the love of your life," I said, while Mom started giggling.

"Of course I will, hun, I am praying for you that God will bring the man who is after God's heart."

We both hung up, and Mom actually made me laugh and feel special. *Thank you, God, for my family.* I thought to myself how God would send a word at a time when you need it the most. I undressed and soaked in the warm bath; my Jacuzzi tub was such a great amenity to have. The bubbles from the bath water covered my body. But in this moment the bath made me think of joy, renewal, and regrouping.

Yes, that is what God is doing—giving me joy even in the midst of confusion. God was renewing me and regrouping my life. I lay there in that tub relaxing until I thought of Mandy and Brandon. I dried off while I noticed my house was silent, so silent I could hear every creak and crack. I slipped on my soft cotton pjs and decided to roll my hair. I had neglected myself, so it was time to regroup.

Chapter 6

TRUSTING GOD

I had no real dinner plans, but a large hamburger pizza was sitting on my nightstand half eaten. I had cuddled up in my bed hugging my soft comforter watching a movie. If it was not for my mother, I would have not felt so uplifted.

My eyelids were getting heavy, and I could not fight it any longer. The sound of a cooking show woke me up. I realized I had been sleep for about five hours; it was one o'clock am. I went downstairs to put the remaining slices of my pizza in the refrigerator. I had made it to my soft, warm bed. I lay down and could not go back to sleep.

I thought about Brandon and how he was always excited about helping others reach their purpose. Brandon would touch me with purity; he never tried to sleep with me. Brandon was truly a real man of God. So I wondered what happened with Mandy. Did he really fall in her love trap? I noticed my bed vibrating and realized it was my cell phone. I think it is very disrespectful when there are calls after midnight unless it is an emergency.

I checked the phone; it was Brandon. "Yes, what is wrong?"

"I could not sleep. I kept trying to debate on calling you at this time because this is not a decent hour. But I found out late last night about what happened at work today in the staff parking lot between you and Mandy. I could not wait. Is it okay if we talk? Sorry that I woke you."

"You did not wake me I just woke up and could not go back to sleep," I said with warmth in my voice to let him know that I did not mind. Brandon started off with small talk and then he mentioned Mandy. "Look, there's a lot to say. Mandy and I began to hang out more when you and I broke up," he said while clearing his throat. "I was so hurt about the card that I read, I started to imagine so many things about you. London, it sent me in a frenzy." When Brandon said that, I felt his pain.

"I understand, but you never let me explain to you," I said, trying to at least redeem myself.

"I knew you must have slept with this guy, and I felt so angry; it was best for me to stay away from you, not because

I wanted to hurt you but because I wanted you to show me this self-centered guy who used you so I could beat his you know what! I realize hanging with Mandy was not a very good idea."

Brandon kept talking. I still remained quiet; my heart beating began this steady pace because I did not know what he was going to say next.

"Mandy and I had dinner at her place; it was getting late, and she keep offering me too many wine glasses, and I did not realize that I was a little buzzed. I know what you might be thinking that I can't blame it on wine." Before I could say anything in response, he quickly spoke again.

"I am taking full responsibility for that night." Brandon was trying to convince me in so many ways that this moment he shared with Mandy should have never happened. I knew he was going to tell me more, things that I didn't want to hear.

I wanted to disconnect, but I knew the truth needed to be said. I could hear my mother's voice and her words telling me that God can heal anything.

I was nervous again; it was the same feeling I got when I saw him and Mandy hugging when she was at our job.

"Mandy and I slept together, and she—"

"Wait, I cannot hear any more. Look, just you and her have a great life together and raise your baby together!" I yelled.

"London wait calm down, let me finish," he said.

"Okay, I am sorry, go ahead," I said while tears rolled down my face and my voice trembled.

"London, please don't cry, listen," he said as if he could see me through the cell phone. Brandon finally revealed that Mandy and him had sex, and Mandy confessed that she loved him.

"London I am so sorry. I understood how you felt," he said, looking for some sympathy.

"Two wrongs don't make a right," I said.

"Well, I thought it made sense that Mandy and I had been friends for a long time maybe she could be the one," Brandon said, but he quickly spoke again. "I realize that I did not love her, and I told her it was not going to work because I was in love with London."

Brandon lowered his voice and said, "London, I love you. I know that you are supposed to be in my life. God has a plan for you and me. Look, trust me, I don't think I am the father. I used protection, and she told me that it could be a possibility that the baby was somebody else's."

"Brandon, I don't know what to say. The fact remains that you could be the father," I said while taking a sip of my water. Brandon and I had been talking for an hour now. I was getting sleepy.

"London, please can you give us another chance," he said with hope in his voice. I wanted to say yes, but what if what we had done outside the young relationship was just a sign that we are not ready. I needed to pray.

"Well, Brandon, I know I love you, and I think maybe we both did too much to just pick up from where we left off," I said. Before I could say another word, Brandon blurted out, "Don't give up on us now! Maybe God is trying to tell us to heal first."

"At least let's just start over with being friends," I said, thinking that was a good idea.

"I want you to pray about this, and yes I would like that only in hopes of a relationship," Brandon said with confidence.

"Okay, Brandon, so we will see each other after work," I said, giggling because it was about two o'clock am.

"I have a better idea. Are you down?" Brandon said with a small chuckle of laughter in his voice.

"I don't know yet. Down for what?" I said, wondering what kind of plan he had in mind.

"Down to skip work and have breakfast together then go to the park for lunch and then have dinner at Houston's."

"Brandon, you have a breakfast, lunch, and dinner date plan. Sounds great," I said. I had butterflies in my belly. This was joy that I was feeling; I could get used to this. We said our goodbyes, and he said he would call me around nine in the morning.

I lay down to at least catch up on some sleep before nine in the morning. The sunlight graced my face with a welcoming, warm touch. I rolled over in my bed and grabbed my pillow to block the sunlight to try and fall back to sleep. The buzz from my cell was alerting me to get up. My body did not want to roll out from under these nice, soft covers. I looked at the phone; it was Lisa. "Hey, sis," I said, my voice still cracking and breaking, trying to search for my normal tone.

"Where have you been? I have not been able to talk to you," Lisa said.

"Lisa, just so much has happened, and I did not want to tell you about all my crazy drama when you and Tony were expecting!"

"Well, sister, we are having a girl and more great news!" Lisa said while her voice sounded perky and alert.

"Okay, tell me!"

"Well, London, Tony and I want to relocate and move the business to Dallas."

I was so happy because I missed not having my sister. "Yeah, sis, I am happy and cannot wait. What are your plans?"

"Well, Tony and I we will be visiting for Christmas, and that will give us about a week to stay and search for place to live, and then I am going to visit doctors that my doctor recommended to start assisting me for delivery in Dallas."

"Does Mom know about this?" I asked.

"Yes, I told her a week ago, and I told her to keep it a secret from you," Lisa said while laughing. I could tell my little sister was so happy. "So, London, what is new?" Lisa said, sounding curious.

"Well, Jason came down about three months ago, and he came over we talked and then we did some things that should have never happened!" I said, feeling the same guilt all over.

"London, wait you and Jason hooked up! No, no get out of here!"

"I let my emotions and feelings and flesh blind me from the fact that I loved Brandon." I really did not want to tell Lisa all of this. But I needed to confide in someone that I trust.

"Brandon, the guy you always talked about from your job?" Lisa asked, trying to put the pieces together.

"Yes, well, Brandon and I started talking after we went on a date, and we began to really like each other. Lisa, it was like being with someone who gets you. Brandon treated me with gentleness, and he loved helping others." Talking about him reminded me that I needed to be getting dressed for my breakfast date.

"So, Brandon and you started dating and getting to know each other. Than Jason comes down to visit you at your house?"

"Lisa, yeah I know, I should have met him at a restaurant or somewhere public since it was at night," I said, feeling convicted.

"London, you let your guard down and hopefully you learned your lesson."

"I did, trust me...after Brandon found the note that Jason sent with roses to my job, based on what the letter said Brandon realized I had been involved with a man that night... the same night when I told him I had a lot of work to do," I said to Lisa, just remembering how horrible I felt during that time.

"See, London, lies will not get you far. It only gives the devil opportunity to come in and take over. But we serve a good God. Pray and God will turn it all around for you, sis," Lisa said while she began to share her moment in her life that did not go so well. "My relationship is not perfect. Trust me! Tony and I started off kind of rocky too, but let's not go there."

I was hoping she would be more transparent then that, but at least she was willing to admit things were not all perfect.

"Girl, we are talking about your drama," Lisa said while dishing out a laugh.

"Lisa, what if I told you that Brandon ran into another woman's arms because of the break up and slept with this woman and now she is pregnant and the baby might be his."

"What?" Lisa said, trying to get a word in.

"Lisa, just listen. Brandon and I only started dating for only one or two weeks then the day he and I made it official was the day Jason arrived and I messed up," I said without elaborating on details.

"Brandon had this friend Mandy who knew him since college, but they had only been just friends. You could clearly tell that she liked him more. Well this was the lady he goes and cries on her shoulder while she gives him wine and then for him it led to having sex. But Lisa, he said that he used protection and doesn't really believe that baby is his. He thinks she is only doing this because right after their sex he told her he did not want a relationship because he was in love with me."

"London! Please! Do you really believe him? Didn't Jason do you the same way? Sleep with you and send some card in your roses making up some dumb excuse why he did not want to stay in some kind of relationship with you?" Lisa sounded very furious with the shenanigans that us grown people were involved in.

"Look, London, Brandon should have known that this girl liked him, but then as soon as he felt like he was dissed by you, he runs into her bedroom after being friends with her for all these years?"

"I do not think that Brandon planned to sleep with Mandy. I believe he let his guard down," I said. Maybe I was taking up for Brandon, wanting to believe his story. "Jason and I did the same thing, so I can't judge Brandon," I replied.

Lisa paused. I could hear her take a deep breath. "Lisa, just listen to what I am saying. Because I did the same thing, the situation was the same. I had been friends with Jason, and I had never slept with him until that night in my apartment. If I could just erase the memories."

"Girl, that is true… wow you and him both broke your values before God and cheated on each other in the same way. That devil got you both outside of the will of God to keep you guys from trusting the Lord and allowing God to be the center of your relationship." Lisa was preaching to me now!

"Look, London, you both will need to give up your flesh, meaning your lust and greed, in order to please God with a God-fearing relationship," Lisa said while chomping on the phone, eating. "It only points out that you both had to hit the bottom hard, and if you can forgive through all of this, then you really do love each other."

Lisa had made a very good point. I told my sister everything, and I felt free in some way to share my failures instead of masking the truth. It is something powerful when you dance in the truth that really will set you free!

"Well, Lisa, thank you for your advice. I am meeting Brandon for breakfast this morning," I said.

"That sounds great. Make sure that you guys watch the time because you and Brandon should not be alone because both of you already have proven that being alone at late hours is not a great idea. So set your boundaries and stay strong."

"Just so you know, we have been separated for about three months now, and I have gone through the process of healing, and I fasted and prayed. But, you are so right… no matter how saved you may think you are, you can still get caught up in someone's bed," I said.

"Yes! Sis, that is what a real true conviction would do; it will send you on your face before God and allow you to see things from a realistic point of view. Look, let me go before Tony get jealous of me spending too much time on this phone, girl!" Lisa said, laughing .

I noticed it was 8:45 in the morning, and I was running around my room trying to make a choice on what to wear. I found this knee-length peach sweater dress that hugged my shape and put on my black flat designer boots. I took the rollers out of my hair and let the bouncy curls just fall down while I finger-combed my hair. I could not leave without putting on my makeup. Brandon was here. I could hear my doorbell buzz while I grabbed my cell and purse. I quickly picked up and sprayed my favorite perfume that lingered in the air.

I closed my front door behind me as I walked out to his car. Brandon was wearing a black sweater and black jeans; he was handsome just like the last time I saw him, only this time I was in his arms.

"You always look like a diva, girl!" he said while hugging me while we stood in front of his car door. He was such a gentleman.

"Thank you, Brandon," I said, smiling. He released me from the hug and placed his hand on my hand and said, "Look me in the eye."

I looked up at his brown eyes. Brandon wanted to tell me something. I was hoping he was not going to pop the big question so soon! It was too early in the game to say yes.

But he did not… He simply held my hand and gave it a squeeze, smelling his manly, strong cologne that somehow intertwined with my perfume. Brandon was telling me that he had made an oath to put God first and never give his body to anyone but his future wife.

"London, are you listening?" he said while kissing my cheek.

"Yes, I promise that I will put God first no matter what!" I said. Brandon grabbed me and began to laugh. "Let's go, girl," he said while opening the passenger door, and I jumped in his Infiniti. Brandon's vehicle had nice, black, soft leather seats, and he had the new car smell. I sat back and tried to forget that Mandy could be giving Brandon his first child.

I wondered if I would always feel like Mandy was the chosen one, the first one having his first baby, and he would always be grateful for her. I thought to myself, *Can I handle this?* I pushed those thoughts out of my mind only to focus on Brandon and me. Brandon arrived uptown, and he took me to this organic restaurant called The Belgians that served fresh vegetables and fruits, club sandwiches, fresh soup and their favorite breakfast food. I sat down at the small table for two. I could hear the chatter of conversation and laughter that was coming from each table.

I enjoyed staring at the small babies sitting in their high chairs sucking on their scrambled eggs while their parents tried to keep their small, chubby fingers from rubbing all over the table because of germs. I saw the mothers pulling out germ guard wipes to wipe off the tables and their little hands. The smell of waffles and toast and fried chicken, bacon, and coffee filled the restaurant.

The waitress handed us a menu.

"Thank you," I said.

"Would you like a cup of coffee or water?" she asked, while we both scanned through the menu to order something great and delicious.

I knew Brandon was a godly man, but even men of God will drop the ball. That is why Pastor Jeff always preached, saying don't put your trust in man but in God.

The sunlight beamed in the restaurant like a ray of happiness sent by God. The waitress brought cups of hot chocolate with whipped cream.

We both ordered, and she took our menus. "The weather has been great this morning," I said, taking a sip of my hot chocolate. Brandon agreed while he sipped his hot chocolate.

"I am so happy to be here with you," he said while reaching across the table to hold my hand, only to be interrupted by a phone call. Brandon asked to be excused; because of the clinking and the loud chatter he could not hear.

I wondered who that could be. The waitress came back with our breakfast. She sat my homemade pancakes with strawberries and bananas topped with powdered sugar on the table. Brandon had a platter with crispy chicken wings and thick homemade waffles with powdered sugar.

Brandon sat back down at the table with a weird look on his face.

"Is everything okay?" I asked.

"I just got a phone call from Mandy asking me why I was not at the office, so I told her I was out with you. I tell you, she told me off and hung up."

I could only imagine how she is going to treat me throughout this relationship, I thought to myself. "Are you kidding me? What is up with her lately with this mean streak? I thought she was a very nice lady."

Brandon took a big bite out of his waffles and poured extra hot syrup on his waffles. "Look, London, she was nice, but since she's been pregnant she has turned into this monster," Brandon said while filling his mouth again with another bite of tasty waffles. I felt like I was talking to Brandon about his pregnant wife or girlfriend. *Monster is an understatement,* I thought. I was jealous because he knew her in a way that he did not know me. I ate my tasty pancakes and sipped on my hot chocolate. "I told her that if I am the father, we will be only friends because I am not in love with her," Brandon said with a bit of frustration in his voice. "I want to be with you; she knows this."

I looked up at Brandon. He could tell I was bothered; that's why he felt the need to reassure me. That's why I cared for this man.

"I have to meet her at the hospital for the results," Brandon said.

"What, so soon?"

"Yes, about three weeks ago they took my DNA."

"So that's why she called you?"

"Yes, also to threaten me and talk crazy." He chuckled.

"Well I want to go too," I said, wiping my hands off.

"Waiter, check please," Brandon said, motioning for the young, blonde waiter to come to our table.

"You sure you want to come?" he said with a weird look on his face.

"Yes, I want to hear this for myself."

Brandon looked confused or worried. "I don't think it would be right to bring you; it might make Mandy upset," he said without thinking. I looked up at Brandon and had the flash from the future. I could see him trying to protect Mandy's feelings for the rest of her life as long as she was apart of his life. My ears were hot; I was mad. So mad I felt like if I opened my mouth, fire would come out.

"Okay, look, you are right. It is not my baby. What does this have to do with me?" I stood up from my seat, gave a crooked smile, then grinned and picked up my purse and headed out the restaurant door for some fresh air. I was walking so fast that Brandon had to skip to catch up with me. He grabbed my arm and slightly pulled me back. The light breeze covered us.

"Hey, I am so sorry. I am being selfish by not realizing you are a part of this, especially if you are going to be in my life," Brandon said, looking in my eyes with this blank stare, hoping that I could understand him.

I was silent; I could not speak I was so mad. I could not believe after hurting Brandon with my dumb actions by sleeping with Jason that it would have such a chain reaction that would hurt me and remind me of what I don't have and that is kids and a family of my own. I got in Brandon's car and realized that I still had not said anything.

Brandon turned to me again. "London, I am taking you to the hospital with me. No more protecting anyone. Let's deal with all of the issues together if that is that okay." Brandon knew how to say the right things at the right time.

"Yes, that's fine," I said in a whisper. Brandon patted my hand and drove off to the hospital. The expression on Mandy's face when she saw me coming in with Brandon was priceless. "Hello, doctor, how are you doing?"

"I am doing well," the doctor said. The doctor greeted me and directed us all to the back office. We all took a seat in the brown leather chairs while the doctor sat behind his desk.

"Okay, so who are you?" The doctor asked.

Brandon said, "This is my girlfriend, London."

The doctor look puzzled. "Okay, well as long as we are all family here, that is fine with me to share the results unless Mandy is not comfortable."

"Doctor Robertson, go ahead and read the results. There are no secrets," Mandy

said without a care in her voice; she sounded like she knew that the results were going to be in her favor. "Brandon, look, I just want you to be a good father that's all I want," Mandy said.

"I don't think you will have a problem," he said.

My heart was pounding. I did not know how I was going to react. The doctor opened the envelope, and Brandon held my hands tight. "I think no matter what the results are, I knew everything would work out for the best.

"Congratulations, you are the father, plus Mandy is about fourteen weeks and is in her second trimester!" The doctor said he could not tell the sex yet.

Brandon looked very sad and happy at the same time. I stood up and felt tears fill my eyes. I did not want Mandy to see.

I gave Brandon a hug and whispered in his ears, "It will be all right." Brandon kissed me on my cheek and gave me a half smile. He then turned to the woman who was carrying his child.

Brandon walked up and gave her a hug. Mandy looked surprised, but she looked up at me and gave me the sneakiest grin. She then softly told him, "Thank you for supporting me even if this was not what you wanted."

Brandon let Mandy go from his embrace and held me closer—so close that I could feel his heart beat fast. "Wow, London, I am going to be a Dad," he said as if he won the lottery. I smiled. We all left out the office, and Brandon and I waited in the lobby for Mandy.

I told Brandon about how Mandy treated me at the job and how if I was going to be in this relationship with him, he needed to tell her not to treat me like that.

Brandon agreed. "Mandy, I think we need to talk about boundaries."

"Oh really, you and Miss Kennedy want to talk about boundaries? What do you know about that?" she said as she gave me an evil look.

Brandon saw how she was looking at me up and down while she was talking. Brandon was upset. "Mandy, look, stop talking to London crazy and know that even though you may be carrying my child, this is the lady who is in my life, and I love her."

I was so happy that Brandon spoke up on my behalf.

"Fine," Mandy said, laughing. "Brandon, there will be no need for me to deal with her. I only need to deal with you. London is not your wife yet." Mandy said.

"Look, Mandy, what is wrong with you? Why are you acting like this? Yes, true we had sex, but for the last three years you have always known I had a crush on London before London and I hooked up!" Brandon said while raising his voice. "Brandon, look, let's go. People are staring," I said as I grabbed his hands and went toward the hospital exit door.

"Yes, Brandon, all that time of hearing how successful she is and pretty. She is, but you had a real woman in front of you!" Mandy yelled while we left the hospital room.

"I Swear she planned this," Brandon said. "She caught me at a vulnerable time and I kept drinking that wine. I don't drink, so I was drunk, and I can't even remember having sex, just her kissing me. I was knocked out. I would have never dishonored my vow with God if only I had not gotten drunk!" Brandon shouted then broke into tears and began to mutter under his breath.

I could see the picture clearer now based on what Mandy said, and Brandon's story sounded like Mandy trapped Brandon.

But could Brandon even prove that his best friend, that is a woman, trapped him? I think many would laugh. It may not be true, but it was my theory. I thought about it, but I pushed it all out of my mind.

There are so many women who have tricked men in that way, and I believe Brandon was one of those men. Brandon and I left the hospital.

We returned to my place around 4:00 p.m. Brandon stretched out on my sofa, and the next thing you know he was knocked out. I guess he was so tired from the wait and excitement from today! I looked at the man whom I also had a crush on for three years. I had finally made it into his heart but not on my terms, not in the way I wanted. This was not how I pictured this. I went into my kitchen to see what to cook in my refrigerator.

I prepared two baked lamb chops with a seasoning of rosemary; red chopped onions smothered in gravy, and red potatoes and seasoned them with garlic salt and black pepper. I add a fresh garden salad. You could smell all the different aromas of food that filled the whole house. I could see Brandon being awakened by the delicious smells. Brandon sat up from his thirty-minute nap. "I see you in here cooking, London," Brandon said while making his way behind me, wrapping his arms around my waist while I was stirring in my pot with my smothered lamb chops.

Brandon kissed me on my neck, and I turned around and kissed him softly on his lips. I slowly wrapped my arms around his neck, and we both began to kiss each other, our bodies harmonizing to a slow rhythm. I had to remember what my sister Lisa said about boundaries, but before I knew it Brandon pulled back with a smile. "I am going to your bathroom to freshen up for dinner, okay," he said.

"Yes, baby, do that. I am fixing your plate now."

I was never afraid to whip up a super meal! I popped the already baked dinner rolls in the microwave so they could be soft and warm. The table was set for two, and I turned the surround sound to the soft sound of smooth jazz; the saxophone was playing slow, harmonizing with the soft beat of the drum.

The music filled the atmosphere, relaxing every nerve in my body that was tense. Brandon sat at the table with me. "Wow. You really surprised me," he said, smiling from ear to ear.

"Why would you say that? I asked knowing what he was about to tell me.

"I thought you were high maintenance and cooking was not your thing until you cooked for me that time I asked you out," he said. His smile faded just like mine because we both were reminded how I let us both down.

Brandon broke the silence by saying he loved my food. We both started to talk about the past when we both were kids and sharing funny stories and sad ones like when we lost grandparents. The conversation helped us both move in closer than we were before. I had learned that God had created Brandon just for me. I really believed he was my soul mate. Nevertheless, I had some more growing up in God to do. After dinner we both cleaned and washed dishes as if we were married. I knew that this night was going to end early, but a part of me wanted this night to never end.

Brandon and I lay on the soft floor rug together that was in my living room, and I had my photo album, showing him pictures of my family. "London, I just want to say today has been like a roller coaster. One minute we are frustrated, the next laughing out of control. I knew Mandy had been in my life to hinder me. She never really cared for me. She just likes my title, and I told my Dad the situation and he warned me about her. I thought he had her all wrong. But Mandy really showed her true colors after the fact. I think she wanted to get me drunk on purpose, but hey I am not going to go there. It happened, so I won't worry about it." He said.

"Brandon where does Mandy work?"

"Oh… she worked for that doctor. She is a receptionist for Doctor Robertson," Brandon said.

"I don't think Mandy is that stupid," he said without me saying a word. It was almost like Brandon could read my mind. We were connected. I said, "Well more like crazy! I think you need to plan your own paternity test somewhere else," I said while both of our cell phones started buzzing. I ignored my call because it was my office calling and that could wait. No more being the workaholic trying to win over an account. Brandon's facial expression went from a happy man to a confused one. I could bet money Mandy was calling again. "Babe, I am going to take this in the den if that's oaky," Brandon said. Part of me wanted to tell Brandon no!

I didn't say a word; I just nodded my head, and Brandon gave me a quick smile. He had returned after five minutes. I was watching the old comedy that sent me into a laughing spell.

"What's so funny?" Brandon asked while falling back down on the nice, soft rug. We both were side by side, and he had his arm around my waist. I closed my eyes while we both engaged in the sweetest kiss. That kiss took my wondering thoughts and cast them in the abyss. I sat up and wanted to know how this was going to work out, but I kept silent and did not want to ruin the mood,

"Brandon, you are a great kisser."

When Brandon kissed me, we never kissed in a perverted way. We just kept our lips closed so we could feel the soft touch, of each other's lips. I did not really know the rules on what you should not do in a Christian relationship, because all I do know is not to have sex or anything that could lead you in the sheets. We would put God first. We both were learning.

"Thank you, but let's change the subject."

"Okay, I am still trying to do this celibacy thing." I chuckled a little. I had forgotten that Brandon had to control his desires just like any other man.

"Okay, Brandon, let's play checkers." I pulled out the checker game from under my couch, and Brandon bragged about how he was the champ and was good at the game. "Don't be mad when I beat you!" he said, sounding so confident.

"Okay, but for the record I always win!" I shouted.

I leaned in to set the game up only to see Brandon cell phone light up. Mandy's name appeared. Brandon ignored the call and began to play checkers as if nothing happened. "Brandon, she is calling you again." I could not help but mention it. Brandon said, "Yeah, Mandy has been calling me all day." I had given Brandon this look on my face then blurted out, "Wow, Brandon, she is like a stalker!"

He glanced up at me with a peaceful expression. Then he said, "Let's not let her ruin our checker game. You are going down!" Brandon laughed while taking two of my checker pieces.

"Not fair at all!" I said, smiling from ear to ear. I still could not get Mandy out of my head. Something was not right with that woman!

I thought that dating God's way would be less drama and everything would be perfect. I realized that the only different from dating from the world was that both of us loved God even if we both made ungodly decisions in the past. We both wanted to let God lead us through our relationship and our individual walks with God.

Brandon and I both wanted to get back up from our failures and walk in the right way! Brandon wanted to start back going to my church, and he even talked about how God was leading him to join my church, Loving Temple.

I knew that the time was getting late, and we had played more than three games. Brandon began to laugh because he beat me at all the games. I looked at him and began to wonder how three years ago of having that crush could lead us to a relationship. Brandon looked at me with a stare as if he were thinking the same thing.

"I just want to say, thank you for giving this a chance…" Brandon began to move closer again. Brandon grabbed my hands and looked me right in my eyes. "London, I knew you were with that guy, but I should have never let that be the reason to push me to make the choice to run to Mandy." I could not believe he felt that way. I mean it was great hearing him take responsibility for his actions and not blame me. Brandon made me feel a little bit uncomfortable, because he made me have flashbacks of Jason's hands touching me and kissing me. I pulled my hands away because I needed my space. I felt weird that all of this was happening. I felt like this was done to split me in half on purpose.

Brandon frowned a little and gave me a smirk but didn't say much. I guess he could tell I was feeling weird. "I am sorry, Brandon, everything that has happened just seems crazy, but I know I can handle being in this relationship. God is working on me."

"London, you cannot keep pulling back from me because you are getting upset or frustrated," Brandon said calmly.

"London, if you can't deal with the results, then just tell me you want out…" I looked at him with a very uncertain look.

"I don't want out, I am in this, just give me some time. Everything just happened today!" I said, trying to prove to Brandon that I loved him while he released my hand. I was still on the floor thinking. I knew that I needed time to accept all of this.

Brandon stood up and grabbed his phone and grabbed my hand and lifted me up from the floor. "I know…you are right. You need time to deal with all of this," he said, looking at me with confidence. Brandon gave me a kiss on a cheek and told me good night. I nodded my head while giving him a kiss on his lips. Brandon wrapped his arms around me and gave me the biggest bear hug. I knew I would love his embrace and I thanked God for Brandon. "Well, Brandon, call me and I will see you soon." Brandon smiled and nodded, and he left. I washed my dishes and got ready for bed.

I had to read my Bible for some spiritual food. I began to read about King David. I learned how he was a king and he did not do the right things all of the time. I understood that even when we mess up, we have to give God our whole heart. David made sure he repented, and the Lord still had favor over David.

I found myself sleeping, curled up on my couch in the den. I knew that God was teaching me that life was not always going to be perfect. My cell phone began to buzz. I answered the phone call; it was my mother. When I answered the phone, I glanced at the time on my cell; it was 2am. "Mom, what's wrong?" I said. Part of me was up and the rest was still in dreamland.

Mom's voice trembled, and I knew something was wrong. I rose up straight on my couch, grabbing my soft blanket closer to my neck. "Mom, slow down what is wrong?"

"You were trying to know him… I am so sorry!" Mom kept saying that over and over.

"Mom, it is okay. What happened?" I said, very calmly, trying to calm her down. "Well, London, I got a phone call from a friend who knew your Dad. He told me that your real father died in a car accident last night!"

My body was numb. I was too late. I knew it was a very urgent feeling that I had to meet my Dad, but God knows better. "Mom, did I have any brothers are sisters?" I wanted to know so badly.

"You have no sisters or brothers. You are the only one," my mother said while crying some more. "I wished that you would have waited to tell me this, Mom. Now I cannot go back to sleep," I said.

"I am sorry. I had to tell you because I felt so bad that after all these years. I was too afraid to let you meet him for yourself." My Mom went back to sobbing.

"I guess God knows best. He has the answers to the questions that we can't answer," I said.

I could not believe I handled that so calmly. I know that this may sound very selfish, but I thought she was going to say the Dad that I called Dad was dead or sick. I would have lost it, because Robert my father had been there for me like he was my Dad. I loved Robert like he was my real Dad. I understood that my father was very abusive and when women have lived with a man who would beat on them, the most intelligent and brave thing for that woman to do was to think about her babies and self! My Mom was that brave woman; she removed me out of harm's way.

I was afraid that since I had never been through what my Mom had gone through, I was insensitive to her feelings.

My Mom was still sobbing. "Mom, it is not your fault that you did not want me to be a part of his life, because if he was hitting on you, who would have kept him from hitting me! So you did the right thing, Mom." I wanted to know more about how he died.

"What happened? How did this accident happen?"

Mom cleared her throat as she paused to search for her words. "Thank you, sweetheart, I knew how you wanted so much to know this man who was your biological Dad." My Mom's voice sounded strong and back in control. "Well. they said he had been on drugs for years and had made up in his mind to change and go to rehab. They said he started to go to church and help out in the community. Well, that night he ran into a drug dealer in this bad neighborhood, and he ran from this guy and jumped in his car because he must have owed money. Your Dad was not looking because the dealer had a gun, so based on that your Dad ran into another car while driving off," Mom said, while I could just see everything that my Dad had gone through as if it were a movie in my head. I felt sorry for this broken man who was my father. I thought to myself at least he had changed even though his past came back to haunt him.

"Well, Mom, I am praying that God covers us both and maybe we both can go to the funeral to say our goodbyes," I said, hoping that Mom wouldn't back out of this. She needed to let go of some pain that she was holding on to.

"I will think about it, London." Then she blurted out, "I guess…I will go."

" God has everything under control," I said.

"Thank you, honey, for your encouragement. I thought I was going to cheer you up, but it was you that cheered me up."

" I am going to try and catch up on some more sleep."

"Goodnight, sweetheart," Mom whispered as she disconnected the call. I stretched to the ceiling trying to relieve my stiff muscles. I lay back down on my soft sofa and before you know it, I was sound to sleep.

I started the day with breakfast and a nice cup of hot tea. I loved the taste of raspberry tea. I wanted to just rest today—no Brandon, no family, no business calls at all, so I ignored every call. I played some smooth sounds of worship music while

I googled information about how early someone could have a DNA test.

Something was not right. I had to find out the truth. I realized that even at three weeks you could have a DNA test. They had come out with a new test since 2002. I read up on everything dealing with DNA. I was wrong; you can find out early - very early. I just needed to accept the fact that Brandon was having a baby but not with me.

The phone began to ring. I ran to my phone to answer it.

"Hey, Brandon."

"I have been calling you. What's going on?" he said, sounding concerned.

"I have just been relaxing," I said.

"Well what are you doing today?" Brandon knew that most Saturdays we hang out, but today I was just going to be alone. I wanted to just think.

"I am going to visit my Dad and Mom today." I thought of a good excuse instead of telling Brandon no.

"I can come with you; I have not met them yet."

I knew that Brandon was going to ask me that one day. "I don't think this would be a good idea. See, my Mom just found out that my father, my biological Dad, died last night, so I wanted to just chill with them both," I said, hoping Brandon got the message that I did not want to spend time with him.

"London, sorry for your loss. This would be a perfect time to spend with you so I could cheer you up," Brandon said.

Brandon just did not get it. When I am sad or have a lot on my mind, the best thing for me is to pull away. Brandon began to tell me how he was going to spend time with the guys and play some basketball since I insisted that we would not hang out today. Brandon and I talked for a while and then we said our goodbyes. I got dressed and was now headed to my mother's and father's house. When I got there I could see the pain on my Mom's face.

I knew she was upset over my real Dad dying. I did not know how to feel; there was so much going on my brain that I could not keep up with my own feelings. My father and mother were both in the kitchen cooking lunch.

"Hey, everybody, how are you guys doing?"

"Well, it has been forever since I have seen my baby girl," My Dad said as he came and gave me the biggest hug. I ran to hug my Daddy, and I could feel goosebumps running up my arms. I knew this was a sign that I was going to cry. I needed my Daddy to hug me. He was always my father even if his blood did not run through my veins.

I had tears that I could not hold in any longer. "Thank you, Dad, thank you for loving me and making me feel like I was your daughter just like Lisa and Terry," I said with my voice shaking. My father was "not just a good man" but a godly man.

"Awww, stop all that crying. I loved you because God put you in my heart to love. When I married your Mom, I knew she was the woman I was going to spend my life with. I knew that you were going to be my tiny, curly-headed little girl. Dad said, hugging me back. My Mom joined the hug fest. God had a way of healing each and every one of us with His touch.

My Mom was free; she was no longer hugging us with regret and hurt. She was hugging us as a free woman.

It was like she could feel again. "Okay, we better get back to this food, Robert," Momma said while giving me a wink. Daddy went back in the kitchen with Momma cooking fried catfish and French fries with coleslaw; that food smelled so good! I walked upstairs to my old room and decided to just lie down on my bed. I began to reminisce about school and my high school friends; they moved away and some of them got married and had kids. Just even thinking of kids I thought of

Brandon. I wondered what was he doing, but I did not know what was going to come out of his mouth.

Mandy was acting tacky, just how she looked. I know I wasn't supposed to judge. "London, come here. You've got company!" Momma screamed. Who would know how to reach me? Brandon? I ran down the stairs, and it was Lisa! I could not believe she would be here that soon.

"You look so pregnant!" I said.

"Yes, you look so thin!" Lisa said, smiling with her chubby hands and wide ankles. "Tony, it is so nice to see you; it's been so long." I hugged them both. My sister flopped on the living room couch while Tony unpacked their rental car and brought in their luggage.

"Mom, did you know they were coming so soon?" I asked.

"I did not. She surprised your father and I this morning when she said she was here, but you had told me you were on your way over here so I wanted to surprise you." Mom smiled while she placed the plates on the long dining room table and set the table with hot dinner rolls, coleslaw, and a dish filled with catfish and chicken strips.

"Mom, thank you for letting me and Tony stay with Dad and you until we can move in our home," Lisa said while coming in the dining room.

"Well, Lisa, to have my daughter come home before Thanksgiving and Christmas is just a blessing."

Mom began to fuss at Robert for not watching the batch of French fries. "You burnt them up!" she yelled.

Daddy was laughing and talking to Tony while watching the basketball game. I thought about Brandon; he needed to be here. Lisa began helping Mom in the kitchen while I wandered off to my Dad's study filled with his trophies and I kept tossing the idea of calling Brandon in my head. Finally I called him. I left a message telling him that it would be nice to see him if only he could come by my parents' house.

I walked back to the kitchen; Mom was setting the rest of the food at the table. "Were did you go hiding?" Mom asked.

"I went to use the phone," I said, hoping that Mom wouldn't start getting all in my business again.

"Lisa, I don't know why your sister has not let us meet him yet." Mom knew she was ready to dig all up in my business. Mom called the men to come sit down at the dinner table. When we sat down, Lisa could barely fit at the table.

"I can't believe that I am having two grandbabies. Terry is due any day now. That's why Shon and Terry can't come for Christmas this year." There was a small quietness at the table, but Daddy and Tony broke the silence. Tony was bragging about how his team was going to mop up Daddy's favorite basketball team.

"Guys, hush up and leave all that sports in the living room," Mom said while passing the rolls. Daddy said grace and we all ate. I had Brandon on my mind, but I knew this was my fault again. He practically begged me to invite him over. My sister and Mom talked about baby names and places to go shopping for clothes. I felt left out because Mandy was pregnant by the guy who I loved. I saw Dad and Tony laughing and making jokes up about being a Dad.

If Brandon was here, he would have fit in with my family.

My family would love him. I was still trying to figure out the perfect time for Brandon to meet my family. I wished I had let him come over today, I thought to myself; but I was so lost in my emotions. I finished up my food. It felt like I was not there, like my body was there but my mind was elsewhere. "Anyone want any dessert?" Momma asked.

I wanted to go home because I did not fit in. "No, Mom, I am leaving," I said while getting up from the table and reaching for my purse.

"So soon?" Lisa said. "I thought we were going to catch up on being sisters!"

"I've got a lot of work to catch up on. I will come back Sunday or next Friday."

I really was just ready to leave; I had so many different feelings that were getting the best of me. "Well it was surely a blessing to have you come over," my Dad said. "Dad, I will be back for Thanksgiving next weekend."

"London, next time, bring your new boyfriend."

Everyone at the table began to say oh's and awws! My Mom started it again by making that reply. "Okay, I will, Momma." I grabbed my things and jumped in my car.

I made it home, and Jason was on my doorstep sitting there. Now this was going to get crazy. My heart was beating, and I did not know what was on his mind, but whatever it was he needed to tell me. I walked up slowly to my front porch. Jason stood up.

"Hey, look I know this is weird and I did not call you, but please hear me out." Jason looked like he had not had a good night's rest. I was so mad at him; he was the reason why I was in the mess; or at least part of the reason.

"Jason, I don't want to hear it, just leave!" I shouted. I was tired and wanted to just go to sleep.

"Please, dang it, listen to me!" Jason had never yelled at me, but I really didn't know Jason any more. Jason was dishonest, and he was frantic. I stood there in shock. What was I going to do? Run? Maybe… but he might catch me, and then what? *God, please protect me tonight.* Jason started walking back and forth. "Look, I need to just come in and explain."

"No! I'd rather you'd just kill me out here so everyone would know what happened!" I yelled.

"Look! London, I am tired of your crazy mess! This is all your fault! My wife found out about us, and she left me; we have not been married long at all!

I need you to call her and fix it!" Jason dropped to his knees and grabbed my legs, sobbing into my thighs. I did not understand how she found out about me.

"Jason, pull yourself together. It's going to be okay," I said, trying my best to sound sympathetic. "The truth is what goes around comes around; that's what my granddad used to say," I said. "Look what happened to me! Brandon ended up in the arms of Mandy." I had this question going on in my mind. Did Mandy tell Jason's wife about his affair with me? Mandy knew about the affair. Jason started to tell me what happened. His wife received an anonymous phone call from Texas, and it was a woman calling her to tell her about us."

My heart started to beat fast again because this time the psycho was not Jason. He is just a victim of being the one hurt by love. The psycho was Mandy! "It was not me, Jason, I would never do that. I was so ashamed about it that I could not go to work for weeks and months. Jason, you need to get a room and call me tomorrow. I can't talk to you like this; my boyfriend is really upset with you too!" I knew he needed to know the truth about Brandon.

"You told your man! Oh my gosh!" Jason started to look around as if he were trying to make sure my man was not close.

"Okay, out of respect, I am leaving, but you call me so we can discuss this matter," Jason said while he called a taxi.

"Make sure you walk to the café spot. The cab can pick you up there! I don't want you standing in front of my house!" I yelled while going inside of my home. I looked back before closing my front door to make sure Jason was far away from my yard. I went inside my house and got ready for bed; it was already 9:00 p.m., and Brandon still had not called. I was drained; today had been very interesting. I was happy spending time with family, but too many things reminded me of what I wanted so badly… while everyone around me had their life. I lay down and fell asleep.

The week was almost over and I spoke with Jason before he left for California; we both realized it was Mandy. We could be wrong. But all the evidence that we had pointed to Mandy. Brandon texted me twice but he really had been avoiding talking to me.

I did not see him on Sunday for church, I texted him that my family was having Thanksgiving dinner on that Sunday. I had invited him.. Brandon had the nerve to respond late! Brandon called me on Monday saying he was busy and had to plan for a project that will help raise scholarships for different high school kids around different cities. Happy Thanksgiving!

How could you miss Thanksgiving with your girlfriend? I was upset. But Brandon worked a lot.. In order to be in a relationship with him, you would have to understand that. I was a professional as well. I understood that Brandon and I would not see each other often.

I went to lunch at a restaurant with Kevin where we had to review different accounts that needed to be updated.

Kevin was young and handsome; he was smart and for sure a bachelor. I didn't know why I was acting like I was married. Not saying I wanted Kevin, but I just felt like I was watching myself, making sure I was not saying anything to make this guy think I was flirting.

"Kevin, so do you have a girlfriend?" I was only asking to make small conversation. Kevin looked at me as if I asked the wrong question.

"What did I say? Is everything okay?" I said to break the silence.

"You mean, Sherry did not tell you?" Kevin said with a surprised look on his face. "Tell me what, Kevin?" I said, hoping everything was okay.

"I am gay."

I was taking a sip of my water and it shot out of my mouth on everything on the table. "Kevin, I am so sorry!" I said, wiping my face with the cotton napkins. "You really shocked me!" I said laughing.

"I know that you are a Christian and maybe that's why Sherry never told you," he said, as if he were hoping that I was not going to start condemning him.

"True, Kevin, I just don't believe in a lot of things, but to judge you or hurt you for your lifestyle is wrong!" I said. I am praying that maybe Kevin would see the God in my life and hey, you never know one day he will be sitting at my church praising the Lord as a straight man.

We both started to laugh so hard that people began to stare. I looked up, and Brandon was walking in, being seated at a table with his business partners.

"Well, Kevin, let's call it a day. We can pick up on Monday," I said, trying to wrap this meeting up. "Friday I will not be in the office. I will be taking a day off to spend some time with my pregnant sister and Mom. My birthday is coming soon," I said with a smile on my face, but out of the corner of my eye I saw Brandon's stubborn self.

"Ms. Kennedy, that sounds great. I will also call Mr. Davis back to confirm his meeting for next week," Kevin replied.

"Oh, how are you two doing? It looks like you guys have been working hard," Brandon said as he walked up to the table." I was startled because I was not expecting him to come over so soon. "Yes, Brandon, this is Kevin, and we were just out for lunch looking over work," I said, with a little bit of tension in my voice.

"Wow, you take your work everywhere don't you," Brandon said. Kevin got up from the table and said, "Look you two, excuse me, I see you guys need to talk, so thank you, Ms.

Kennedy, for the lunch," he said in his feminine voice with a two snaps up and a two snaps down. I think Kevin only did that because he could sense that Brandon was jealous. Kevin never acted that way at work.

"Oh, wow was… I that rude?" Brandon said, while feeling ashamed of himself.

"I am sorry we have not been hanging out," Brandon said while he smiled. "I used to have extra time, but when you dissed me I went and met a business man on that Saturday, and I been busy ever since," Brandon said while leaning in and kissing me on my lips.

I missed his soft, warm lips, but that kiss still could not make me forget about him dissing me on Thanksgiving.

But I did start this mess. Now he for sure finished it. I was happy Brandon and I were not fighting anymore. "Look, I hope you did not think the reason why I have not seen you was because I was blowing you off." I gave Brandon a crooked smile. He said, smiling again, "I wanted to come to meet your family on Thanksgiven but I had committed to a load of work."

"Well to tell you the truth …I did call you that Saturday the weekend before Thanksgiving to tell you to come over to my Mom's, because my sister and her husband were in town."

Brandon interrupted me. "So then you changed your mind about needing space and called me to come over.…

that's bull, London! You wanted to show me off in front of family!" Brandon laughed, but he had raised his voice. The other couple at the table had to take a second glance to make sure everything was all right.

"Brandon, no that's not the whole truth," I said while standing up gathering my things so I could leave. Brandon was already standing. He leaned in and said, "Tell me the whole truth." I could smell his cool and clean-smelling cologne. I looked him in his eyes and told him how I felt.

"Brandon, I was at my mother's Saturday and Sunday, but remember my father died; it really hurt me. I felt like something was missing, and I knew it was you," I said, trying to keep my tears from falling, but they ran down my face. "I had been so emotional all week because my father passed away. We did not make the funeral; it was too much for me, and I never got the chance to meet the man who gave me life. I thought it would be easier to deal with my feelings alone."

We gave each other a sweet kiss. "I thought I was getting on your nerves. I am sorry that I did not really understand what you were feeling. Wow, you do love me, London. I missed you too. Look, let me go back to this table before my friends leave. I will call you tonight okay?" Brandon said, while headed back to his table.

I was so happy to have run into Brandon. Brandon just did not know how much I loved him!

The month of November had gone, and the temperature had dropped. We were now three weeks into December and my birthday was soon approaching! I was special to have a birthday before Christmas!

I went home for the day and organized my closet. I turned on my favorite song and listened to the soft tunes of Tamia. I could not wait to see my Mom and sister on Friday. I finished hanging all my clothes by colors and styles; I had completed my task for that day. I called my sister to see how she loved Texas so far.

"Hey, sis, how are you and your husband enjoying Texas so far?"

"Well, London, Tony loves the prices on the homes. Tony and I found a nice home in the uptown district, and it is more like a townhome. The house is lovely… three bedrooms and a small backyard for outside BBQs. I am so excited!" My sister sounded like Texas was becoming her home. Lisa began talking about exploring Dallas.

"I wanted to tell you that I found a doctor who is willing to take me after six months and…..we went ahead and put an offer in for that townhome."

I was so happy that Lisa and Tony was finally making a home for themselves. "I am so happy for you, Lisa. Looks like you will be out of Mom's hair," I said while laughing.

"Girl, I love Mom, but she just worries too much for me," Lisa said.

"Lisa, do you believe that Tony was the man that God chose for you?" I said.

"Yes, London, I do think that it is also a choice that God gives you." While I pondered what she was saying, my doorbell rang.

"Lisa, someone is at the door. I will see you tomorrow."

I went to the door, but there was no one outside. I looked under the door, and there was a letter with my name on it.

Dear London, you have been warned.

I did not understand why someone would send this letter to me. Warned about what? My emotions were taking over, and I could no longer keep playing with Miss Southern Belle and her tactics. I called the police and showed the officer the letter. The tall, dark cop sat down on my couch and said, "Do you have anyone who dislikes you for some reason?"

"Well, Officer Blake, I am dating this guy who used to date this woman who hates me. That same woman came to my job and got all in my face at work telling me to stay away from him."

Officer Blake wrote this information down and said, "What is your boyfriend's name?"

"Brandon Gains."

"What is the young lady's name?"

"Mandy. I don't remember her last name," I said, feeling violated and realizing that this was getting out of control.

"Well, Ms. Kennedy, what makes you feel threatened by Mandy, the young lady?" the officer said while standing up with his paper and pen.

"Well, for one she is upset with my relationship with Brandon."

"Okay, but people get mad all the time; it does not mean she wants to do you harm," the officer said with a dumb smile. "But I will talk with her, and maybe if she knows that police are involved if she did send this letter to scare you, she might think twice."

"Thank you, Officer Blake. I really feel like she is losing it."

The officer gave me a glance like maybe I was overreacting. Officer Blake left, but I would not put my faith in him.

I just did not trust Mandy; she was losing herself. I called Brandon, but I got no answer. I left a message telling him what happened. Just then, Brandon's name appeared on my cell.

"Hey, I am sorry I missed your call, but baby, Mandy called me saying that she was bleeding really bad," Brandon said.

I could not believe this. Brandon was at her rescue by her side.

"I was calling to say that someone sent me a letter saying that I had been warned, and the police came out…"

Brandon interrupted me before I could tell the rest.

"Look, London, have some sympathy for once. Mandy lost my son… she is going through a lot. Brandon said. His voice trembled after every word. I could not feel sad for her… what was wrong with me, am I overreacting? Did jealousy set deep in my heart? Maybe it was keeping me from feeling any sympathy for her. I just felt like something was not right. I thought to myself.

"Okay, look I am sorry Brandon for your loss. Have you talked to the doctors and ask what happened?" Brandon just paused.

"Look, I got out here when she was already admitted," Brandon said. "Brandon please speak with the doctors," I insisted.

"I will London. I will call you later." I could not believe Brandon, that he could care less about my safety. I heard a small whisper. London, let go of your jealousy. Love bears all things, believes all things, hopes all things, and endures all things. 1 Corinthians 13:7. God had to remind me of that Scripture. Lord Forgive me of my cold heart. I need you to fix me, Lord.

I called my Dad and told him everything. "This girl could be dangerous! It is not good for you to be alone in that house."

"I am fine, Dad, just so confused. Something is wrong with that woman, Daddy," I said while fixing me some dinner. "Dad, don't tell Mom. She will worry so much."

"I won't tell your Mom, sweetheart, but just promise me that if something happens again you come over to our house for a while until we find out who is trying to scare you or even harm you. That Brandon is blind. He thinks this young lady is innocent," Daddy said. "Brandon must be going through a lot too, London, he did just lose a baby."

"Well, Dad, that is true. I am just numb right now," I said. "I am going to eat my pasta and try and relax."

"Take care, London," my father said, while sounding really concerned.

I felt like Brandon was not even aware of how I was feeling about all of this. It was like being on a roller coaster ride— one minute you're up, the next minute you're down, but the whole time you're screaming.

"Goodnight, Dad," I said, while disconnecting the phone.

I curled up in my bed watching some TV while finishing up my dinner. I never thought that dating Brandon would come with all this drama. I was frustrated, just knowing that Brandon was at the hospital by her side. I could not believe Mandy was so possessive.

I picked up my Bible and began to read Psalm 91:1 (Whoever dwells in the shelter of the Most High will rest in the shadow of the Almighty). I kept thinking about that Scripture and realized that God wanted me to stop worrying about everything. When I was in college, I worried about making sure I made all A's and nothing less. I also worried if I was not pretty enough, so I entered beauty pageants and loved when I would win because winning made me feel like I was somebody.

You would think a girl with a great family would not need to be reassured to feel loved. When single, I worried about who was going to be my husband and when would I meet him. Now God had sent this wonderful man in my life, but this man came with some issues! I guess I did too. Brandon was supposed to protect me, but when he was not there God was always there with me!

I fell asleep to the sound of the old reruns of the *Love Boat*. I got up in the middle of the night to check my cell phone to see if Brandon called, but he did not. It was about two am and I could not go back to bed for some reason. I scanned through my CDs and found an old one of my Pastor preaching a sermon titled, "You Have to Trust God in the Storm." I was filled with the word of God. This message touched my inner soul. I knew God was speaking to me. In this very moment, I knew I was in the storm. I heard a car pull up, and I heard footsteps leading up to my door. I felt the darkness just like my nightmare, but this was real.

I just began to say a prayer hoping that those footsteps were someone I knew. The steps got louder and louder. I went to my front door to look in the peephole and notice a tall man wearing all black. I could not make out the face. What should I do? Call the police? I was so scared. I called my Dad, but no one answered. The man standing at my door was now knocking. I did not say a word. I stood there hoping this guy would go away. *Who could this be?* The man then started kicking my door.

I yelled, "Go away!" The man heard my voice and started to run toward the back. I thought of my backyard area and the French doors. I ran to it and the tall man busted the French doors down. I ran across my living room to hear his footsteps behind me. I spotted my cell phone, and the man was standing over me. I felt like I was going to faint. Every part of my being had frozen. The man jumped on top of me, and I yelled to the top of my voice. "No! No HELP!" The man pinned me down and began to slap me and punch me.

The man started to pull down my pajama pants as if he were going to take something that did not belong to him. I wanted God to save me; my body was my temple.

This man was my nightmare! I reached for my cell, dialed 911, and I yelled for help! The man and I were wrestling while the man was trying so bad to now pull down my underwear. His hands were cold as ice, and his face was covered by a stocking cap. I finally saw my help and knew God had sent him. My neighbor must have heard the scuffles and my screams.

This man who had lived in my neighborhood for years never spoke to me, but he wacked the man with a bat. The police burst in, yelling, "Freeze!" They began to separate my next-door neighbor from this evil man. I curled up on the couch, and the police arrested the man.

The man was Mandy's doctor! I told the investigators everything. They now took me seriously. It was a shame that it took this nightmare to happen before they believed me. They left for the hospital to ask Mandy a lot of questions. The ambulance arrived to make sure I was okay. I did not want to call Brandon; he should have been here. Mandy was behind all of this. I kept thinking, Mandy set me up! My father got me in the car to protect me from everyone in the neighborhood. My father took me to the hospital to make sure I was fine.

After spending two hours at the hospital, my father took me to their house. My Dad was so upset. "I can't believe that this monster who was supposed to be this girl's doctor was trying to rape you!" Dad yelled.

I could not describe my all of emotions right then. But I knew for sure I was furious!

"I am so upset. This girl must have known that the doctor was some kind of monster," Dad said. I could not speak. My joy was gone. I had been slapped and punched in my face, so the right side of my face was bruised. When I got to Mom and Dad's, everyone was waiting up for me in the living room. I did not want them to see me looking so vulnerable.

I wanted them to just leave me alone. "Oh my gosh, my baby was attacked by some crazy person!" my Mom screamed. I looked up at Lisa and Tony; they had terrified looks on their faces. The doorbell rang; it was Brandon. My Dad answered the door.

"Look, young man, you know that my daughter has been beat up and almost raped by the doctor of your friend, ex… whatever you want to call her. Son, something ain't right!" my Dad said, while letting Brandon in.

"Hello, I am so sorry that you have to meet me under these circumstances. I had no idea that this would happen. I am sure Mandy did not know that doctor was going to do that. She was in the hospital. She lost my baby!" Brandon said, trying to make sure my family knew that Mandy was innocent.

I felt like this was his way of protecting her. "I hope you understand that, London," Brandon said while his hands were trembling. "I just have to thank God that God was there with London to protect her," Brandon said while he walked over to sit by me and put his arms around me.

Lisa came to Brandon with a welcoming smile. "Hi, Brandon, so nice to have met you even if this was a horrible night. God has a way of making everything work for the good."

Tony came and shook Brandon's hand. "You take care of my sister-in-law." Brandon smiled and nodded his head.

I was still in shock.

"Look, Brandon, you need to stay with her tonight. We can fix you up on our couch," Mom said as if she had known Brandon for years.

"Thank you, Mrs. Kennedy, I am going to take you up on that offer," Brandon said while his eyes shifted back to me. My Dad was too upset and went to bed without talking to anyone.

"Look it's my fault. Mandy was crying when she found out what happened to you. She was devastated and wanted to tell you that she was so sorry for being rude and trying to come between our relationship. I am sorry that you had to go through this!" he said.

Brandon looked in my eyes and realized that I was staring in space as if I had tuned him out. "I am sorry, London, you were right… Mandy had no business dating that crazy doctor and disliking you!"

"Mandy was wrong because she had neglected her son as well. Mandy's Mom took Raymond to live with her. Mandy had gone through a bad break up and that led to her partying and throwing herself at a men and dating that doctor! This is just so crazy!"

It was driving me crazy to hear Brandon talk about Mandy, but I still said nothing. I just watched him pace the floor.

"I guess she wanted to make me suffer!" he said. "I am so sorry, London! I should have listened to you when you called." Brandon began to cry. "I should have left that hospital. I knew that something was going to happen when we hung up! I did not listen!" He began to cry again; his face was no longer confident like the man I had always known.

I realized I had not said a word to anyone. I had the image of that man touching my legs with his cold hands, his breath breathing down my neck, his hands touching me in places that were only meant for the man I loved. My eyes just gazed at my familiar surroundings. Brandon placed his arms around me, and then he kissed me on my lips very soft.

It only reminded me of that nasty man… "Don't do that, Brandon," I said while gritting my teeth.

"Baby I am so sorry. Look, just relax okay? Remember he did not get the chance to do what he tried. Okay, that's the good part."

I felt like if Brandon were there, this would not have happened. If Brandon had trusted me, I would have never experienced this. "Brandon, if you would have been there for me instead of Mandy, I would not have been attacked by that crazy loser!" I yelled.

"Look, just lower your voice okay? Everything is fine, London, I am here now. I promise I won't let them get away with what he did, baby." Brandon held me tighter like he did not ever want to let me go.

Something inside of me felt safe in Brandon's arms. I calmed down while laying my head on Brandon's chest. I knew it was not all Brandon's fault because he was a victim too. Brandon also just lost a baby; I knew he was hurting. We fell asleep on the sofa holding each other.

Chapter 7

LOVE AND JOY

The sun came through, and I could hear my grandmother laughing. She was wearing her beautiful blue dress and her hair was all in long curls. "Hey, London baby, you know you need to let God heal you. When God heals you, then you will be able to love that man. God is love, London Kennedy!"

My Grandmother's perfume was like a sweet honeydew melon. I looked at her and wanted to hug her, but she kept walking in the kitchen where the gold sunlight shined in. I called her name, but she never looked back.

I woke up; it was only a dream. I could feel my warm tears fall down my skin. I was reminded of how my grandmother loved telling me how my grandpa and her had met. I would love to sit up close to her and listen to her stories; Papa died when I was just thirteen years old, but Grandmother died when I graduated from college with my master's; she was my Mom's everything. I wanted to have at least met the right guy like Lisa did. Lisa had her wedding before Grandmother passed away. Lisa was just eighteen; she and Tony were young and in love. I was happy to at least be the bridesmaid. I wanted Grandmother to see me walk down that aisle. I was too flirty and dating the wrong men.

I knew that God allowed me to dream of her to remind me to not fear. God was letting me know that I needed to let go of the pain. This was going to be hard, but I know there is nothing too hard for God! I looked at Brandon holding the pillow in his hands while he was sleep. Brandon was snoring, and it was kind of cute. I forgave Brandon for not being there for me last night, but God was there for me and helped me fight that creep.

I also prayed for Brandon. God allowed the both of us to go through the storm. However, God knew Brandon and I would survive.

I knew now how so important it is for women who have been abused, whether the abuse came from their husbands, boyfriends or even a stranger that it should never be tolerated.

I am a new London Kia Kennedy. My life is not a game because I know that we only live life once. I was no longer holding any grudges with people. I wanted to give everyone who wronged me a clean slate, including that monster. I wanted him behind bars, but I didn't hate him. My Mom came in the living room in her pink robe. "Hey, baby girl, you okay?"

"Yes, Mom, I am more than okay. I dreamed about Grandmother, and she said to forgive and let go of the pain so I could love."

My Mom came closer and said, "See, you had an angel protecting you, sweetheart. Some women are not that blessed; they don't live to see the next day."

"Mom, you are right. That's why I know now I have a purpose greater than just falling in love but doing God's will to help women who are just like me. Maybe we look different and our stories even might be different, but so many women are looking for love, and they have no clue that love is not found in the arms of a man, but it is found in giving your heart to God and loving him."

My mother stood there as if she had seen a ghost. "Baby, you have really matured." My mother gave me a hug. "Well I am going to fix all of us some breakfast. Go and relax. Oh, yeah Brandon really loves you. I think he is a keeper," Momma said while smiling at me.

I smiled back while looking at my handsome boyfriend. I realized that life can be difficult, but God has a way of bringing the truth out.

God wanted me to understand how to love. Brandon had pretty much done what I did to him, but I could not deal with it because the idea of him having a baby on the way was really not okay with me even though I kept saying it was. Brandon was just being the strong man that he was by helping Mandy while she was supposed to be carrying his baby.

Brandon had failed to ask more questions; he just went along with her story because he trusted Mandy. There is a time to trust, but make sure you ask all the right questions. I knew I was going to speak out against abuse and helping women with low self-esteem; this was now my purpose.

I sat down against Brandon who now had both feet propped up on the sofa. I wrapped my arms around him and kissed him on his forehead. Brandon's eyes slowly opened up. "Hey London, you're smiling. My prayers have been answered." Brandon began to hold my hand. "I love you, London."

My Mom's breakfast was waking everyone up.

"Look, I can't stay. I need to go down to the police station, and they will need you to press charges. Are you ready for that?"

"I just want to get it over with," I said, ready to move past this nightmare.

"I want to talk with your Dad, so I will be back later this evening. Maybe your Dad will be more calm later," Brandon said while stretching.

"What are you two whispering about?" Lisa said while holding her round belly. "Well, I need to go with Brandon to the police station to press charges against that monster," I said. My voice was shaky at the thought of it, but I was strong enough to put this guy away.

"Well, they don't need you to go since the guy was caught in the act," Dad said while coming out his bedroom.

"Well hello, Mr. Kennedy," Brandon said. My father just waved his hand.

"Well look, London, you don't need to go right now. Maybe later. Stay with your family and I will call you later."

I did not want Brandon to let me go; I really felt safe in his arms. "I don't want you to leave me; I feel so needy right now. Do you promise to come back?" I said while clinging against Brandon's coat.

"I promise to come back," Brandon said while walking in the dining room with Lisa and Tony and my father. They were all getting ready to eat Mom's homemade butter biscuits and her gold brown hash browns with crispy bacon to top it off. "Well, it was nice of you guys to let me stay the night over. I swear that couch was softer than my bed," Brandon said while laughing.

"Well, sweetheart, you sure you don't want stay for breakfast? That police stuff can wait," my mother said while setting the plates on the table.

"Look… Son, stay. She is so right, plus, London, really needs you," Daddy said. I knew my Dad would finally come around. "Well, I sure hate to turn you all down. The food smells real good too. I will come back for dinner and take you up on that offer of sleeping on that soft sofa bed tonight if that is okay?"

My father's face was priceless; his mouth was wide open.

"Well, of course you can stay over tonight; we can all enjoy each other's company." Mom spoke before Dad could say anything.

I was so happy and felt warm inside. God knew I was always independent, and I would never slow down, but this time I had to.

"Sounds like a plan," Brandon said while hugging me one more time. He began to leave. I watched him walk out the house, and then I ran to the window and watched him jump in his car and drive off. I watched until I could see him fade off in the distance.

I sat down with my family and ate breakfast. This was the first time in a long time to have almost my whole family there at one time. Terry and her husband were still in LA. I realized I was not worried about things that were useless like what

I did not have. I was enjoying my family for the first time in a long time. I went up to my old room after breakfast. I felt so safe and surrounded by family when a week ago I felt alone. It was amazing how your emotions could trick you and have you believing a lie. It was so important to have a healthy perspective of yourself.

I knew that Brandon was going to work everything out.

I got a phone call from the officer. "Hey, is this Ms. London Kennedy?" the officer said.

"Yes, speaking."

"I wanted to tell you that this guy is going down for more than eight years - a very long time. The young lady who was involved with this guy claimed that she had no idea that he was going to do that to you. It seems like she may be just innocent."

The police officer went on to say Mandy would not face any jail time unless there was new evidence showing that she was involved. That crazy doctor also would lose his license to practice medicine or work in any health clinic or hospital; he would be banned from practicing anywhere!

"Believe it or not, that man said he had followed you from work that day when you had that fight with Ms. Mandy Shaw. He knew were you lived and planned to assault you. It was his fingerprints in your home that matched the prints that was on that letter. Well, young lady, you are pretty lucky!" the officer said.

I politely said, "I am blessed!"

I was so thankful that everything ended well and I could move on. Lisa came in my room. "Hey, you have always been the strong one," she said while touching my hair.

"Thank you so much, sister."

"I love Brandon. Do you think he is the one?" Lisa asked, giving me the giggles like some teenager.

"Yes, Lisa, I do think that God made Brandon just for me and everything happened for a reason." My sister held me in her arms and started to cry. "I know it was God who sent me to Tony," she said while still holding me in her arms. Lisa always acted as if she was the big sister or somebody's Mom.

"I am so happy that you are fine. That bruise that was on your face looks a lot better than last night." We both smiled as she gazed in my eyes as if she could see right through my soul. "Good," I said with a side grin. "I thought the same thing. What was meant for evil God turned all this around for my good. I know the Lord really loves me!" I said out loud.

"Well, lets go downstairs and watch that movie while the men are in the den watching the sports channel."

My sister took my hand as we both headed to the living room. My sister replied, rubbing that belly, "Okay, looks like we both will be sister bonding tonight." We both sat down to enjoy this moment. It had been years since I enjoyed my sister. Brandon had not called, but I knew he probably was getting everything ready to come for dinner.

Time had passed so fast. It was now 8:00! I sat down in the living room on Mom's soft couch and enjoyed hanging out with my sister. Lisa sat there and put on a love story movie; we both were suckers for love stories.

"Robert! Go get that chicken dinner so I won't have to cook! Robert, us women are on strike. We don't want to cook!" My Mom was yelling at my Dad in a playful way.

"Okay, boss lady, you don't have to cook as long as you give me a kiss," Daddy said while holding Momma around her waist while giving her a kiss on the lips. "You guys cut that out," Tony said while grabbing the keys to the car.

"I will meet you out there, old timer. I see you later, sweet lips," Daddy said while hitting Momma on the behind.

"OMG! You guys need to get a room!" Lisa shouted from the living room while laughing. I just smiled, because these were family moments. This was what family was all about. The only thing we were missing was my baby sister, but Terry and her husband would soon be here.

My Mom had loved my Dad; she had been through the worst kind of abuse, or so different family members told me; but Mom never talked about what she went through. If my

Mom could let go and enjoy her life after the storm, I knew I could do the same.

There was a knock at the door. I knew it was Brandon; he knocked three times, I could tell how his knock was. I pulled my curly locks into a ponytail since my hair was not flat ironed. I got to the door, and I said while looking out the peephole, "It is Brandon." I opened the door and jumped into his arms.

"Wow, you must be so glad to see me," Brandon said while bringing in his black bag. I open the door wearing my comfortable cotton shorts and a tank top. Mom and Dad had it very warm in the house. It felt like summer time.

"I am so happy you made it," I whispered. "I have never seen you so, so…happy," Brandon said while waving his hand saying hello to everybody.

"Come take a seat, Brandon. We are watching a very good love story. Now when Dad comes back with the food, they will try and steal you and pull you away into the den where the sports are on," Lisa said, shouting from the open space living area. Brandon's face lit up with excitement.

"Oh yeah! The football game! Got to find out the score!" Brandon reminded me how he is a football fan.

"Well, I am not letting you go tonight," I said as I leaned in to kiss him. Brandon quickly pulled away to say hello to my Mom while she set the table. Brandon gave me a, awkward glare. I thought it was funny. "Mom almost caught us sneaking in that kiss," I said. Brandon laughed, and my Mom came back in the family room to tell us to get ready to eat.

"Your Dad just called me and said he was pulling up, so let's all go in the dining room; the food is now here," Mom said.

Dad came in with a smile on his face, and Tony sat the fried chicken on the table. The food smelled like southern cooking in big mama's house on a Sunday morning. Too bad my Grandmother was in heaven, but Glory's Fried chicken dinners made you feel like you were eating big Momma's southern cooking.

"Robert, honey, bless the food," Mom said while everyone sat down at the table ready to eat. Dad blessed the food and said a special prayer to God for keeping me safe. We all laughed and ate like a big family; even Brandon was part of this family.

I felt so happy that he could spend this moment with my family and me. We all stuffed our faces with delicious food. We had game night; we played dominos and card games and checkers, and I enjoyed seeing my sister Lisa hi-five Dad, boasting about how she was going to beat everyone at all the games.

Brandon was sneaking peeks at me at every turn, and blowing kisses at me when no one was looking. After the games were over and everything in the kitchen was cleaned and the food was put up, everyone headed for bed. I grabbed my coat so I could relax outside on the front porch to see the stars shine. It was something about the stars that I loved so much. I had left Brandon in the house on a business call. I sat out on Mom's porch just gazing at the night sky.

I was thinking about how God gave me that dream about my grandmother so I could connect to the places in me that were hidden. I realized after my attack that it made me value my worth and my life. I thought about Mandy and how I had always thought that Miss Southern Belle had it made; she seemed so confident in herself and like she had beauty and respect for herself. How could one man lead her down a road of manipulating and being dishonest in everything just to get Brandon's love?

Mandy did not have the love of God. When you are missing the love of God, you will feel empty and broken. Those types of people will also do almost anything to get that type of love, even if they go about it the wrong way. But the sad thing about Mandy is, she was desperate. I felt a warm arm around my shoulder and the smell of cool, crisp men's cologne.

"Why are you out here? It is thirty degrees out here!" Brandon said while sitting next to me holding me. His warm breath touched the back of my neck.

"I wanted to see the stars, and so I came out here to just think on the things of God, I mean look, Brandon, the night sky looks amazing. God's creations all around us are just so wonderful!" The sounds of the night life like the crickets and the sound on the streets had settled in. The streetlights were on, and the cars were parked in driveways. It seemed like everyone was asleep except for us.

"Look, let me tell you this. I never thought I would meet such a strong woman like you. I remember the Ms. Kennedy 'I am fine and you know it'," Brandon said while laughing.

I gave him a nudge with my elbow. I giggled. "No, that was not I; I did not think I was so fine. Well, maybe that was me in the beginning," I said while thinking about how Tina and I would get in this stupid competitive war with each other. Maybe I was that girl who thought I was number one! It is amazing how Jason and how Brandon both came into my life to push me outside my comfort zone. I was then pushed out of my box when the attack happened.

I was pushed out of my box to live and to have a purpose. "Hey, do you want kids one day?" Brandon asked me out of nowhere.

"Yes, I have always wanted to have a family. I just needed that husband," I said, smiling at the thought of a family.

"Well, I am freezing my behind off, so let's go in," I said, while pulling Brandon's hands to have him to pull me closer to lean in for a soft kiss. If I could sum up how Brandon's kiss really made me feel, it was like my life was changing. We both went inside to a warm and cozy home.

I looked into Brandon's brown eyes and saw a glimpse of my future: my husband, and the father of my kids. Brandon pulled out his sofa bed, and I handed him some warm extra blankets. "Brandon, you should be warm enough tonight," I said.

"Yes, London Kia Kennedy, I will be super warm tonight especially after that sweet warm kiss."

I blushed. "Don't say that loud. You know Momma don't play that. We are not married yet," I said with a whisper.

"Yes you are right, goodnight sweetheart," Brandon said. I walked upstairs to my room and jumped in my old bed, reminding me of when I was back in high school. My sisters and I were like the three musketeers. I was thirty years old, and my life was never this complicated until I met my love. There was a lesson behind this relationship. I think it is so important to be a healthy loving single, before you can love another person in your life.

The next day Brandon and I had to go back to our homes. I was no longer the same London Kennedy. However, I was determined to live my life with faith, and peace.

I was now in this happy place even though the storm had rocked my boat and I thought it was over. I closed my eyes to see his face and his hands touching my body all over. My heart began to beat so fast that it felt like my heart was going to jump out of my chest. I was having a nightmare that seemed so real. I jumped up and realized I had only been asleep for two hours. I prayed to God to give me peace to keep the image of that monster out of my dreams.

I struggled to get back to sleep. I knew that being back at home was going to be a challenge. The night was hard, for me; but it was time to face my fears.

Walking around in my silent house brought back the screams, only to remember that the screams were my screams. I told myself that I could do this no matter what. My life is not my fight, but my stage to overcome to love, to live, and enjoy!

I kept saying that over and over until my own words drowned out my victim screams. I thanked my mother for cleaning up my house and making it smell like fresh lavender. I called Brandon while I was at home; I knew he was busy working. Brandon told me he was at work making plans and signing deals. I contacted Kevin right after speaking to my

Bran, and he had me set up for a meeting this Monday. I had to wear the perfect black Vera Wang suit and my red high heels.

I was ready to jump back into the workflow. I was off for too long—a week was too long! I headed out the door on my way to the coffee shop. The traffic was not so bad on this Monday morning. I jumped out of my car, and a handsome gentleman gave me a smile. I smiled back, but I knew my heart was taken. God had my heart, and my Brandon was in it. I got in my car and headed to the office to meet with Kevin and the CEO of Marketing Connections. I felt brand new and I was ready.

I walked in the office and there was a crowd of smiling faces and balloons. I had gone through so much turmoil, I forgot that my birthday was today! Just five days before Christmas, December 20th. Brandon was standing in his Armani suit looking handsome as ever. My coworkers, even Mr. Wallace, had big, bright smiles. "HAPPY BIRTHDAY!"

Balloons of all colors where let down from the ceiling, and a big pink cake was waiting for me.

"Thank you, everyone, I can't believe you guys would spoil me like this," I said while everyone was smiling from ear to ear. The owner of the company, Dan Lou, marched down and shook my hand. "We want to thank you for your many years at this company, winning all the major accounts and building this company's name and our brand!"

He handed me an envelope, and inside were two tickets to the beautiful Maui Beach. An all-paid vacation. Everyone was clapping. I could not believe that even in my pain I had stood and was happy and others now celebrated me. Brandon came with this great big box. I wondered what was in this box! It was the new handbag from Christian Louboutin. I hugged Brandon and told him I loved him. Brandon gave me the biggest hug, and everyone said "Awww." Everyone had a nice piece of cake and went back to work. I was now thirty-one!

I loved being thirty-one and was ready for the world!

I went back to work and told Brandon I would see him later. It was time to get back at working hard. I went in our conference room to wait on my client. He was on his way. The meeting started right on time as soon as he came in. I showed him how we could take his brand and build it as high as the stars. The CEO of Marketing told me he would think about it and give me an answer by email.

I was not worried. They all play hard-to-get in the beginning. I called it a day after checking emails and talking to several clients. I gathered my gifts and many cards and took them home.

Brandon had meetings to attend to, and he said he would call me later; we both had to catch up with work. I knew it was time to start that vacation after I took this new account.

Kevin was doing a great job with everything. I got home and relaxed after a hot shower; I had pizza and called it a night. I could feel the fear trying to creep back in. This was my second night at home, but if I could stay on Sunday night, then I could stay on Monday night. I turned my alarm on this time. I had a house alarm, but that crazy night I forgot to turn it on. I was in my soft nightgown and realized that somehow in the crazy moments, the uncertain moments, God brought out the best in me.

I played some soft Christian music and rested. I thought about church last Sunday. Brandon and the family had spent the last day with each other, and the best place to do that is at Loving Temple Church. My church family really prayed for me and wanted me to start a woman's ministry at our church. I knew God was now giving me that platform to share my story and pray for women. I closed my eyes and let the sweet sound of praise and worship music heal my soul.

My Mom and Dad called me and woke me from my snooze!

"Happy Birthday! We have been calling you all day!" Mom said while Dad and the family was in the background yelling happy birthday.

"What are you doing?" Mom asked.

"I was sleeping."

"What? At this time? It is only eight o' clock, my love," my Mom said. "Well we want to bring you food and cake and gifts!"

"Mom, I don't mind. I am just so sleepy," I said.

"Okay, my darling. We will save you a piece of your own cake."

"Love you, Mom, thanks!" I said while my Mom disconnected. I was knocked out.

It was Christmas Eve and everyone was preparing for dinner at my Mom's. We had a special guest, my baby sister and her husband, who were now in town. Brandon and I were dressed in all black, and I could not leave out my shockingly beautiful red pumps. Brandon and I arrived on time. My Mom's house was filled with all kinds of Christmas decorations and the fireplace mantel was covered with Christmas lights. Their Christmas tree had beautiful red ribbons and white lights; the smell of pumpkin pie and Daddy's favorite smoked turkey were going to be the highlights of the night.

Brandon brought his famous pecan pie, and I brought my cream cheese pie with sprinkles of pecans. My Daddy was all dressed up, and everyone had a joke to tell. My baby sister, Terry, came running up to me with her small tummy. She was expecting a baby as well; she was not that far along from Lisa.

Shon, her husband, was very quiet; he would usually just say two or three words for an entire night. "Mom, you look so pretty. Love your curls and your beautiful red dress."

We all sat down at the table.

My Mom had mac and cheese, greens, mashed potatoes and yams, black eyed peas and can't leave out the best cornbread dressing. And Daddy's smoked turkey. The deserts were chocolate cake and Brandon's pecan pie.

I was ready to eat, but we had another surprise guest! The doorbell rang. "Lisa," I whispered, "did Mom or Dad tell you who was coming?"

Lisa nodded no. I heard a lady's voice and a man; it sounded like an older couple. I looked at Brandon; he had that blank stare. "Brandon, do you know the guests?" I said, but before he could answer, Brandon moved away from the table to hug the older couple. The lady was about fifty-five and very fair skinned, and the man was very light brown skinned with gray eyes.

"Hello, Son," the man stated as he hugged Brandon. I joined them, but I had butterflies in my stomach. This was a very big surprise.

"Hello, you must be the beautiful London," the woman said while grabbing me and hugging me so tight that I could not breathe.

"I am London. Nice to meet you, Mr. and Miss Gains."

"Likewise," his father said while they both took a seat. Brandon's Mom, Mary, scanned the house with her wandering eyes. I guess she wanted to check out how we lived.

"Mary, you are a lawyer, right? Brandon had told me you practiced law when he was growing up," I said to make conversation.

"Well, London, I stopped practicing ever since Brandon graduated from high school but yes, I loved it. I went to Harvard, and I really had to study. As an African American, nothing good is free!"

I could see why Brandon talked very little about his mother; she was so cold and stiff. I did like his father; he was down to earth, laughing with my Dad about his fishing days and how maybe one day they could plan a fishing trip. My Mom did not like bourgeois women, so she would try and smile and say less. "So, Linda, what college did you graduate from?" Mary asked.

I was taking a big spoonful of my potatoes, hoping the more I chewed I could void hearing my Mom's response.

"Mom, now come on we are here to celebrate, not investigate," Brandon said. He was looking more uncomfortable than I was. Everyone began to finish up dinner, and Brandon's Mom was just talking a lot. My Mom gracefully smiled.

"I went to a community college and received my associate's degree and then went on to a small university when my kids where in grade school and got my four-year degree in teaching and started teaching. I fell in love and started my family. That was my biggest purpose to love and be a great Mom and a well-respected role model."

My Mom said that very well.

"I like a woman who honors family," Brandon's Dad, Mark, said while eating the food on his plate as if he could not get enough.

"That's why I married her. She was not a self-centered woman," my Dad said.

"Oh, please don't think for a minute that I disagree. I was always a workaholic and missed out on a lot of Brandon's grade school days. But I admire a woman like you, Linda."

Mary smiled as if she knew she needed to stop talking.

"You have a wonderful home," Mary said, pushing her plate away from her and pushing her chair away from the table while walking to the living room with my Mom.

"Thank you, Mary, it is always great when family can reclaim their room," Mom said.

"Mary, I am headed to the den with the fellas," Brandon's Dad said while heading back to enjoy some male bonding.

Lisa and Terry and I joined Mom and Mary after putting up the dishes.

"So, how did you and Brandon meet?" I smiled from ear to ear because I loved sharing this story.

"Brandon was the young, handsome, intelligent man at our company, and he was not afraid to let people know that he was a Christian, so we met at company parties and finally he asked me out! I knew he was the one."

Mary smiled, and even though she seemed uptight I could tell she loved her son, and she liked us. She just ran with a different social class of people, not just money, but people who bragged about things that we would not care about!

We all walked into the living room.

"I would like to thank you for inviting us to your home, Linda. Your daughters are lovely!" Mary went on and on talking about her sorority sisters and her new ideas to change low-income communities. Anyhow, watching Mary speak was like watching Brandon. I realize that Brandon and his Mom were both passionate people.

"I am so glad to have met you and your husband," I said while standing up. "I am going back for some pie… would anyone like a slice?" I asked.

I heard a deep voice from behind me saying, "I do." It was Bran. I had not called him that in a long time. "Look, before you go in and get a slice of pie, I want to tell you something." I had butterflies in my stomach. The last time Brandon said that, he was telling me about Mandy's crazy behind.

I looked up, and all the men were in the living room; my sisters and my Mom began to smile. Brandon dropped down on one knee. My eyes filled with the warmth of my tears. My heartbeat started to make that frantic beat again. I was so shocked. God had blessed me with this moment that came in a place of redefining my worth and value. I no longer wanted to rush in the idea of marriage; I was too busy enjoying the idea and the facts about how good God was.

God was so good; he gave me a family that loved me, and now a husband. "Brandon, oh my gosh!" I yelled.

"London Kia Kennedy, I love you even when you question yourself. I still think you are beautiful even when your makeup is off and you look a mess. I know in my heart I found a wife. Will you marry me?"

Everyone in the room clapped and cheered. I said, "Yes!"

But this moment was like I was in slow motion. I saw Brandon's Mom crying with joy. My Mom and Dad were in tears of happiness; my sisters and their husbands were cheering for us!

God reminded me of my dream of my grandmother telling me to let go. It is amazing how God wants you in a place where you finally can see that it is not you who will make it happen; it is God who will bring all things to pass. God is really looking for a people to go after his heart, not the simple pleasures of life or the gifts. Because if God give you over to the gifts or the pleasures, you will begin to worship the things, and not God! I held Brandon so close I could hear his heartbeat. We both just held on to each other. The ring he slipped on my finger was sparkly and a princess cut and a four-carat diamond. Brandon really outdid himself. But I would have married him even if he tied a yarn around my finger, because I knew the call was great to be a wife and walking in my purpose would cost the most!

Chapter 8

I SAID YES

Iwas sitting in my mother's living room helping Lisa and Terry clean up all the wrapping paper from our gift exchange. Christmas was fun, and I was thankful to have had a birthday; then Brandon purposed to me on Christmas Eve. Brandon and his Mom and Dad were staying at this nice condo not too far from my Mom and Dad's house.

I talked to Brandon all night like a teenager. I kept saying things like, "I love you too." Brandon was my future husband; I could not believe it.

"Terry, Lisa, so did you guys know that this day would come for me?" I asked, smiling.

"London, I knew God was going to bless you, and what a great birthday and Christmas gift, but Brandon is a strong man who really wants to walk after the plan of God!" Terry said.

"So, I can see you both in church speaking and having a great influence on others by sharing your story," Lisa said while putting Brandon's and his family's gifts under the tree. I knew that God was going to use our story to inspire couples and singles that did not have the perfect story to tell.

"I feel the same way, Lisa," I said.

"Well I just believe God is bringing all the family together to really get closer to Him more, just look how Lisa and her husband moved to Texas to stay, now Shon and I are thinking about moving here," Terry said with a smile.

I yelled out loud, "Now I will get to have my sisters!"

"I can't wait to plan this wedding!" Lisa shouted.

"I know we are all going to have to fight about this and that with Mom because you know how stubborn she is," Terry said. We all looked at each other and busted out in high-pitch laughter! My Mom came in the living room in a black dress and high heels. All the sisters looked at her with a smile.

"Mom, where are you going all dressed up?"

"Thank you, my darlings, Merry Christmas to you all!" Mom said while she modeled her beautiful dress that Dad got for her. "Your Dad is taking me out on a date for Christmas dinner! We go out on dates every other weekend."

Lisa said, "Mom, I don't go out that often, so you get all dressed up for Dad?"

"Yes, once you get married you can't lose the spark! You must make sure he knows you still got it!"

"I am taking notes, Mom," I said, while Dad came out in a dapper suit; his cologne filled the living room.

"Yea, I love taking my baby out!"

"Lisa, your Mom and Dad have more fun than we do!" Tony said while laughing.

Mom and Dad left. I knew Brandon was coming over soon and my sisters and their husbands and I, would have the house to our selves. "So everyone, let's do game night," I suggested.

"Ok, only if I get to pick the games this time because you picked all the games last time. "Tony said.

"Wow do I smell a sore loser because as I recall you lost all the games? Lisa, get your man, girl!" I said, while giggling." Lisa and Tony laughed out loud.

"That's ok, let's play against each team. We will team up with our spouse or partner and see who wins!" Terry said

"Sounds like a deal," I said .

We all agreed. There was a knock at the door. Shon opened the door. They both greeted each other with a handshake.

"Brandon you made it," I said. Brandon sat at the table in a seat next to me. . "Ok, what's going on? All I see are board games: Connect Four, Checkers, Scrabble, and my favorite, Monopoly!!" Brandon said. Brandon was already excited!

"Brandon we are a teaming up with our significant others. So Brandon you better bring your A game," I said, while smiling and adoring his brown eyes. "Oh, ok well that means, we are going to kick their butts!!!!" Brandon said, while giggling.

"See, I knew you were going to rise to the occasion," I said. Brandon gave me this warm kiss on my cheek.

"London, where are your Mom and Dad?" Brandon asked, looking around trying to make sure that he did not get caught kissing me, too funny.

"Oh they went out on a date," I replied.

"This is why I love your Mom and Dad. After all these years, they still have this fire. I want to make sure I learn something from them both," Brandon said, smiling.

The night was special; we all had dinner together on Christmas Eve, so on Christmas night our parents were having their own celebration. Our parents have made their relationships last long," Brandon said, while holding my hand. "Yeah, you are so right, Bran. I think because they keep it hot and fresh, but most of all, God first."

"Okay, are you two lovebirds going to talk all night?" Terry said.

"Wow, Terry, I thought you were sweet and innocent, but it looks to me like you want to be the boss!" Brandon said while settling into his spot at the table. I sat beside him; the games had started. We had music in the background playing. All of us were singing along to the popular tunes from the nineties. Those songs were oldies but goodies.

Brandon and I won almost all the games. I had so much fun!

"Brandon, it is time to exchange our gifts!" I said while reaching under the tree and handing him a big box. Brandon smiled and began to rip in the gift. He looked inside and pulled out a football jersey from his favorite team, the Cowboys. Brandon screamed and picked me up and twirled me around the room. "Merry Christmas!"

"Okay, here is your gift from me." Brandon pulled out a gift box that said, *From Mary*.

"Look, open my gift first!" Brandon shouted, waiting with excitement. I pulled back the sliver wrapping paper and opened the box. I had my own diamonds, but the earrings were priceless. They reminded me of a princess! I loved the earrings.

That Christmas was a night that would be remembered as one of the best Christmases that I'd ever had!

Chapter 9

BLENDED FAMILY

Brandon and I spent the month of December and January blending our lives together and learning more about one another. The New Year had came and gone, and my family and Brandon's parents all spent time getting to know each other from movie nights and special dinners at my parents, church, and just loving on each other. I can say it was the perfect time to bond and blend our family over the holidays. I knew everyone had to go home and back to work. I was going to miss Brandon's parents. I had a very special connection with his mother for some reason.

My sisters had their babies—Terry had a boy and Lisa had a girl; the babies were such a gift from God!

I knew that Mom was going to give me grief, but I loved every minute of her excitement about planning my wedding. Brandon and I were sitting down at Gimonta Cake and Bakery, and they brought out twelve different slices of cake for us to taste. I loved the red velvet cake, and the creamy French vanilla cake was my favorite. Brandon loved the cream chocolate cake and the strawberry cake better; we both began to debate which cake would be better for our wedding cake.

I had no idea that weddings could be so complicated.

"Well, have you guys came up with which cake you want to have for your wedding?" The tall, blonde hair, lady replied while taking our samples away.

"Well, I think we should have two cakes, one for the groom and one for me, the bride."

I smiled while taking selfies with my Bran. I never do that, but since I was engaged and I knew in my heart that this was the man God sent in my life, it made me act like a love-crazy teen. Brandon and I had been through hell and back, but God somehow kept us together.

"Okay, sounds like a plan. I want my cake to be the German chocolate cake," Brandon said while eating one of the samples before she could take it away.

"I would like the French vanilla cake for my cake," I said while grabbing my purse and cell phone.

"Brandon, sweetheart, I've got a meeting with an investor, so I will talk to you later."

I beat the traffic and made it to my office. I was meeting with an investor who was intelligent and had great ideas for marketing and making a brand.

"Hello, James Hilton," he said.

"So glad you were able to meet with me," I said. "I would like for you to meet Kevin, my assistant."

"Hello sir," Kevin said while presenting the PowerPoint for our interview. Mr. Hilton smiled all the way through the meeting and he didn't say a word. I was a little nervous because it seemed as if Mr. Hilton was not sold on my ideas on how to turn a million-dollar company to a billion-dollar business. "Ms. Kennedy, thanks a lot. We'll get in touch with you and let you know if I would like to invest."

I smiled but could not get a word in because Mr. James Hilton was out my office so fast. "Don't worry, Ms. Kennedy, you never know… he just might invest. Go home," Kevin said, "Don't work too hard. You have to plan that wedding."

"Okay, I will try and rest, but man it feels like I have a ton of stuff on my plate."

I left work and headed home. The freeway was not as bad. It was five o'clock and I was halfway home.

I could not get James Hilton out of my head. I had never failed at getting an investor to invest. I was losing it. I answered my cell; it was Terry.

"Hey, baby sister, what's going on?" I asked.

"Mom is driving me up a wall. Lisa and Tony have moved out, but they left me with Mom who is overbearing at times, trying to take over! No, Terry, he does not need formula. Breastfed is the best way to go. Well, I wanted to tell Mom, well you breastfeed Shon Jr.!"

"Wait… breathe calm down, Terry. Mom is just trying to help. You just need to let her take him and get some rest and then know that you and Shon will be moving out soon."

I could hear Terry breathe much slower, and she sounded like she was back here on earth. "It is so easy for you to say that, London," Terry said. "Remember that I was the only daughter who lived around Mom for a long while." I said.

"Yes, and I don't know how you,…"

"So I know how Mom can be, Terry, and last year was the only time that I saw Mom for who she is."

Terry calmed down and realized that Mom was only trying to help.

"Terry, try and get Mom to babysit for you. I would but I am too busy. Take Shon out on a dinner date just the two of you," I suggested.

"I will take your advice sister," She said.

"Goodbye sis." I made it home and walked in my house, and the first thing I did was get in the shower. I slipped on my silk pink pjs and put on some nice tunes. I relaxed on my soft bed. I could not believe that this was a new year and my life was changing. *God, thank you so much for blessing me!*

I started a group for women. I knew that God was still healing me, so this group was to benefit me as well. I felt God strongly telling me to be more active in my church. So I started these meetings every Thursday night so that women like my mother and me would not feel ashamed of our sin.

This group would provide a safe place so we could share our testimonies and the love of God.

I was so thankful that my mother joined the group and was able to tell her story. I had been told nothing about her past, but God really moved on my mother; she told all the young ladies to never put your trust in the idea of love but put your trust in the one who is love and that is God! In these meetings no judging was allowed.

I knew that next Thursday would be my turn to share my story how God taught me how to wait and believe in Him, even when things are not so perfect. God had showed me that if Rahab the prostitute was spared, then I knew, according to Joshua 6:17, that God would spare all women. God would save and love women who were struggling with all kinds of hurt and pain. I was so excited. I found myself thinking a lot about helping other women.

I found myself lost in dreamland.

"Brandon, Brandon," I said while half asleep.

Brandon called me in the middle of the night.

"London, hey, I am so sorry that I called you this late, but I would like to tell you I love you."

"Brandon…. I love you too," I said while the butterflies danced in my belly just at the sound of his voice. I had been the girl that men used, and now I was the woman that this man loved!

I knew that Brandon really loved me because he really loved God!

"Look, baby, go to sleep, and I will call you tomorrow."

"Brandon," I said in my sleepy raspy voice, "I miss you!"

"Hey goodnight. I miss you too. Soon we will be sleeping in the same bed," he said.

"Goodnight, Bran," I said while still thinking about what he said last. I could not wait. Trying to maintain celibacy was really hard. But we both wanted to honor God and each other. I finally went back to sleep.

Chapter 10

NEW DAY, NEW THINGS

Kevin came in my office with this great big smile. He had burst through the door. "Ms. Kennedy! You will not believe this, girl. He wants you! HEEE wants you!"

"Slow down, Kevin. Who are you talking about?"

"Well, Mr. James Hilton said he wants you to handle his accounts. Not just one but all of them!"

Kevin began to yell and jump up and down. I was excited too, but somehow I was not feeling like this was going to work out, working with this big-time millionaire who is very intelligent and handsome.

"Okay, Kevin this is great, but calm down."

Kevin still had that big smile, "So, Ms. Kennedy, he wants you."

"Don't look at me like that, Kevin, I am a soon-to-be married woman!" I said with a very serious tone.

"My name is mind your business, but I am just saying it looks like you have more than a business account… you are getting a secret admirer because he sent you these." Kevin went back out in the hall and came back with a big bouquet of beautiful white tulips.

"How did he find out that I love white tulips?"

"I don't know, but this bouquet is super big!" Kevin yelled. "Let's read the card!" "Kevin, stop right there, no no no. I have no need for you to read my card. I can read my own card."

I said giggling at how noisy Kevin was being.

"It says, 'London, you are a very brilliant woman. I love the way you think… I can't wait to work with you!' James Hilton."

"Kevin, see its just business," I said. But my intuition was telling me something different.

Kevin is making hand gestures like some teenager.

"Wow… Do you know that this is THE Mr. James Hilton? You are a bad woman!!! Uh Man, I have to give you your props!" Kevin said.

"Okay, Kevin this means we have to work hard, so start setting up those PowerPoint slides and cancel my lunch date with Bran.

"Ms. London Kennedy. Are you sure you want to cancel that lunch date with your future husband?" I turned around, to face Kevin, "Yes, Kevin chop! chop!"

Wow! This meant more work and more money!

I spent all day with Kevin working on ideas and PowerPoints to present to Mr. James Hilton. I realized it was 6:30 and we had been working and eating in the office all day long. It was time to shut it down.

"Kevin, look, I will see you bright and early tomorrow morning."

"Yes, Ms. Kennedy," Kevin said while we headed to our cars.

I realized I missed about five of Brandon calls. I returned his call while driving on the crowed freeway. "Brandon, so sorry, but guess what I just got? James Hilton's accounts… all of them!"

"Wow, that is great, baby!" Brandon said, sounding excited. You are on the ball! Hey how are you going to plan this wedding if you have taken on such a great workload?"

"I will manage, Bran, do not worry."

Brandon began to tell me how his day went and how he wanted to meet up for dinner.

"Brandon I had pizza and a salad with Kevin," I said to let him know that once I got home I was working some more.

"London, we have not seen each other in about a week. I miss you and I want to see you." Brandon sounded so cute.

"Bran…" I said while pulling up in my garage and walking inside. "I am telling you, I will make sure we see each other for lunch.

"Yeah, but since you are going to be working for Mr. Hilton, you will be dedicated in working to the max, which means no time for lunch or me," Brandon said, sounding pitiful.

"Awww, Bran, I will promise that lunch date belongs to you," I said while getting ready for a shower and bed.

Chapter 11

TAKING ON MORE

The next morning was hectic, and everyone seemed like they wanted to call me for this and that. I had thirty voice messages, and my coffee was not hot enough; I knew this was going to be a long Thursday. Kevin came in the office looking well groomed and handsome. I would have never thought that this nice, handsome, smart, intelligent man was gay. Kevin was a hard worker; I was so happy that Sherry did leave and replaced herself with Kevin. Don't get me wrong, I loved working with Sherry, but she was not as educated and diligent as Kevin. "Ms. Kennedy, he is here!"

"Who is here, Kevin?" I said, not sure why Kevin was acting strange. He was never nervous around clients.

"James Hilton, your secret admirer," he whispered in a joking way. I did not find that very funny. I looked up and saw James Hilton walking into my office. I could hear the women chattering, giggling and admiring his handsome looks. I also knew that these women also knew he was a millionaire.

"James...I'm sorry, I mean, Mr. Hilton. Did we have a meeting at this time?" I asked, wanting to know why was he coming to my office without scheduling an appointment. "Look, I wanted to get to know the woman I will be working so closely with," he said while scanning every part of my body. It made me feel awkward.

Mr. Hilton came closer to me, so close I could feel his body heat. James looked me in my eyes, and I could not help but to notice how nice his dimples were. James's eyes were gray with brown speckles and reminded me of the guy I dated in high school. He was a jerk and a cheater.

"Look, I have heard a lot about you, Ms. Kennedy. You are strong, smart, and you are a workaholic, and that is what I need, somebody like you... so what's next?" Mr. James Hilton was confident, smooth, and somewhat cocky. I liked that about him; it was almost looking at me in a male version.

I was not falling for his handsome features and his alluring charm. This was only business, at least that was what I kept telling my flesh.

"Mr. Hilton, we should start by showing you our ideas for your marketing company, the Ad Store. Let's start by changing your brand to what you stand for. If we can do that, then we can target more consumers from different demographics," I said. Moving past Mr. James Hilton made me feel weak in my knees, not because he was handsome but because of the way his eyes followed my every move.

I spent the day with Mr. Hilton and realized he was not so bad; he was just passionate. Mr. James Hilton and I were in my office laughing about how he grew up thinking that pig feet was on the tables of everyone in America like McDonalds until he got to grade school. "This chicken and mashed potatoes is so good… I wish we would have meet sooner," Mr. Hilton said.

I was too busy eating my fried okra and baked chicken mac and cheese and cornbread…Judy's cooking has the best southern cooking in Texas.

"Mr. Hilton, you have to taste Glory's fried chicken dinners. Man they are super good!" I said, because if Mr. James Hilton thought Judy's cooking was good, he would fall in love with Glory's food.

"So tell me about your husband," Mr. Hilton said. I was flabbergasted that Mr. James Hilton wanted to ask me about my personal life.

"Mr. Hilton, …"

"Call me James, I prefer that you call me James," Mr. Hilton said.

"Okay - James it is. On the other hand he is not my husband yet, but really soon and I cannot wait. We met here at the job. He works in a different department."

"So, do you believe that he is your soulmate?" James asked.

"That's a very good question. I know that every part of my being belongs to this man. We are already one." I did not know why all of the questions, but it did not take a rocket science to figure out he was into me. This conversation was not really professional. But I figured as long as I do my job, then everything would work out right.

"In all honesty, …this man is a very lucky man."

"I prefer to say blessed. I don't believe in luck," I said. James glanced at me with a smirk.

"Ms. Kennedy, Brandon is on line two," Kevin announced. I was saved by my fiancé's phone call.

"James, we can catch up tomorrow."

"Okay," he said.

"Sounds good. Enjoyed working with you!" I said while James grabbed his to-go plate of food and walked out my office.

"Brandon, hey baby, how are things going?" I had to turn Brandon down for lunch again. "Sorry, baby, James and I ate in my office." I did not want to keep canceling our lunch dates and dinner dates, but I had taken on a large workload. Brandon of all people should understand how it is at our company.

"Okay, London you have been so busy," Brandon said. By the sound of his voice, he was not happy.

"I know. I will make it up to you," I said before we ended the call. The day had now come to an end, and I was headed home.

I called Brandon to apologize when I made it home.

"Look, London, it is cool, work is work," Brandon said in a dry tone.

"I am so happy you understand. I would meet you for dinner, but I have that meeting at the church for the women's ministry. I will see you later. Maybe we can have dinner tomorrow night."

"Look, whatever, London…just call me when you have some time."

Brandon was very upset.

He just hung up without saying I love you. I knew he would get over it. I knew I needed two more weeks with working with James and bam! It would be done!

I arrived at my church, Loving Temple, and Pastor Jeff Ramon and his wife, Cindy, were leaving, "Hello, First Lady and Pastor," I said, greeting them with a smile.

"Now when are you and that Brandon going to set the date?" Pastor asked.

"I have been planning everything. I have been wanting to call you about using the church for some time in July for the dinner rehearsal," I said, feeling so unprepared, not really knowing what Brandon wanted.

"Well, that is not that far away, so you need to really set up a date because in July we have church picnics and revivals," Pastor said while heading to their car.

"Okay, Pastor you two have a good night."

I walked into the second sanctuary. All the ladies had showed up again. I somehow was getting butterflies. The church was filled with a lot of young ladies and older ladies. Minister Shoranda was talking to my Mom.

"Hey, ladies. Mom, how are you?" I said.

"I am so happy that everyone decided to come back and they brought friends," Mom said while taking her seat. Minister Shoranda prayed for all of us. I was sitting in my seat thinking about everything I had been through and how wonderful God was. I was so blessed. The feeling in that church was warm, and joy filled the room!

I knew that God had showed up.

"I would like for you to give a hand clap for this lovely lady who started this meeting and she has the grace and integrity to stand here tonight to talk to all of us about her journey!"

Everyone began to clap. I stood up to walk to the microphone and realized that I was nervous, but I knew God did not bring me this far to not share my story with passion.

"Hello, everyone. I am so glad that you guys came out." Looking at all the faces, I could tell they wanted to hear the truth. They wanted to know how God could move in their lives. I began to tell my story about how I never really felt sure of myself because of all the missing pieces and how that led me down a road of chasing love.

I told them how I had so many failed relationships and how I found true love and how God began to teach me how to love him and myself and how I found self-worth under the clutter and the mess of my life. God was right there! God taught me how to love again. "I just want to say this before we leave… God has ordained these meetings. I have come up with a name for us… Daughters of Hope!"

Everyone cheered, and I saw my Mom in the crowd cheering and smiling. She was now living just like I was. We both were free! So many women came up to me that night and just cried on my shoulder and told me how much they needed to hear my story.

"Hey, sweetheart, you were great," Mom said, as she gave me the biggest hug. I looked at my Mom; she was fabulous and fearless.

"What happened to Lisa and Terry?" I asked. Mom looked at me while waving goodbye to the ladies.

"Terry and Lisa, they both were just too exhausted with the babies and trying to balance their lives, so they could not come. I am telling you, they wanted to be here."

I knew that my sisters wanted to come out, but maybe next time. "I know, Mom, but tonight was great because God really used all of my broken pieces to make me a whole woman. God will use what is broken!"

Chapter 12

THE BIRTHING GROUND

I had finally birthed my pain and watched God use it for his glory. I was so happy walking in to work with a new attitude. James Hilton was sitting at my conference table looking over a few folders we had put together. When I walked in the door, he began to clap.

"My super star!" he said looking tall and handsome. I scanned the room and notice it was only the two of us.

"Thank you. I did not know I would be greeted with a standing ovation," I said, smiling and feeling so happy.

"So tell me why are you glowing," he said, watching me again with those eyes.

I wanted to tell him, but I don't like to share my personal life and my beliefs with my work partners, but James might need some God in his life.

"I started this program at my church called Daughters of Hope, and we had our meeting last night."

"Really, sounds very interesting, you seem so passionate about everything that is in your life…. You know, that is why I am glad to have you over my accounts!" He said while walking over to the oversized desk.

I smiled and felt so honored that James thought highly of me. "Look, as a matter fact, let's start this program and turn it to a nonprofit! I will be your first sponsor!" James had said something that God had already told me to do!

I could not believe that Brandon did not think of this first because he was the expert in starting nonprofits.

"Wow!" I yelled and jumped in James's arms while James embraced me with a gentle hug and looked right in my eyes. I felt like I wanted to kiss him, and by the looks of things he wanted to as well. But a small, weird feeling came over me as I stared in James's eyes. I felt that James gave off a very familiar vibe. We both were interrupted by a knock at the door, and my handsome fiance came in the office.

Brandon was looking at me and back at James. James quickly released his hands from around my waist. Brandon laid down his bouquet of roses on my desk.

"Hey, Bran! I am so happy you came," I said, still startled a little bit from that hug. I was glad that it had not ended with James kissing me. Boy, this would be ugly.

"Hello, my name is Brandon, and I am her fiancé," Brandon said, standing tall and confident.

"Yes, I heard a lot about you," James said, with a smug grin.

"Well, I cannot say the same for you," Brandon said while staring at James over from head to toe.

"I told you, honey… James hired me for all his accounts."

"Yeah you did, you been so busy I have not been able to celebrate," Brandon said while giving me the side eye.

"Well, it was nice meeting you, man. I will let you to enjoy lunch. It is always a pleasure working with your fiancé," James said, giving Brandon that smug grin again.

"I don't understand why you are so upset," I said, giving Bran a big hug.

"I am not mad, but I just did not like that guy all over you," he said, while wrapping his arms around my waist.

"Brandon, I only have eyes for you," I said, smiling.

" That guy clearly likes you," Brandon said, while we both headed for lunch. Brandon and I arrived at Lou Bay Lunch and Dinner where they served Jamaican food.

I sat down at the nice small table for two, listening to the low sounds of Jamaican music playing in the background.

You could smell the aroma of curry chicken and red beans and rice. I loved island food. It was spicy and delicious.

"What are you going to order, Brandon?" I asked while taken a sip from my glass of water. The waiter poured Brandon a tall glass of water as well.

"I would like to order, curry chicken, red beans and rice, cornbread and an ice cold tea." Brandon said. "I would like the same, I said." Brandon was a little bit distant and awkward. I think that Brandon was still thinking about James.

I wondered if Brandon trusted me.

"So, London you seem really busy lately. Have you had time to plan this wedding?" Brandon asked, trying to seem calm and cool, when you could see he was frustrated.

"Brandon, no, I had to make four different PowerPoints for James and I went into his files for several different accounts to change the name on one of his businesses and then we worked on his marketing his brand.

"I don't understand why Kevin is not working with you guys. And why are you calling your client by his first name?" Brandon said while taken a mouthful of rice and beans. "Because James only wanted to work with me directly, and for the simple reason that James asked me to call him by his first name," I said, hoping that Brandon will not jump to conclusions.

"See, that's what I mean. Clearly this guy is pushing up on you, and you are being too naive to see it! Brandon raised his voice to a higher tone then normal.

"What? Too naïve? Wait… I am going to pretend you did not say that!"

I was so mad at Brandon. "Brandon, look for the record I can be trusted, okay?" Brandon jumped up out of his seat. "What? Trusted? I need to remind you about what happened the last time you were alone with a handsome, successful man… the panties came off!"

I could not believe Brandon and I were having a serious fight! We had never been this mad since we broke up.

"Look, I am done… you can fight by yourself. I can call a taxi to take me back to work," I mumbled.

"Yeah, go head and leave, run back to James, your boyfriend!" Brandon yelled while I left him at the table acting like a high school boy. I walked to the front of the restaurant and called my Mom, but there was no answer. I remembered that Mom always said to never run away from your issues, stand up to them.

I knew that Brandon was being overly jealous, but he clearly had not gotten over the pain of me cheating because he was yelling and Brandon never yelled unless he was super mad. I walked back to the table to find Brandon with his face in his hands.

"Look, Brandon, I don't want to cheat on you. If you don't trust me, then how can we move forward? I think we both need a break from each other so we can really make sure that this marriage is what we both need right now," I said, with tears in my eyes.

"Look, I don't need space. I do need to trust you. I did not know that I would act like that," Brandon said while looking up at me. "Maybe you are right, we do need some counseling, but if we keep on breaking up every time something happens, then we should not be together," Brandon said, while leaning in towards me. "I can promise to love you but I cannot promise that I won't never make you mad," he said.

There was truth in what Brandon said. I knew that it was going to be bad times just like this, and if you claim to love someone, you should not run away. "Brandon, if we stay together we need to love each other enough to go to a counselor before marriage. We have been through so much. For this reason we should definitely seek godly counseling," I said, trying to be very optimistic.

"Sounds like a plan. Now come and sit down and finish up your lunch," Brandon said. I glared at him, and we both began to laugh. I felt like he needed that confirmation to know that I loved him. I leaned in and gave him a warm kiss on his lips. Brandon's eyes lit up; the kiss had caught him off guard.

"Brandon, I want you to know that I have grown since then, and God is my first love, but he brought you in my life, so I will never hurt you like what I did before." I said.

"London, I am sorry too. You have been missing in action lately. I just missed you, and since both of those situations happened before, I am more nervous over the guys than thinking that you would cheat. I want to protect you," Brandon said, while taking a sip of his water.

"I understand you want to protect me," I said, smiling. I knew that Brandon loved me so much!

Brandon dropped me off at my office and gave me a kiss on the cheek. James was waiting in my conference room.

"Hey! You are back. Hope you are ready for this… We got to go to Canada to meet with two business owners who are connected with one of the accounts. They want to hold off on changing the name of the business until they meet you, so I plan to book a flight for this weekend, and we will be back on Sunday night."

Brandon would not like this at all, I thought.

"Mr. Hilton, this is so sudden," I said, while plopping in the soft plush chairs. "Look, London in order to work with me you have to be ready for anything at any time," he said, while leaning in close to me. I could feel his hot breath. "London, I prefer for you to call me James. I thought I cleared this with you. See you this weekend London."

I slumped down in the chair while he walked out the room.

I was so tired and could not wait to go home and take a hot shower. I talked with Kevin before the day was over and told him to take care of other accounts and meetings. I told him that I would be in Canada this weekend and to make sure everything was taken care of. I made it home; my house was quiet as always.

After my shower I put on my black silk pjs .

I began to reminisce about the conversation I had with Lisa the other night, and she was telling me her story of being a new Mom. I was so happy for her. I checked my messages, and Brandon had called. I was kind of scared about telling him that I was going to Canada with the guy that he did not trust at all. But this account meant everything to me. Brandon's name popped on my cell phone screen.

"Hey, Bran, what's going on?"

"Well, I missed you and I wanted to tell you that I found a counselor. It is Pastor Ramon and his wife!"

He began to fill me in. "They want to meet with us for dinner this weekend." Brandon sounded so happy. How could I tell him that I was not going to be able to go? What do I say to a man who was ready to end this separate home living arrangement soon?

"Brandon, I have to tell you that I have this amazing opportunity.... and I have to go to Canada for this business meeting with James on Friday, and I will be back on Sunday night." I said it really fast with a lot of energy, hoping that my fiancé would not feel neglected.

"What, baby, are you kidding me?" Brandon's voice was low, and I could tell he was let down hard.

"Bran, Bran, I will be back. I have to meet the other partners who are over the account that James and I are changing the name," I said, trying to convince him it was just business.

"Well, I will need to call and reschedule. Next time I will consult you first, London, sorry about that." Brandon sounded so mature. "I want to have lunch with you tomorrow okay London?"

"I would love that, Bran!"

"London, I'm looking forward to see you again for lunch. Love you, baby!"

"Love you too! Have a good night!"

Friday went well, and the lunch date with Brandon was awesome. We both hugged each other and reassured each other that we loved each other. I landed in Canada after a long flight. I went to my hotel room, which was a fancy suite. The room had one queen-sized bed and thick, gold Egyptian-thread sheets. I loved the room service. I had a lovely vase of tulips in my room. I smiled because I knew who had sent them. It was nice of him to send me flowers. But James was being very discreet about his flirting. I knew it had to stop. I lay down after I ate. James was calling my cell. I was still halfway in dream world when I answered.

"James, hey, what's wrong?"

"Nothing. I wanted to make sure you made it safely."

"Thank you."

"London, if you need anything I am in the room across from you," James said while I hung up. I knew deep down in my heart James was pursuing me.

I was trying to block it out because this account was big.

The sun beamed in my amazing suite. I watched the sun rise while I was having coffee, which I don't drink often. I just need the caffeine to wake me up.

I had on a black and white striped blouse and a white suit; I looked very cute. Vera Wang always saves the day. My hair was straight and my red lips were definitely glowing. I wanted to make a great impression. I walked in the meeting that was being held in a conference room in the hotel.

The two men were in their late 70's; they never smiled when I greeted them. James Hilton was sitting there, looking as handsome as ever. He was confident. I presented the Power Point slides, telling the partners that the best thing for the firm was to recreate the company. I was offering the company a makeover that would change the business to a billion dollar firm. James and I both left the meeting smiling.

"Whoop!! You did it!"

James grabbed me picked me up and turned me around! I was so happy because I reached a higher level in my career and James helped me.

"Look, miss lady, I am going to take you to the best dinner tonight!"

Really, is this James' way in getting me out? I will let him take me out just for dinner.

"James, is there another meeting on Sunday? Because if not, I can leave for home tonight."

"What!! No, you can't just leave! No, that was the only meeting," James replied with disappointment.

"Ok, I will stay tonight for dinner but I will leave on Sunday morning."

I went to my room and changed into a nice long sleek black dress, with gold pumps. I pulled my hair from my face and dashed to the bar in the hotel. The single women at the bar were desperate and overrated. I could not believe that they were throwing themselves at all the professional men. I had a flashback and I thought of myself; I used to be those women. James sat on the side of me, looking handsome, like a model.

I realized that this was a dinner date and not a business dinner. I began to daydream….thinking about Brandon, and Jason. I thought that Jason was everything, but I could not see him for who he really was - a cheater! Brandon, I knew he was a godly man from the start, I mean he was a little cocky… but he loved God. You could tell by the way he carried himself and how he respected me from the start! I looked up at James and that crooked smile he had; he wanted to take me out on the town. But I could not help but remember Bran's face, when I had been so busy working on accounts with James and I was not spending any time with my man.

"Hey, everything ok?" James asked.

"Yea, it is. It's just that I do not want to hang out with you, James, when I could be on the phone with my future husband."

As I said that, the weight came off of my shoulders because I was now standing up for what I really wanted.

I realized it was not about my job or how much money I needed, it was about the man that God created for me.

"Wow, you're dissing me. Look, what's wrong with you girl? I am single with no kids; I am rich and handsome, and everyone at this bar would jump at an opportunity to have just one conversation with me."

I could not believe James was not playing it cool and his real feelings were surfacing.

"Wait a minute James!" I said loudly.

"No, you wait!!" James responded louder.

James' true colors were showing; he was acting like the devil himself.

"I hired you because you are fine not because you are good! I was hoping you were good in bed!"

I blurted out before James could say more. "Oh no! I am leaving tonight, and you can pay me what you owe me; I quit!" I said while walking away from this jerk. James knew what he was doing; he was trying to keep me busy on purpose to make Brandon mad. That is why it is so important to pray!

I went to my room and packed my things and flew out of Canada that night. I arrived in Dallas at midnight. I called Brandon. Brandon was half asleep and he could not believe I was calling.

"Baby what's wrong?" He asked.

"Nothing baby just… that James he ….let's just say you were right about him." "What the hell happened??" Brandon yelled.

I knew Brandon was really upset because he does not use language like that. "Brandon calm down!!" I said, knowing that Brandon already went through the worst with men hurting me.

"He did not do anything but yell at me baby…. I will tell you in the morning," I said, while pulling up in my driveway.

"I need some rest; I am at home now." I had to calm Brandon down to get him to disconnect the call.

I rested the next day. I had already called Kevin and informed him on what occurred. Kevin thought it was crazy; he thought this was a movie scene. I finally got the nerve to call James Hilton.

"Hello," I heard his voice and was lost for words.

"Look, I hope you had the chance to calm down." I said trying to soften the blow. "Oh, it is Miss Kennedy. Look, I took care of everything… I decided to talk with your boss and let him know that I had to let you go, because of our personal spat we had over drinks. Your boss did not like the idea that we were at a bar and turning a business meeting into something personal."

I could not believe this handsome, devilish man!!! I was so mad at how he discredited my name.

"I see where this is going." I said very politely.

"Don't worry, Tina is picking up from where you left off," he said.

I did not say anything to Mr. Hilton; I just disconnected the call.

I called my boss and explained to him what happened. I was told to take my vacation and relax.

"Don't worry about James Hilton; he is known to be a pain in the, you know what."

I was officially on vacation. I guess the good Lord knew that I needed to prepare and plan for my wedding as well as being a wife. Soon I heard a knock on the door. Somebody was at my door. It was Lisa and Terry with their babies! "Yeah!!!!" I screamed. "You guys made it!" I said, jumping up and down like a two year old.

"We just wanted to stop by and see how things are going. You've been missing in action, girl," Lisa said.

"I love your townhome," Terry said as she sat down on my couch. Lisa had a girl and Terry had a boy. Their babies were so cute.

"Well, we are so glad that you took time off from that job of yours. We don't get the chance to see you. Terry and I both moved to Texas to spend time with family," Lisa said, while rocking her baby girl back and forth.

"I know…I am taking a vacation and I am off for four weeks."

"I cannot believe that you get all those days off! Man, your job has all the perks!" Terry said while feeding Shon Jr.

Someone rang the doorbell.

"Well, I think that is Brandon." Lisa said, while opening the front door.

Brandon stood there.

"I am not going to bite," he said while I stood there, not knowing what was going on in his head.

Brandon reached out and gave me a warm sweet hug.

"I missed you Bran!!!" I said, feeling really loved.

"Hey, Terry, you both are looking great!" Brandon said while smiling, and his brown eyes just lit right up. Soon he started playing with both babies.

"Look out, London… from the looks of things Brandon might want a big family!" Lisa said while elbowing my arms.

"I thought you ladies were leaving? It is time for Lisa to go! Thanks for using my body as a punching bag!" I said, joking around. My sisters left with their very cute babies. One day that will be me soon. I was so happy to have my sisters here with me; my life was coming together and was unfolding right before my eyes. I could remember the dates and the lonely nights and long days at work. My thoughts used to always stay on the ideology of marriage. "Is that him?"

"Could that be my husband?"

I always had questions and worries, and I never really slowed down to smell the roses. It took almost losing the man that God gave me to walk out my life and run into the arms of another woman for me to realize that I needed to make some changes. I mean, the worst part was that woman whom he ran to was the reason why I was violated and abused.

Then, God worked everything out. He started with the inside of me. Wow, I like that, I just might write a book and call it ,"The Inside of Me." You never know what is in store.

Brandon plopped on my sofa and started flipping through the TV channels.

"Bran, did you eat?" I yelled out from the kitchen. Brandon is not a big screamer; he hated raising his voice unless he was upset.

Brandon walked in the kitchen with me and wrapped his warm arms around my waist. This was the second week in February and today was Valentine's Day! With me being busy from work and all the gifts from my birthday and Christmas I was overwhelmed. So February was just going to be a night in.

I loved being in the kitchen cooking for my man while he embraced me. We both have been celibate and that's why we could not entertain each other too long with the sweet warm kisses, the touches and too many hugs can trigger the need for more. I can say we both knew when to draw the line. Brandon was still holding me, while I seasoned my chicken breasts and placed them in the oven.

"London, baby I am so happy that you know how to cook for your man; I prayed for that..ha ha." Brandon said while laughing.

I broke the embrace with a crazy look. "Why are you laughing, is that a laugh for I think I can cook, but really can't?" I said, pushing Brandon lightly away from me.

"Girl, no you can cook!" Trust me, if you could not cook, I would have told you!" Brandon said while licking his lips.

"Happy Valentine's Day!" I said.

"Well, I made a nice garden salad and fresh French bread so we will be eating in about 20 minutes," I said, as we both moved toward the sofa in the living room. "Sit down London, you are always moving…."

Brandon was right; I always had to be doing something. I sat down on my sofa while Brandon sat next to me.

"Happy Valentines Day to you too!!!"

Brandon and I did not do anything extravagant. We just had a simple night with Valentine's Day cookies and he bought me a cute stuffed animal. I just cooked for him. We searched through the channels to find a great movie. Brandon was just gazing at me. "Look, I am so glad you finally got a break from work and we both can plan this wedding. Time has passed so fast; we are already in the second week in February, on love day," he said, with my head on his lap. I smiled and said, "For sure, Bran." I was now connected to this movie. The movie was about a couple that wanted to have a baby and the wife was nervous about trying again because she had a miscarriage. It made me think about what women had to go through and the beautiful feeling of being a mother!

Soon I said, "Brandon the movie is over and it is time to eat, eat, eat!" Brandon jumped up and walked slowly to the table, he turned around so he was facing me.

"London, one day we will have us a bunch of babies…" Brandon said, while tickling my belly.

I laughed so much…

"Stop Stop Stop!!! Ha ha!" I laughed some more.

We both sat down and ate while catching up with each other on work and projects. "Brandon, I know I should have listened to you when you mentioned that James Hilton was a rich, up-to-no-good type of guy," I said while taking a mouthful of my crispy, tasty salad.

"Just know that people are so selfish they will try anything to break up a good couple," I said.

"Don't feel bad. Look at Mandy!"

We both had not mentioned her name in a while.

Brandon regretted that he brought her up. But I was over it; she was no longer the lady that could hurt me.

"I am sorry, but she should be the last person that I should bring up," Brandon said while stuffing his mouth with juicy, seasoned chicken.

"This chicken is so good, London," Brandon said while shaking his head in slow motion, from side to side.

"I am glad you like it."

I knew I could make my way into his heart with my cooking. I thought to myself remembering when Brandon first had some of my cooking. Brandon and I finished up dinner and we both headed to the living room. It was about 9pm. I did not like this part; Brandon had to leave.

"London, sweetheart, I need to go home and make some connections before bed. "I'll see you later, ok?" We both now were standing by the front door. I felt so sad, like my best friend was leaving.

"Why do you look so sad; you make it seem like I am going out of town or something," Brandon said while putting on his leather coat.

"I know…it's getting to me that we don't live together."

Brandon reached out and pulled me in his arms and squeezed me like he was never ever letting go.

"Bran, I love you, and the fact that I had to take my vacation for sure was God! I needed to work on those wedding plans."

Brandon smiled like the sunrise, then he leaned in and gave me the sweetest kiss on the forehead that made me melt like chocolate.

I knew it was time for him to go!!! But how I wished we were already married. This courtship, I meant engagement, can be hard, when you are really trying to stay pure before the wedding.

"Love when you do that," I said, sounding dreamy.

"Well, good night, and make sure all the doors are locked. Call me if you hear anything strange."

Brandon gave me the rundown like that every time he would leave. Brandon did this ever since my attack.

"Ok, Bran…..goodnight and I'll talk to you soon!" I yelled while he was already getting into his black Infiniti.

Chapter 13

EMBRACING LOVE FOREVER

I last saw Bran three days ago. I enjoyed our counseling session with my Pastor and his wife. They were so transparent that it was delightful. We were already moving into planning our wedding.

After the session I was at my mother's house, reflecting. I was so thankful that Brandon and I took the pre-marital counseling with Pastor Ramon. Brandon and I had only one more night to meet with him and his wife for dinner at their house next week. I was so excited. My mother and I were in her second living room looking at so many wedding dresses. This was my fifth book.

"Look, London it has been already two months since this Bran has asked you to marry him. You need to find a dress and a venue fast." Mom said.

"Mom who told you that you can call Brandon, Bran?"

"What! Girl, that just rubbed right on to me since you always say, 'Bran this, Bran that!!' " Mom said in a funny, nagging voice.

"Well I don't sound like that!" I said while she laughed and went in the kitchen. I wanted this wedding to be over already.

"Mom!!! I am calling a wedding planner."

My Mom came out the kitchen with two hot cups of my favorite tea.

"Well, London, you'd better call one soon because time is ticking."

I had called about 100 wedding planners and they were already booked. I was so tired of hearing, "No, I am booked."

Finally, I called this wonderful lady, Amber Smith. I decided to meet with her today, Saturday. I left to meet her at the coffee shop around the corner from my Mom's house. I waited and finally she walked in 15 minutes late for her meeting with me.

My father use to always say never show up to a meeting late you will start and end up being late in the end. "Hi, so sorry I'm late; I'm not really familiar with this side of town, as I am from uptown."

Amber was wearing all black; skinny jeans and leather Coach boots with a very fancy Vera Wang long sleeved blouse, and she smelled amazing. Her blond long locks fell to her shoulders. She was a very beautiful wedding planner who dressed like me. She was the Caucasian version of me.

"I always have said that when I see someone who dresses well, they take pride in their brand."

"Well, nice to meet you. Oh, I love your Louis Vuitton bag!" She screamed. "Thank you! It is my pleasure to meet you, but hope that you are more timely in the future." I said.

She smiled and shook her head. Amber told me she had a team and an office uptown. Amber talked about locations and venues and how she had connections to the Museum of Arts and that having my wedding during the first week of April would be great but since we were almost in the second week of February and we needed to move fast. I had a few great options for venues. I was so impressed! I told her next time I will meet her at her office. I wanted to see what her office looked like and how she managed her office. It was cool how she started her own business. She was looking to giving her company a makeover and was looking forward to my interior decorating services after the wedding. Since I had this time off to plan, I also thought that this was a great time to start my own company! New Year, new things! When the meeting was over, I headed over to Lisa's house for lunch, wearing my long maxi dress in a beautiful tiny red floral print and my black finned shades.

"Lisa, hey where is that cute little princess?" I asked while entering. I was looking for Megan.

"Here she is," Lisa replied, holding Megan in her arms.

Megan's legs wiggled and squirmed.

"Ok, Lisa, why is your baby moving like that?" I asked, making the fish face to her.

"Oh, Auntie London is a fish face crazy girl," Lisa said while getting ready to feed Megan.

"Lisa, don't say that about me! That is not nice!" I shouted while walking in the kitchen to raid her refrigerator.

"London, don't eat Tony's steak. You know how he feel about his food!" Lisa yelled.

"Well, I am hungry, I thought you would have cooked lunch since this was our lunch date."

I walked back into the living room where Lisa was now burping little Megan. "Well, Lisa let's go to a restaurant because girl I am hungry and your refrigerator is empty!" I said while touching my stomach.

"Oh, man!!! You'd better not be preggo!" Lisa screamed.

"How dare you, Lisa! You know I am not playing that!" I said, while Lisa gave me this weird look.

"What do that mean?" I said, hoping that she did not think I was the same easy girl. "Lisa, what do you mean by that face, sister?" Lisa was laughing but realized I was not.

"Look, dang, girl, I was just joking!"

"Ok, fine you were just playing around with the thought that I am sleeping with my boyfriend! Lisa, I started Daughters of Hope; do you think I would play around about sleeping with Brandon?"

"Wait, before this get blown out bigger than what I wanted," Lisa said, trying to find the right words to fix what she had said.

"You know what, it is time for Megan's nap, so Melinda please take Megan and get her to sleep." Lisa said while the nanny picked Megan up and they both disappeared upstairs.

"Lisa, look no matter what, somewhere in your head you think that I am still that girl!" I said picking up my purse to leave.

"Ok, so you're leaving? This is not the way to solve a disagreement," Lisa said, while I headed for the door.

She followed me. Lisa was upset, as she walked frantically to the front door. "Wait, I am sorry, you are so right I had no business joking about you having a baby and sex," Lisa said.

I felt so sorry for Lisa, I was not that mad at her… but I wanted her to sweat a little bit…lol.

"Well I am leaving anyway because I am buying lunch for the both of us. Next time you'd better cook or buy take out!" I said, with a bright smile.

I did not want to get so upset with my sister that it would cause some kind of split between us so I let it go. Lisa hugged me and said, "Better yet, let's go out while the nanny is on the clock."

We both left to go to a nice restaurant that was close to her home. I enjoyed my sister, but it was time for me to go home and complete my business plan.

Chapter 14

NEW BEGINNINGS AND LOVING LIFE

I was so excited about typing up my business plan and seeing my brand new business on paper! It was amazing how God would use the same gifts that He blessed you with to turn around and bless others! I have seen God restore every area of my life! Working for the best firm and being blessed to get million dollar accounts was awesome. It was good, but God had another purpose for my business skills! I was now my own boss!

I had been so busy with planning the wedding and working on my business plan I had not spent much time with my love and my best friend Bran! I was sitting at my desk at home printing my business plan when my Dad called me.

"Yes Father," I said.

"Well, I wanted to know how's my baby coming along with those wedding plans," Daddy said while having that cough again.

"Dad I thought you had that cough taking care of," I said, feeling really concerned. My Dad tries so hard to keep us women from worrying.

I always wondered if he wanted a son because being around all of us women had to be a challenge for him.

"Well, I went to my doctor with your Mom. I am just fine; it's my allergies that got me coughing up a storm," he said, while hacking again, sounding like an old smoker's cough.

"Ok, if you say so. Well the wedding plans are coming along great! I already have the location. We are going to have the wedding ceremonies at the arts museum and we have the best caterer that will serve the best entrees.

"Great… I am so happy that you are marrying that Brandon. He is truly a great man," Dad said, barely getting his words out.

"Thank you Father…I am glad you trusted that God was going to bring a true man in my life to love me and even though Brandon made some bad mistakes you looked past them," I said, thinking back when Brandon had moved on with Mandy and getting her pregnant and bringing her into his life without praying about her first. But I knew that I had done my dirt. We both were not perfect, but we both were forgiven!

"Yes, God he knows that we as humans are going to make mistakes," Dad said, hacking again, but this time he sounded like he could not catch his breath!

"Dad you need to go back to your doctor," I said, hoping he would take my advice.

"Look, I am going to call you some other time."

"Ok Dad," I said, while filing my printed business plan. I had already begun to type an offer letter to Amber for branding for her company.

My wedding date was April the 4th. In the first week in April I was going to lose my last name! God's love is so pure and true, but I can't leave out that sometimes you will have to trust even when you cannot see the whole story!

Brandon and I were meeting for dinner that night at a fancy restaurant inside one of the coolest uptown hotels. I had a busy day hanging out with Mom and meeting with Amber. After that, I

had lunch with my sister Lisa. I was definitely making my rounds. I had on a gold form-fitting sleeveless dress and gold stilettos. My hair was blown out with big soft curls and I even decided to color the ends blonde! Yes! I knew the season had changed and spring was almost here.

I was escorted to my table. When I arrived, my heart was beating fast as if this was the first time I was seeing my man! I scanned the restaurant and noticed a very familiar woman. This woman was classy; she wore a red dress with black red-bottom heels. Her skin was a nice soft brown, and her dark brown hair was hanging past her shoulders in big curls. With her bangs swooped in the front of her face, it was hard to see who she was. I had an overwhelming need to know who she was. The mystery woman was sitting at the bar from across from me. The lady laughed softly while tipping her wine glass to her mouth to take a sip. Two handsome men in suits stood on both sides of her. I could not remove my eyes from her. I mean… could it be possible that this classy woman (who was possibly rich, based on the rock on her ring finger) be somebody I know? I ordered a glass of white wine while the young lady turned around and glanced at me as if she could feel someone staring at her. I turned away as if I was looking for someone.

I then heard my Brans laugh. How could I forget a laugh like this? I began to scan the room again, and I noticed couples laughing and holding hands. I knew tonight was special because it seemed like everyone had love in their eyes!

My eyes stopped scanning the room once I saw him. My Bran was one of the men standing by the mystery woman. He did not see me as he was laughing and smiling while he gazed at her. I could not move my legs; so many emotions were going on in my head. I wondered, was I jealous! I was getting married and my man was a not just a good guy, he was a godly man! I wondered why he was not looking for me; he knew we were supposed to meet up tonight.

I walked slowly to the bar and tapped him on his shoulder. He looked startled but gave me this big hug!

"Bran, I have been waiting for you for about fifteen minutes!" I said as my voice rose. I caught myself and lowered my voice.

"I am so sorry, I thought you would call my cell phone to let me know you were here," Bran said with a half grin.

"I told you… I was going to sit at our same table!" I said, while rolling my eyes. Brandon looked at me as if he was taken aback, based on my ongoing attitude. "Look London, hey, calm down," Bran whispered while embracing me in a nice warm hug.

I needed that hug because I have not really seen Brandon in a while. We both had been working really hard. I looked up in his light brown eyes and realized I was overreacting.

"I am sorry, Bran…I should have called your cell phone to let you know I was here." I whispered.

Brandon took me by my hand and politely turned me around to face the handsome young man whom I saw Brandon talking to. The young lady who was dressed in red was still sitting down sipping her wine, but the way she was sitting I still could not see her face.

"London, meet my friend John Miller; we went to college together."

I glanced at John. He was well-dressed, and his dark brown skin was smooth with a million dollar smile. I shook his hand and smiled. The restaurant was a little bit loud as everyone was talking, eating and laughing.

"It is a pleasure in meeting you, London. My good friend, Brandon, talks about you all the time."

I never heard of this John guy before, but John knew about me. I reflected while John and Brandon were giving each other advice on business deals.

"Really, wow that is good to know that he talks about me." I said smiling from ear to ear.

The lady in red was quiet and she finally spoke. The mystery woman turned around slowly to face me, and it was her, my worst nightmare!

"Hello London, it has been a while."

It was Mandy. She was beautiful, and her makeup was perfect. Her clothing was very expensive. I was just shocked. I could not speak. Mandy began to speak again.

"I am so sorry about everything that happened between us. I hope we can just put the past behind us."

The lady in red was my number one enemy. How could this be happening?

I still could not speak. I just stood there. John looked puzzled at Mandy's apologies to me.

"Look, London this is my wife Mandy Miller.... Now I did not know you guys knew each other," John said, while taking a large gulp of his wine. I still could not speak, and my legs were numb. Bran was searching for words and it seem to me that everyone was talking in slow motion and I felt as if I was being tricked. "Look, London we could leave, I did not know that Mandy married John Miller. I just found out," Brandon said while whispering in my ear.

I suddenly had the courage to speak my mind.

"Look, John Miller…It is a pleasure meeting you but, your wife…"

Before I could speak, Brandon came over to me, grabbed my arm and told his friend that we needed to talk alone. Brandon took me to the back of the restaurant. We both were tugging, something that Bran normally would not do.

"Look….Baby, please don't tell my friend about this thing with Mandy."

I could not believe that my soon-to-be husband was asking me not to expose this woman who, first tried to hurt me by getting us involved with that crazy doctor! I wanted to leave, but all kinds of questions were going through my mind - like why is Brandon still taking up for Mandy? And why is Mandy married to Brandon's good friend?

"Why Brandon's friend?! Why?!"

I yelled at him, but this time I did not try to lower my voice. I was just remembering how I experienced a horrible attack, and had to deal with Mandy's bad attitude. Now, this was supposed to be date night, now this night has become a nightmare! Brandon grabbed my arms and pulled me close, he looked in my eyes as if he did not know me anymore.

"London please listen to me…Mandy had nothing to do with that doctor coming in on you," he said in a soft voice.

"I know you blame her because she was so mean to you during the time she was carrying my baby." Brandon wanted to make everything better, but he was making me feel worse.

"London, she was not the reason for that attack by that crazy doctor who plotted to rape you!"

Brandon was staring into my eyes, hoping that I would just let this go. Brandon was such a good guy; he was always willing to forgive.

"But Brandon what about me?" I asked, hoping that Brandon would come to his senses.

"Look, London, Mandy and John were here when I got here. John told me about them getting married. So let's go back to the bar and just act calm and then we can leave."

Brandon was trying his best to make sure that this night didn't get out of hand.

"Ok, fine with me," I said, not looking up at Bran.

"But wait, I need to tell you what Mandy said to me once John left to the bathroom. That is when Mandy told me that she was so sorry that she treated me like that and she really wanted to be married so bad that she started to do things that she would never do, like sleeping around with men and with me knowing that I was drunk. She said it was a mistake, she said she knew I loved you. She even went as far as dating her boss who was abusive to her as well. She said when she had heard about the doctor breaking in your house, that's what really woke her up. She changed her life around and gave her life to God."

Brandon kept talking and he would not give me a chance to get a word in.

"She wanted to forget about the past and asked me to forgive her for being mean. Mandy did not tell John about what happened because John would be heartbroken. She wants to tell him after her baby is born. You see, they dated when we all were in college. London, John would be very upset if he knew that Mandy and I had something."

I was listening to Brandon, and it seemed so unfair that all of this was happening on our date night.

Mandy is married already and now pregnant again so fast. I thought to myself that this woman is for sure crazy. It seems as if Mandy ruins everything!

"Ok, look Brandon, I understand, you want me to not speak up and put Mandy in her place! So I am leaving right now…and she's pregnant and drinking wine??" I asked while heading for the entrance.

Brandon then let go of my arms, and he put his hands up in the air and just stared at me as if I was the one that just did not get it.

"Ok, London, do what you do best - just walk away!" he yelled.

"This is what you do best!"

Brandon dropped his hands down and walked away from me.

What is going on? How could Brandon think I had the problem? Brandon was being stubborn and not understanding of the fact that I don't like her at all. I debated in my mind to run after him, but why should I? He should have let me tell her off! I marched towards the parking lot, that night the breeze was blowing my hair back. I was very upset and replayed the entire evening in my head. Mandy can afford name brands now - wow! I thought she did a good job by marrying rich!

I heard a faint voice behind me.

"London," Mandy called, while she was coming behind me. I turned around and looked right in Mandy's face. Mandy was beautiful. It was amazing what money could do for a person. But Mandy was always pretty, I thought.

"What do you want from me Mandy???" The look in Mandy's eyes were unforgettable, she was standing there, wanting another chance. My body was so full of hate and I did not want to give in to her plea of forgiveness.

"Stop London, I have not been the best woman, but I am not the only one who has made mistakes before," she said with such tenderness in her voice.

When Mandy said that I could not help but to think back on how I cheated and how I wanted a second chance with God and with Brandon.

"Look, yes I did sleep with Brandon and yes I thought being pregnant could control him," Mandy said, while the night air whipped gently through her long, flowing brown hair. Mandy looked like a model on the outside but she was now telling me what was in her heart.

"London, I did not plot for that doctor to break in on you, please understand. I knew he was crazy but not crazy enough to do that," she said.

I wanted to punch her right in this parking lot. I did not because I am a lady. I wish this happened during my college days, because I would have slapped her. "Mandy, you just don't know how many nightmares I had after that night!" I screamed while tears flowed down my face. I was standing there feeling broken all over again. I did not want to let her see me cry.

"Maybe you did not know, but I had to go through a lot!" I said.

"What do you want from me now?" I asked, while wiping my tears away.

My heart was so filled with emotions that I needed to go home.

"Look, just stay away from me Mandy!" Mandy could see the hurt in my face.

She stood there, and before she could speak, I shouted out telling her to stay away from me and jumped in my car. I drove off leaving Mandy standing in the parking lot. I got home quickly; thankfully the freeway was clear. Brandon had not called to check up on me; that was not like him.

I took a long shower and got ready for bed. It was only nine o'clock and I still had not eaten anything. My phone rang; it was Brandon. I did not pick up the phone; I just let it ring. I lay down and covered up with my tan silk sheets. I could not believe Mandy… Brandon was calling me again. I ignored him and turned on the soft tunes of worship music. My Lord is my help…played over and over in my head while I fell into a deep sleep.

The sun shined in my bedroom window. What a beautiful morning, I did not want to get out my soft bed, but I did not want to miss church. As I stared at my bare face in my bathroom mirror I realized that I just needed to let go of the anger that I had for Mandy. Could I really forgive her? Daughters of Hope was a place for all women who had made mistakes and who have been hurt. How could I form such a group but could not bring myself to a place to love Mandy unconditionally? I got into the shower and allowed the warm water to run down my body, hoping that my pain could be washed away. I got dressed in my navy blue dress with matching heels. I let my hair down and made sure my makeup was just a light, natural look.

When I arrived at church I saw my Mom and sisters sitting in the third row. I sat by Terry and Shon. Terry was beautiful, dark brown and about 5'5" and she was holding my nephew in her arms. I enjoyed watching Shon Jr wiggle and squirm around in her arms,.

"Girl, why is my baby wiggling in your arms, Terry?" I asked, smiling.

"Look, he has gas," she said, while making a stinky face.

I giggled. "Well, I will love him from a distance," I said.

Pastor Ramon's older daughter Tasha came out on stage and began to sing. I looked around the room and noticed that the church was packed. I saw Brandon; he was in back of the church in a nice suit. I thought he was going to another church, but I guess he wanted to come to my church.

Brandon loved Pastor Ramon. Pastor preached a sermon on, "The True Meaning of Love" and how Jesus died on the cross for everyone, including those who hurt Him. I knew that this message was for me. After the sermon was over, my mother walked over to me. She looked flawless in her black fitted dress and her gold pumps.

"Baby, hey how are you?" Mom asked.

I was standing looking over Mom's shoulder at Brandon talking to Pastor and his wife.

"Mom, I am just great!" I said, smiling and wondering to myself what Brandon was saying to Pastor Ramon and his wife.

I hoped he was not telling Pastor about Mandy and me.

"Well, this coming Thursday the women are all meeting here at 7pm for dinner," Mom said, while patting me on the back.

"Ok Mom that sounds great! Who is serving the food?"

Mom turned around and hugged one of the ladies.

Brandon was making his way over towards me.

"Hey, Brandon," Mom said, smiling.

She loved Brandon. He walked over and gave my Mom a big kiss on the cheek. "Hey, Mom! Is it ok to call you that?" Brandon asked, while he flashed a smile.

I was standing next to Mom, looking down at my shoes.

"Brandon, you are family, sweetheart! Well, look, I need to go back home and take care of your Dad, London," Mom said.

"Wait, Mrs. Kennedy what is wrong with Mr. Kennedy?" Brandon asked, looking concerned.

"Mom, I thought he was doing fine!"

"Well both of you calm down. He has asthma; he will be fine. All these years and now in his late 60's he develops asthma. But he is not coughing like he was, and he needs to start working out so we will both join a gym, for sure."

"Well Mrs. Kennedy that is good to know. We need you both in good shape for our wedding." Brandon glanced at me and smiled.

"Yes, Mom, tell Dad I love him," I said.

"Ok, love you both and I am late; I have to go and cook for my love. See you both soon."

Mom left the church running to Dad.

"So cute; your Mom and Dad really love each other," Brandon said while looking into my eyes.

"Yes, they are both still in love after all these years."

"London, let's go to the park and hang out!"

I was surprised that Brandon did not mention anything about Saturday night. "Ok…I am down. So we are going to wear our church clothes?" I asked.

"Yes," Brandon said.

As soon as we stepped out on to the church parking lot, Brandon carried me to his car.

"Brandon!!! People are watching!" I yelled. "You know how church people talk," I said, while Brandon placed me inside his car.

We drove off. The sun had gone down and the night was just perfect!

This Sunday was wonderful! Brandon and I sat on the picnic bench watching the stars. I leaned back onto him and rested my head against his chest. The park was empty. Watching the empty swings reminded me of when my sisters and I were small kids, running to get on the swings to see who could go the highest. Brandon and I gazed at the night sky; it was just the stars and us.

"London, do you trust me?" Brandon asked.

His voice was mellow and smooth, but it made me uncomfortable because sometimes I ask myself that question, but could never answer it. I did not want to respond, but I knew Bandon wanted an answer. I still could not speak.

"London, sweetheart, do you trust me?" Brandon asked one more time.

"Well, Bran I do love you and I know you love me too, but sometimes I just feel like you are such a good guy and just for the sake of doing the right thing you will take someone else's word over mine which makes me feel like you are putting them first instead of me."

Brandon sat up and we both looked right in each other's eyes.

"Look, I am not trying to ignore you and put you last," he replied.

"Maybe you are right. I have been the good guy, trying to make sure that everyone is happy, but in the end somebody gets hurt," Brandon said, brushing my hair out of my eyes.

"Time is moving fast and the wedding is around the corner. We need to trust each other, London."

He tilted my head and I looked away. My eyes were getting lost in the stars and my own daydreams, on how life would be when we were finally married and living together. I wonder if I would be that wife he dreamed of. Am I really ready to be Mrs. Gains?

Brandon called my name as if he could tell that I was lost in my own daydreams. "Look at me baby," Brandon said.

"I don't want to cheat… and Mandy is not who I want. I don't believe that she is a godly woman. I want you to forgive her and pray for her because we are past that drama."

Brandon made sense.

"Brandon you make sense. I do want to forgive her. As a matter of fact, I have forgiven her, but when I see her it does not mean that I won't be upset. Brandon that does not mean that I have forgotten about what she did. You need to understand, Brandon. I still need time!" I said it very loudly, feeling very frustrated.

Brandon pulled back because he does not like it when I yell.

"This is what I am saying, every time you have to deal with something that bothers you, you feel the need to get upset," Brandon said, while looking around trying to make sure no one heard me.

"I dislike that about you; you start to get loud or scream, and you walk away from me," Brandon said softly,

"I am sorry," I said, "I know I have a lot to learn. I love you so much; I don't want to lose you." Brandon was stroking my brown curly locks.

"You won't; I know in my heart that God brought you in my life. I am thankful for what God has done. The young men that I mentor they are so happy for me. Spending my life with a woman that God has chosen for me is truly a gift!"

The night air was getting warmer and the season was changing. Spring was almost around the corner.

"Well, let me take you to your car," he said, as we both walked slowly to his car.

When I got home, I was extremely tired and I still had some work to do for my business and our wedding. I thought to myself that God really loves me to bless me with a man that loves me so dearly. He is not perfect, but he has the heart to love me like Jesus! He is patient, and he loves me from the inside out!

"Lord, thank You for him. I pray that you keep him and bless him. Send your angels to protect Brandon," I prayed.

I took my shower and got ready for bed. My soft black nightgown felt so smooth against my skin. I lay down and drifted off to dreamland. I dreamt that I was walking in this dark house and all the doors were closed and I tried turning on the lights but I could not! I began to hear someone crying hysterically. I ran to the front door of this house and could not get out. I realized the doorknob was missing. It was so dark in the house so I thought it was nighttime. Suddenly I thought of a way to get out of this house; I broke the door down! I had so much strength inside of me that I broke the door down with no problem! The sun was shining and I was no longer trapped inside. I was free!

I awoke to the sound of my alarm clock. It was time to start my day off bright and early so I could meet Amber at the location for my wedding!

I got ready. The weeks were passing quickly and we were getting closer to my wedding day. I pulled my hair back in a ponytail; today was my sweats and tennis shoes day!

Amber called me to fill me in on the details about the wedding.

"Hey, you!" she said, sounding bubbly and happy.

The weather was perfect. The sun was glowing through my window and the birds were chirping. Monday was a new day to start new things!

"Hey, good morning, I am Ok!" I said, excited about life.

"Well, everything is taken care of; no more details to handle. London Kia Kennedy, your wedding day plans are over! There is nothing to do but wait until April the 4th!" Amber said with joy and excitement.

"You will have two wedding rehearsals, and the invitations have already been mailed. The cakes have been ordered, and the caterers are already prepared for your dinner menu. Small details, like your white tulips, will sit on each table during the dinner and you will have cocktails one hour before dinner. All of this has been noted. And I have not forgotten about the butterfly ice sculptures. They will be placed everywhere during dinner. I have everything covered! You have just four more weeks before your wedding. This is the second week of March; you are getting so close for the big day, girl!!!!" Amber said excitedly.

I was so happy; I could finally breathe. My wedding day was around the corner, my sister and Mom and I had been shopping for the best wedding dress and bridesmaids' dresses and we found them. Bran and my brothers-in -law and Dad and Bran had their suits. We were all set for this great moment.

I reminisced on the last dinner we had with Pastor Ramon and his lovely wife.

We were at their house and they prayed over Brandon and me. They gave us the best godly advice that I have ever heard. (Loving each other was not based on what we felt, but it was based on the Love of God and keeping God number one!) "Thank you so much, Amber for everything!" I said.

"Thank you London, you are a special woman. I thank you for bringing me more business and giving my brand a facelift! Thank you London!!!"

"Amber, thank you for working hard in such a short time. You had two months to pull this wedding off and you did!" I said. My voice was shaking and I could feel the tears forming to fall down my face like a waterfall.

I could not believe that I had made it to this moment in my life. Everything that hurt me or had made me angry was far from my mind. I could only think about my Brandon, the man I had crushed on for three years before he even asked me out. Brandon, the man who had the heart to love me no matter what I had done or gone through. Brandon was not perfect, as he had made some mistakes as well. But God had taught us that we did not know everything about real love until we met each other. Some people joined themselves with someone just for appearances or based on who they knew or how much power they had. I loved Brandon because of his heart! I wanted to surprise Brandon and show up at his house. I really did not visit his home much, because we didn't have accountability at his house. My family will call or show up at my house all the time. Unlike me, Brandon has pure freedom. There are no interruptions from family or friends. Speaking of family, his family would visit every blue moon. Well, today I wanted to see him. I knocked on his condo door. His neighborhood was busy as he lived downtown. I had bagels and cream cheese for him. Bran opened the door and he had the biggest smile!! "What are you doing here London??" Brandon's eyes were brown, and when the sun hit them his eyes lit up.

"Bran!!!! I will soon be your wife!" I said over and over like a song on repeat. Brandon grabbed me and held me close.

"Look at what I brought you! Your favorite bagels," I said, smiling from ear to ear. I was happy that I could surprise him.

"Come in, baby!" he said, while taking my hand.

I followed him into his two-story condo. Brandon's home was lovely but a lot smaller than my home. He had a two-bedroom home, which is why he plans to move in with me after the wedding. Brandon had granite countertops throughout the house, in his kitchen and bathrooms, and he had wood flooring.

"Sit down while I get us a plate for our bagels and cream cheese."

He was playing some Luther in the background. Brandon was in a t-shirt and basketball shorts. He only wore basketball shorts when he was relaxing or getting ready to play some hoops with his friends.

"Bran, did I catch you at a bad time?" I asked.

Brandon was coming back to the living room with the plates and a butter knife. He spread the cream cheese on our bagels.

"You know, I was going to meet John Miller at the park on this Monday you know, since I'm off until after our honeymoon is over. That was a great idea. I am just happy to be off." Brandon said, moving in close to me looking in my eyes as if he wanted to kiss me and he did.

Brandon did not just kiss me he started in for more. Brandon kissed my face my cheeks, my lips.

"Brandon, Bran…." I said, trying to get out from his love grip. Brandon wrapped his arms around my body and gave me the deepest kiss. He then pulled back, and looked at me in my eyes.

"I have a few more weeks left of being a single man and I know that you are truly a gift, I know for sure I don't want to mess this up baby! Your body is not mine yet, so I will wait until our wedding night. Kissing is not good because it can lead to other things, so I will just kiss you one more time."

"Brandon no nooo!" I said, smiling from ear to ear.

He had just said the most heartfelt words and he kissed me so passionately that I had to say, "No more kisses my love! I cannot take it! Too much love!! Brandon, I love you." I said, with a mouthful of bagels and cream cheese.

"But you are right, no more kissing on the mouth," I said.

"London, I love you too," he said, taking another bite out of his bagel. Brandon's cell phone was ringing and he answered it. Brandon said a lot of yea's, sure's and nodding his head.

"Well, London, baby, John Miller is at the park; he is waiting on me."

I did not want to bring up Mandy, because Brandon and I were having such a great time. Brandon must have read my mind before I could say a word.

"Hey, why such a long face? You are too beautiful to make that face," Brandon said, as he got closer to me, so close that our noses were touching.

"I just want to know - did you tell John Miller?" I asked, looking up at him. I wanted him to see that I just wanted him to be careful, to not be in the middle of Mandy's mess.

"I did not tell him; Mandy told him and he was fine. London, I talked to him afterwards and told him everything. He was thankful that we told him the truth."

"I did not want to tell him until Mandy built up the courage to tell him. Mandy had played a lot of people during that time she was carrying my baby; you see, she was talking to John over the phone when he was in New York."

I wanted to tell him how that hurt me to the core that Mandy was the first one to carry his baby, and not me. I remained quiet, watching him clean up. Brandon was wiping and cleaning his coffee table and threw away the bag our bagels came in. He was always like that, making sure things were clean and in its place.

"London, John knows I would never had gone for Mandy if I was not drunk," Brandon said looking up at me as if he knew again I was reminded of how Mandy acted and how she stalked us.

"London baby, God has restored us and he has brought us out of the storm! I am glad that Mandy has turned her life around!"

I looked at Brandon, still quiet.

"Brandon, do you really think she has changed?" I asked.

Brandon replied, "Yes I do."

"I really want to invite them to our wedding," Brandon said.

Everything in me exploded!

How could I marry a man that just doesn't get it?

"Why would I want to see Mandy on my wedding day, Bran??" I thought I was thinking it, but it slipped out.

"London, I told you about yelling. Do you know how to address issues without acting like a two year old?" He asked in a stern tone.

"It only lead me to feel so in love one moment and then to feel anger, rage the next moment. This is not what it's supposed to be."

I did not say anything for about ten seconds. But my rage had risen so high; I was now ready to unleash my rage!!! But I thought about if I shouted at him and called him names then what good would that do? He is not hearing me at all; he is not seeing what I see. So I stood up, gave him the biggest hug, and kissed him on his cheek. Instead of yelling, tears filled my eyes and I began to cry a river. I could not look him in the eyes. I wanted to say that Brandon, Mr. Know-It-All could not see that I just wanted to have him to myself and not be reminded of how special Mandy was and how Mandy and I went to war with each other over Brandon. I did not want to walk down the aisle and see her face in the crowd knowing that she got my boyfriend drunk and had his baby. It was too much! I walked past Brandon and headed for my car. Brandon thought I would yell or scream like that two year old but he was right! I decided to act like a woman who loved herself with or without Brandon. I got in my car, and before I could drive off, Bran was at my car window.

"London, baby, we should not fight over this."

"You are right Brandon, we should not. Look, I am going out of town because I need some time to think; so I won't be answering my cell phone for a while. So, if you love me you will understand that I need space to pray and think," I said in a soft voice.

My heart was broken. I was now tired of the up and down relationship and getting mad over this one woman.

"London, baby, what does space mean? What is wrong? You have this look in your eyes."

I hesitated before answering him. "Brandon, no matter what, I do love you, but I don't know if you really understand me," I said, with tears rolling down my face. "Brandon, I feel like I have to fight with you so you can understand the simplest things like… Why would I want to see this Mandy woman at my wedding? The same woman who you got pregnant; the same woman who lied and fought with me, tooth and nail? Why would I want to see her at my wedding????"

Brandon stood there with nothing to say. I began to start my car.

"Wait…baby I feel like I am like a broken record, I am always making you so upset that you have this look in your eyes as if it is over!" Brandon said, while wiping tears from his eyes.

I had never seen Brandon look so sad.

Brandon began to explain, "I am always thinking that you are so above this drama and you are so strong that you can teach others even those who hurt you that they never got the best of you!"

Brandon really wanted me to understand his passion for forgiving and giving people a second chance. Brandon was still speaking.

"I am missing the point that you are trying to make," he said.

"I just want you to be happy, baby," he said, reaching for my hand and grabbing my hand and never letting it go.

Brandon, he would always get me, but by the time he gets it, I am mad or heartbroken.

"Its fine Bran, look, I love you and I just need to relax and you enjoy your basketball game," I said as I drove off before Brandon could say anything else.

I drove until I arrived at Lisa's house. I sat in my car because I was so drained and tired. I rested my head on my steering wheel. Lisa's husband Tony was getting out of his car with groceries. He knocked on the car window. I hurried and tried to wipe my tears away to keep him from noticing that I had been crying.

"Tony, hey, how is my sister Lisa?"

"She is fine. Come inside and stay for lunch."

"Ok, Tony," I said, while I closed my door and headed into their home.

When I walked in I could hear the sound of Meagan crying. Lisa was surprised to see me.

"Sister, your wedding is coming so soon. We need to plan your bachelorette party!!!! Tony, did you forget the eggs for breakfast for tomorrow?" Lisa asked, while holding Meagan in her arms.

"I am having a play date tomorrow with Terry and she is bringing Shon Jr. over." Lisa went on and on with her husband. I sat down at the kitchen table and watched Lisa fuss and nag with Tony about almost everything.

Tony was used to it; he seemed like it did not bother him one bit. I was so stressed and hurt.

"Ok, Tony where are you going, baby?" Lisa asked, nagging again.

"I'll see you two later; I am hanging out with Brandon and his homeboys. We are going to shoot some hoops… so I am going up to change. Good seeing you London. Brandon just called me; he did not tell me you were headed over here," Tony said.

"Well, I did not tell him where I was going."

"Oh, Ok… that is between you and him," Tony said, while giving me a weird look.

Tony jogged upstairs to get dressed. Lisa glanced my way as she put the top on her pot of spaghetti for lunch.

"What's wrong, London?" Lisa asked.

"Well, uhm….I just don't know were to start," I said.

"Lisa, check this out, Mandy has come back into Brandon's life, because she married one of Brandon's best friends from college."

Lisa's mouth opened wide. She was shocked.

"Ok, so Mandy claims that she had nothing to do with the doctor coming in on me and she said that when she found out that he did that, she gave her life to God and let go of her bad habits. She said that back then she was a big drinker and she would get so drunk that her Mom had to take her son! She said she did not care for anyone but herself. She went on and on trying ask for forgiveness."

Lisa, interrupted, "Well she talks as if all of this happen two years ago, but it has only been about five months ago."

Lisa was telling the truth.

"Yes, Lisa, I know, and she is pregnant again so fast." I added, picking up my story about Mandy.

"But she stood there wanting me to forgive her. I screamed at her and drove off."

I could tell Lisa was shocked.

"Well, do you want the truth or the fake truth?" Lisa said smiling.

"Lisa, what is the fake truth?" I said.

"Well the fake truth is a lie!" We both began to laugh out loud.

"Look, Lisa you still don't know the whole story."

I began to spill everything to Lisa. "Brandon and I met up for dinner, and guess who I saw – Brandon, John and Mandy at the bar laughing like old buddies." "London…. But you told me that John is his old friend!" Lisa blurted out.

"Lisa, chill out, let me tell you the rest of the story," I said, while pouring some lemonade into her wine glass. Lisa hated that; she gave me the look.

"Ok –so, John Miller has no clue that Brandon slept with his college sweetheart and got her pregnant. Mandy never told him and she convinced Brandon not to tell her new husband about it until she told him herself. Brandon, "Mr. I want to do the right thing" always seem to mess every darn thing up!!!!! He agreed to go along with the shenanigans."

Lisa was now shaking her head in shame.

"Lisa, this guy has no clue how much I cannot stand "Mandy," the woman who fights with me over him when we got back together and to top it off…"

By this time in my story, I was screaming at the top of my lungs and did not realize how mad I was.

"Mandy, who does all the dirt, she wants to be forgiven," I said in my baby voice. "Mandy who sleeps with Bran get knocked up by him, he runs and cater to her every need… and now she went and married his good friend and now she is pregnant again!! By John Miller, the Lawyer!! GOOD ONE MANDY!!!"

By this time Lisa stood up and grabbed me and hugged me. I thought she was joking but she was not she hugged me without letting up.

"Lisa I am fine!" Lisa kept me in her warm, strong embrace. I knew something was about to happen.

"London, it is ok to be upset but let it go," she whispered.

"Let it go," Lisa whispered again.

She began to tell me that it was okay to admit that I was jealous of Mandy having Brandon's baby, and being the first woman to carry his child.

"You can be mad, sad and hurt. You don't have to be strong all the time."

Lisa finally let me go and kissed me on my cheek. It was true; deep down in my heart I felt like Brandon loved Mandy for that one reason and that was because she had carried his first baby.

"I love you London, and Brandon did not see the whole picture."

Lisa said, "You are mad because Mandy had his baby first and that she took a part of him that caused him to feel connected to Mandy. Just the thought of her carrying his baby really sticks with you!" Lisa said.

I think Lisa was right.

"I mean …everything else with Mandy's ex and this guy following you home, that just happened. Mandy did not have anything to do with that or gained from that, plus she had lost the baby that same day. So sis, you need to let go of her having a part of Brandon and not you," Lisa said.

Lisa was right; that was the point of my pain, which was rooted in the fact that she had a baby by Brandon.

"See, sometimes us women we can be territorial," Lisa said.

"But you have all of Brandon and he wants all of you, there is no need to worry about what happened in the past!" Lisa said, grabbing my shoulders.

"But are you saying that I should forgive her?" I asked, knowing that Lisa was holding all the answers at this very moment.

"Yes, London, because you are the one hurting, you are fussing with your man, and this kind of anger can mess up any relationship."

Lisa was right.

"Lisa, have you ever had to face this kind of drama?"

"Trust me, Tony had not always been perfect, but just know that you can't keep running away and always ready to let the relationship go. Be willing to let the pain and the anger go. Because at the end of the day, Mandy has her husband; she moved on. You must do the same," Lisa said.

She was right.

I picked up my things and gave Lisa a kiss on the cheek.

"Look, I need to go home and rest, thanks for the talk."

"Love you sis, no problem!" Lisa said.

It seem as if Lisa was my twin, she knew I needed to hear her words of truth.

I headed home. I noticed that Brandon had left roses at my front door steps with a card saying *I love you, and I am happy for my soon-to-be wife. Love Brandon.*

I called him.

"Hello, London! Sure is good to hear from you today, I miss you," Brandon said. "Well, thank you for giving me space," I said, feeling relaxed, set free and happy.

"I love the red roses, hun!"

"Look, I want to love you, and no matter what I have your back, London!" Brandon said, while his friends and my brother-in-law were in the background, saying, "Love makes things happen!"

They were clowning around.

"Do, you hear these crazies?" I could just imagine them jumping around at the basketball court, acting silly.

"Well, what are you doing for dinner tonight?" Brandon asked.

Brandon and I both said "Pizza" at the same time; he knew me…hahaha.

"Brandon, I love you, are you coming over?"

"I can't because it's getting too hard to come over your house at night, and since we got in to this nasty fight early today, I think it is best for me to go home. I am telling you London, just because I am a youth Minister does not mean I don't have those weak moments. So I will remain in His will," Brandon said, while his voice shook a little when he was talking about showing his feelings for me. It would have been too much for us.

"So true Brandon, so I'll see you in the morning!"

"Yes, breakfast or lunch date at your house. Love you London!" Brandon said.

I knew we both loved each other, but we also knew that I needed to be freed from that dark rage and that hurt that came from a place where I needed to be healed. I keep saying I forgave but I was still not letting go. I went to take a relaxing warm shower and while the water covered me, I could not help but think about my dream. God had gave me that dream to warn me that I needed to push my way out of these unhealthy feelings. I remembered in the dream that I was trapped in the dark house but could not get free, until I busted the door down. Then I was free!

"Thank you Lord for showing me that this battle has nothing to do with Mandy; this is a spiritual fight! Brandon was very smart but I was ready to diminish him and talk to him in such a rage. I thank you Lord for allowing me the grace to just leave."

After my long warm shower and thanking the Lord, my pizza arrived. I was wearing my fun polka dot pjs. I gave my tip to the pizza guy and locked my door. It was about eight thirty and I relaxed in my bed and scanned through the channels. All of a sudden I received a phone call.

"Yes, London is this a good time to speak?" Her soft voice trembled while she was trying to make conversation.

"Mandy, what do you want?"

My feelings were everywhere but rage was not one of them. To tell you the truth I was afraid that she might be a really good girl underneath the drama, just like I was. She just made crazy choices because like me, she did not know how to love herself. I slept with Jason although he had a fiancé and I knew it. How could I judge her? Believe it or not, when I first saw her I thought she was a southern belle church girl with no problems in the world. The truth was she was screaming for help, but no one could hear her; she was a silent screamer!

I know how to scream in silence. My lips were not moving and my voice was not heard yet. I was screaming inside for help too!

"Well, London I just need time to explain myself to you." She said.

"I always loved Brandon as a friend. I used to have a crush on him when we were in high school, but trust me; he looked at me like family. So, time went on and I grew to respect Brandon, he dated other girls I dated other guys," Mandy said, sounding very confident in what she was saying.

"But we both went on to college and I met John, Brandon's good friend. This was when I knew he was my husband. It was then that my heart stopped. There's nobody like John. Not even Brandon made me feel like this!"

Mandy made me laugh, because all this time I thought she felt like that for Brandon; I thought, while eating my pizza. I tried to chew softly to keep her from noticing. "Everyone knew that I was in love with John, but John's rich family wanted him to date young ladies who came from money. I was just a southern girl, that came from a broken family and my Mommy never kept a job, and my Dad, well, he moved on with a new family."

Mandy trusted me? I could not believe she felt like telling me all of this; was this even necessary?

"Look Mandy, you don't need to tell me all your business," I said, interrupting her before she could complete her story.

"No! You need to understand me, and know me so you and I can at least move on to a good place," Mandy said.

"London, God is everything to me, and He wanted me to humble myself, let go of my ways and start a new life!"

Mandy was making a lot of sense. I thought to myself while I said, "Ok, Mandy go ahead."

"Thanks London. You see, God has a way of changing the hearts and when he changed mine, I just have to do what he called me to do and that is walk in truth and love."

"So, my family was not rich and although I was smart and had scholarships to college that did not impress John Miller's Mom. She made it hard for me to date him. She would invite me for a family dinner and I would dress casual because she would say, 'Just wear your regular clothes hun, this is just a casual dinner.'

I would show up in jeans and a nice blouse and everyone at the table would wear gowns with crystal beading. I would stay and pretend that I was not embarrassed. So when we graduated from college, he left without telling me that he was moving to London to finish preparing for law school.

I was so heartbroken. So Brandon was a good friend, and I watched Brandon put his heart in being successful to only give back to the neighborhood kids. He also loved God. I started to pull away from all that church stuff and I met this guy who was abusive. He was in the entertainment business. There were wild parties with drugs and alcohol. I had my son, and when he started to beat me up in front of my baby, I knew I needed to leave. I packed my bags and did not go back to him. London, you probably thought I would have started making wise decisions, but when I heard that John Miller was engaged, it hurt me to the core. It had been six years since I seen or heard from John, but by this time you and Brandon had this love connection. He talked about you all the time. When I met you I was so jealous, because it looked like you had everything that I did not have."

Listening to Mandy tell her story made me see her perspective. I had always made her the one on the pedestal, but she did the same thing to me. It is amazing how we all judge people based on what we see or think, and the sad thing is, they are doing the same thing. We discover that the truth is always somewhere in the middle.

I tuned in again to hear her go on about her life; she answered a lot of questions that I had.

"London, you had the great job, the money, the house and everything; now you had my best friend who I had shared most of my life with. Brandon was not the one I was in love with but he was the one who was always there to pick me up and give me advice. Everything was about to change because of my selfishness. I took Brandon to a bar when I knew he was heartbroken over you. I knew he must have really cared for you because I had never seen him like that."

Mandy went on to tell me more.

"London, Brandon was not a drinker at all but that night he was."

"We both made bad decisions that night and it was all my fault because he was really drunk," Mandy said.

"I am sorry, but he never came on to me. I felt bad but my selfish ways convinced me to believe that it was not fair for him to leave me, to give his heart to a wonderful woman!"

Mandy paused a bit as if she was taking herself back to that moment.

"I did not love Brandon in that way, but he was the closest person to John Miller. Brandon told me that he could barely remember that night, and if something happened he hoped it did not because he was in love with London Kia Kennedy. I was so upset that I was losing my best friend and that my life was a wreck; I wanted to kill myself. Then to top it off, I found out that I was pregnant; there was no way that I wanted this baby. Brandon convinced me that we could raise the baby as friends and move on with our lives separately. Brandon, the good guy, did not know the pain I was in; he just wanted things to go back to the way they were with me as his sister and friend. I was so caught up in my own pain that I forgot that he lost a friend in me. I was now his enemy. I was extremely mad at him for not treating me like crap so I could have a reason to hate him; Brandon treated me like a lady. But London, you see, Brandon's heart is so big that he forgave me! I could not believe that after all the hateful things I did; he still had room to forgive.

I started dating the doctor, and we would drink and I would get drunk almost every night. I was not being a good mother to my son or to my unborn child. My mother took my son from me, and well, you know the rest of the story. I lost that baby boy and that same night I found out what that jerk had done to you! I am so sorry London!"

"Look, Mandy, I forgive you. I am happy that you are telling me your side of the story."

"I told this to Brandon but he was so furious with me that it took a lot of times trying to tell him this story and how I am so sorry! For about a month, I stopped drinking, but sometimes I had a glass of wine for dinner. I stopped drinking uncontrollably. I also started going to church and asked my Mom, my family and my friends to forgive me. You see, London, I hurt more people than just you and Brandon. Most of all, I hurt myself. Well, a month after losing the baby, I received a phone call; it was the guy whom I had loved all those years; John Miller. He and I reconnected and I did not want to lay all my bad news on him at once. I waited and I just could not find the time to tell him. I finally found the nerve to tell him how I spiraled out of control. I just never told him that Brandon was the guy that got me pregnant. So that's why Brandon did not want you to tell John that night. I had asked Brandon not to tell John until I spoke to him first."

"I thought John didn't know anything," I said. I realized that Mandy and I had a lot in common.

By now we had been talking for about an hour.

"Mandy, wow, I can relate to you in so many ways. My life for sure has not been perfect. My Dad is not my real Dad, but I love him like he is! I had accomplished a lot in my life but I worked hard for everything," I said.

I felt like Mandy and I were becoming friends. We both began to laugh at the wild moments we had and the hardship of growing and maturing into women of God. "Well, London, when I told John my story he did not care; he loved me no matter what I had did. He really knew the real Mandy, the Mandy who loved helping others. Even though I have never really been a religious person, I always had morals. But, over time, I threw my morals away while trying to get what I wanted, when I wanted it," Mandy said, while laughing.

"John said that he was young, and after his ex girlfriend dumped him for an A-list celebrity, he realized that he was tired of allowing his mother to control his life. So he went looking for me! London, God did not give up on me, so I beg for your forgiveness. God has been too good to me, even when I was living my life out of control and recklessly," she said.

Mandy broke down and started to cry. I could feel her pain and her joy at the same time; it was almost as if she was describing me. We were in the same season. "Look, girl, I understand how you feel," I said, knowing deep down inside of me, that God wanted me just to listen to her.

"London, I am in love. Once I told John about everything except Brandon, he asked me to marry him. We had a small wedding. His Mom was there! Can you believe that? My Mom was so happy for me. I mean it went from one month I was sobering up and giving my heart to God, to this! Who would have thought that God would move so fast! Now, I told John about Brandon right after we all met in that restaurant. John was a little bit disappointed in me, but he said that was the past and let's leave it there."

"Well, Mandy I agree; from here on out, I choose to put all of this in the past and thank you for sharing your story with me. I needed to hear your story because I never really got to know the real Mandy," I said, feeling more free than ever from my feelings of pain and rage. It was as if Mandy had taken something from me. All along, Mandy had lost herself, but thank God that Mandy found the true meaning of love.

"Mandy, would you speak at my women's meeting at my church on Thursday? I really would love for you to come," I said.

Mandy cleared her throat and said yes.

"London, I would love to share maybe not my long story, but at least a part of my story, as long as someone's life would be changed by it," Mandy sounded excited.

"Look, London, thank you for the second chance. I have started a non-profit as well, named, "Second Chance.""

"Wow, you are moving fast! Look, I would love for you and John to come to my wedding."

I was feeling so happy about feeling free that I had to ask her.

"I am so glad you asked, I would love to, it would be a honor to see my friend marry such an extraordinary woman!"

" Aww, thank you Mandy."

Mandy and I said our goodbyes. Bran, I knew he had good judgment, but for a while I thought he was slipping when it came to Mandy. I had already eaten four pieces of pizza and was ready to go to sleep. The night was no longer young.

Chapter 15

LOVING NEW BEGINNINGS

It was now time to celebrate my bachelorette party with the girls!!! They had planned for a pink Hummer limo to pick me up, and I was dressed in my leather black dress with black red-bottom pumps with my diamond earrings, ready to party! I arrived at Lisa's house; Terry and Lisa looked like sexy, hot Mommas. Lisa's hair was cut in a sexy bob, and her outfit was a long maxi black skirt with a form-fitting red top. Her makeup was soft but beautiful! Terry, the youngest, wore a nice gold maxi dress with gold pumps. Her hair was pulled up into a high bun.

"Ok, ladies, who is babysitting because I know your husbands are with Brandon hanging out," I commented.

"Ha!" Lisa said. "You know that my nanny is babysitting. She just loves Megan!"

Terry replied,, "Jenny from church has been babysitting for me. She is a sweet girl. She is still in college, majoring in psychology."

The Hummer drove off to pick up my Mom. She jumped in and was so hot! "Mom!!" We all yelled.

Mom was wearing black leggings with a long red sweater shirt and her gold pumps with gold bracelets. Her hair was long and flowing.

"Dad let you out of the house like that?!"

"You better know it!!!" Mom said, while smiling.

The Hummer then stopped at the house of Kim, my old classmate. She was wearing a sweater dress, black with vertical green stripes and green heels. She was working those heels and was six months pregnant.

"Congratulations London!!"

The Hummer filled up with friends with whom I went to high school and some college ladies that I keep in touch with from time to time. We all arrived at this loft in uptown. The loft was jazzy and cool. The floors were a beautiful dark wood. As we entered in the loft, we heard music from a retro DJ. Food covered one end of the tables that were set up; lots of finger foods, and desserts including strawberries and chocolates.

The ladies had a princess crown for me; they placed it on my head and then they all screamed while a big red box was pushed in front of me. I was thinking, I know my sisters did not get a stripper! The box began to move and it popped open. The box opened it was a young lady wearing a white dress. She was fully clothed and was holding a box in her hand.

"You guys tricked me!!!" I yelled.

My Mom and sisters were laughing.

"You thought we got a stripper."

The music stopped playing and the 52-inch flat screen came on. Something was happening and then Bran's voice was on TV.

"Hey, London, I know you are enjoying your party but wanted to tell you that I have another gift for you! I hope you like it. This gift has five bedrooms, two guest rooms and four full baths, a media room, an outside basketball court and a tennis court! I love you London!!!"

Everyone in the background started to scream and yell!! The lady who popped out the box walked up to me with a small black box in her hand. I took it and opened it and there were the house keys!! Wow!! I was in shock. So many questions rushed through my mind, like, where is it located? I cannot wait to move in! Brandon and I had the original plan that he was going to move in with me after the wedding. I guess he decided to do something different.

"I am so blessed," I said, as my voice trembled and I tried my best to hold back my tears.

The TV went off and the party games began. The food was so good. I was so happy! I wondered what Brandon was doing and how his night turned out! I looked around the room at the ladies dancing laughing and my Mom smiling. This was a celebration that would never be forgotten!

The night had to come to an end. We were all taken to our homes. We said our goodbyes until next time, the rehearsal dinner. When I went home, I took a shower and went to sleep. Time was passing and April 4th would soon be here.

The next morning Brandon called me.

"Hey London, did you love my surprise?"

I was still half asleep. My voice was raspy.

"Hey, baby, yes I loved the new home!!" I was so amazed that he had bought a grand home.

"Brandon you have been giving me gifts since my birthday before Christmas. Wow, you are spoiling me!" I said as I sneezed.

"Baby, are you getting a cold?" Brandon asked with concern, as I rolled over and hugged the soft sheets.

"No, just my allegies."

"I cannot wait until you are Mrs. Gains," he said.

"By the way, Amber called me. She wants to make sure that there are no last-minute guests for our rehearsal dinner next week," he said while I sneezed again. "Ok, Brandon I will contact her later today. Did you and my father make sure that your tuxedos are going to fit?"

"Yes, London, everything is taken care of. Hey, don't worry; God is taking care of all the details that we may have disregarded."

"John and Mandy Miller told me that you made your peace with Mandy."

Brandon said their names and I rolled my eyes while I tossed and turned in my bed. I finally felt like I understood Mandy.

"Well, I needed to hear her story and I found out that she just needed a second chance." I was so proud of myself that I could finally let go of that heavy weight that I was carrying for Mandy.

"I am happy you did that," Brandon said, sounding so humble and so patient.

"So Brandon, are we both wearing white at this rehearsal dinner?" I asked, so we could change the subject from Mandy and her new husband.

Brandon cleared his throat. "For sure!"

"Well look, I've got to head off to the office," he said.

"I thought you were on vacation," I said.

"Well, baby that is true. I just need to close some files down and make sure everything is done," he replied.

"Well too bad, I would love to see you!"

Brandon giggled. "Well next time London. I'll see you soon."

I jumped up and got dressed for today the day. I had so many small things to do. I also had another client. I was now in business. I received my first check from Amber and she referred me. My new client is Steven Shaw; he is a designer from Dallas and New York. He wanted me to work with him on his websites and PR stuff, giving his business a new look. I was not going to start taking clients until after my vacation. I was just preparing now so that after my honeymoon there would be additional income.

I gave Amber a quick call. "Amber, hey, you…"

Amber sounded happy and excited. "You have about two more weeks until your wedding. Are you excited??" she asked, while sounding so bubbly.

"Yes!! Girl it has not really hit me yet," I replied.

"You guys have a photo shoot like, the day before your dinner rehearsal." My phone buzzed.

"Look, Amber, I have to get this call. We'll talk later."

I disconnected from Amber. I could not believe that I was starting to see my business grow.

"Yes, this is London."

The person on the other end of the phone sounded heavy breathing.....

"Hello…"

"Hello?"

"Look, she never lost the baby," The voice was a voice that I could not recognize. It was a lady's voice; she sounded older.

I know they are not talking about Mandy. I know Mandy would not lie to us again.

I did not feel too good; it was like I was facing the lies and the pain all over again. I knew if I told Brandon he would only get mad. I kept this to myself. I knew it was time to bring in a professional to help, like an investigator.

Chapter 16

SECRETS IN THE DARK COMING TO LIGHT

I walked around all that day, tired of the secrets that people could keep! I had my meetings with Steve Shaw and with Amber for the details for the rehearsal dinner next week. I also went to visit my Mom and Dad. I was relaxing on the sofa just looking in space, thinking that Mandy was lying to me, but maybe somebody is tricking me. I needed to get to the bottom of this!

"Hey, London," Mom said as she sat by me, placing her hand on my leg.

"London, is something wrong?" she asked, looking at me with a look of concern.

I was wondering should I tell her or keep it to myself. I had decided to keep it to myself.

"Mom, everything is great. I've just been working hard."

"Oh, ok…it just looked like a lot was on your mind. Well, the Daughters of Hope is canceled until next week, and I told Pastor we will be canceling all the sessions until the wedding is over."

"Mom, you should have consulted me first," I said, snappily.

"I am sorry; I tried calling you but no answer."

I realized I was not acting as my usual self.

"Well Mom, I will call you later when I get home. I have to meet Brandon for dinner at this fancy restaurant at about 7pm. I have to get dressed. Love you Mom!" I knew that my Mom could see pain in my face.

I made it to the restaurant, which was appropriately named Fancy. The theme was of Paris, with pictures of the Eiffel Tower as part of the décor. The food smelled wonderful. I was escorted to my table and my handsome man was waiting for his future wife, me.

"Hey, beautiful," he said, while the waiter poured white wine. I took my seat and looked at the people. There were couples in love chatting and the wonderful aroma of raisin bread, roasted chicken with garlic herbs, smoked lamb chops and Greek salad lingered in the air.

"Hey, babe… So happy to see you Brandon," I said.

Brandon was smiling; I could tell he was happy. I was still debating if I should tell him about my phone call.

"Hey, did you realize our name is like, almost the same?" Brandon said.

Brandon could be really serious at times, but for the most part, while hanging out with him, he was very funny!

"London, Brandon," I said, with a sly grin.

"Naw…. I don't get it babe," I said, as I repeated our names.

"So when my Mom and Dad are in town, they will meet us at the church for the rehearsal dinner," Brandon said.

Before I could speak, Brandon asked another question.

"Well how many people will make the rehearsal dinner?"

I responded, "I think there will only be about 30 guests for the rehearsal dinner; it will be mostly the wedding party and family. But at the wedding, we are going to have about 200 people. I think that is a good number."

Brandon smiled while he placed our order and I began to talk about everything. I was so excited about the fact that the wedding day was coming soon.

We both laughed. Finally, our food arrived. I knew that Brandon was special when I first met him. He was just so focused on trying to live his life, but for the most part he gave back to the community. I looked at him, and was just watching him, as if everyone in that restaurant was not there.

"Hey, London what are you thinking about?" Brandon asked, while he took his first bite of steak and pasta.

"Oh Bran, nothing. Just thinking of how the big day will soon be here."

Brandon smiled. His phone rang; he had to take a phone call. I thought to myself it must be a good phone call, because he was smiling from ear to ear. I thought back to that phone call and thought to myself, should I tell him, but it would probably put us both in a bad mood. I mean, that call could have been from a person with bad motives that somehow has it out for Mandy for some reason.

"Well, soon-to-be Mrs. Gains," he said, while grabbing my hands.

"I can't believe we have been through so much!" he said.

"I was just thinking that too," I said.

Brandon and I were holding each other's hands while gazing in each other's eyes like two lovebirds.

But Brandon was right; we had been through some dark challenges that almost ruined our relationship, but it was God who brought us through the darkness.

"Well, my parents have already bought their airline tickets and they are ready!" We both began to eat. The restaurant was so beautiful with the Paris theme and the wonderful food.

"Man, this food is so good, baby," Bran said, as he enjoyed his creamy pasta.

"We should have had Fancy to cater our wedding," Brandon said with confidence. "Well, Bran I hate to eat and run, but I have to go…. I am working on another project for work and I think I have another account, so more income! Yeah!"

"Wow girl, you started off with million dollar accounts and now you quit that job to start working for yourself! You are for sure a woman of excellence!"

When Brandon said that, it really made me feel very honored; no-one ever said that to me before. I smiled and gave him the biggest hug, like I did not want to let him go.

"Baby, I cannot breathe," Brandon said.

"I am so sorry, it is just that no-one ever told me that before!"

"Aww baby I love you," he said, while hugging me back

"Well London, go ahead and I will talk to you soon."

"Ok, I will call you to let you know I made it home."

My car was waiting for me at the door of the restaurant; I got in my car and headed home. The night air was cool and my black leather couture jacket was definitely needed. The radio played softly in the background.

I was still unsure about the phone call that I received earlier. It was just crazy!!! I contacted a private investigator because this story was too much for me to handle or tell anyone. My family would only think that I was trying to start something up again, but the truth shall come to light. When I got home I wanted to call Mandy myself. I was not going to grill her yet or tell her about the call. When I had my shower was dressed for bed, I decided to call her.

"Mandy!"

"Hey, so good to hear your voice!"

Mandy sounded puzzled, but was happy to hear from me.

"Well, I wanted to know how far along are you?"

Wow, that sounded so blunt, I did not want to come out like that.

"Well, what I mean… is I want you to make sure that you invite me to your baby shower."

There was a pause and I could tell that Mandy was feeling a little bit curious. "Look, I already know that my mother-in-law called you. She told me she was going to get to the bottom of this so-called mess! She was looking for you to call her back and gossip."

I was so embarrassed; Mandy must really think that I was trying to snoop. Well, I felt so guilty, but who would not want to know the truth.

"I am sorry; look, when I got that call I just thought maybe it was true."

Mandy paused, as if she was tired of going back and forth telling her truth.

"Look London, I am so sorry you had to go through what you did, but hey, next time just come out and be honest by asking me," Mandy said, sounding very disappointed.

"Ok, look you got to admit… you got pregnant and married right after you lost your baby, and you never had a funeral for the baby so it was kind of weird." "Well, Brandon and I both thought it was good to donate the organs and then cremate the baby. We did not want our families to be a part of the process of saying goodbye. Brandon should have told you, but at that time you had been violated and he did not think it was best. We said our goodbyes and went our separate ways," Mandy said. I could tell Mandy just wanted this to be over.

"Look Mandy, I am sorry," I said. I really was sorry.

"No need for apologies. My mother-in-law had no business trying to start this with you! Ok. So lets forget about this ok," Mandy said.

"I will see you on Thursday."

"Ok Mandy, but we canceled the meeting until after the wedding! When Brandon and I come back from our honeymoon then I will let you know."

"Ok then, that sounds great. I cannot wait to see you both at your wedding," Mandy said right before we disconnected.

I could not believe it. Mandy was telling me the truth after all.

I crawled into my soft bed and realized I did not want to work tonight. I needed to take a break from working for myself until after the wedding, which was the reason why I went on vacation from my previous job. My eyes closed while my mind wandered into dreamland. I began to dream about this little baby girl smiling at me; it gave me the best feeling in the world!

Chapter 17

MY NEW LIFE

Everyone was sitting down at his or her assigned tables. We had all of the wedding party and their families at the tables. The Pastors and ministries were all here and my sweet wedding planner Amber Smith; I just love this woman! Amber has been amazing. She took me as a client and even made my dreams come true by putting this wedding together in three months. My Mom and Dad were sitting down at their table with Brandon and his Mom and Dad. I felt blessed! My outfit for this special night was a white long sleeve dress that was form-fitting and at knee length, with black pumps. My hair was pulled back in a high bun. I wanted my makeup to have a more of a natural look. My sisters and their husbands were here. I was scanning the room and there was my soon-to-be husband! I could not believe I still got excited like a teenager when I saw him. The chatter from everyone laughing and talking was echoing in the room. I could hear my favorite song playing in the background. My church family had been great at preparing such exquisite decorations and flowers for my rehearsal dinner.

Brandon was talking to almost everyone in the room. Brandon was that man: strong, friendly and an awesome businessman! Wow, he spotted me and he was coming my way. I know for sure if my love could be transformed into light, I would have lit up this entire room alone. I smiled as he came up to me, looking at me with those almond-colored eyes. My heartbeat had picked up speed.

I was soon marrying this man.

"Hey, beautiful," Brandon said, while taking my hand. He began to turn me around and around. I felt like his model for that moment.

"Why, thank you, Handsome; you look really great," I said. Brandon wore a white v-neck collared shirt and a couture white blazer with black jeans. I can tell you that this man looked like he stepped off a runway. He should have been on a cover of a magazine.

"So, did you get the chance to see Mom and Dad?" Bran asked, while smiling.

You could tell he was so happy. "London baby, Mom and Dad was just going on and on about you! They have been bragging on you since they arrived," Brandon said, while we both looked at each other and he kissed me right on the lips.

"Hey, buddy, you still have some days to go before you can kiss my sister-in-law," Tony said, while laughing.

Well, I know most of the Christian couples have been holding out from kissing until their wedding day, but we had kissed each other all throughout this relationship. Since we had no knowledge on how to date Gods way, we had to learn by trial and error. So, we never stopped kissing, but we did set boundaries. We will preach and encourage other couples that are courting or dating Gods way to not kiss until the wedding day. We went through a lot of emotions, so if you set your boundaries and are strict in keeping them, it will keep you in God's will. Kissing awakened some emotions within Bran and me, so sometimes we would spend weeks not seeing each other. But God taught us how to really love. "Hey, Tony I have already kissed my beautiful girl, but that is all," Bran said, while blushing.

Tony smiled and said, "I know Brandon. You are a good guy, and a God-fearing man!"

"Thanks Tony," Brandon said.

Amber came out on the stage that was decorated beautifully.

"I am so thankful that everyone made it out," she said in clear tones on the microphone.

"I would like for the soon-to-be bride and groom to sit at this special table that was made for a King and a Queen!"

Everyone clapped while Brandon and I walked up on the platform to the special table that they prepared for us and we sat. Amber gave Brandon the microphone, while she excused herself from the stage. Brandon stood up to share his speech with the audience. Brandon began with his hand in his pocket while pacing the stage as if he was a game host.

"I would like to thank my Mom and Dad for coming out. They came a long way just to support me and my future bride."

Brandon spoke very well, with passion and thankfulness in his voice.

"Thank you, to my future in-laws for creating such a beautiful daughter from the inside out! My new family has embraced me: Lisa, Tony, Terry and Shon, Mrs. Kennedy and Mr. Kennedy. I love you guys like you were my own family."

Everyone clapped and cheered while Brandon was still talking. I drifted off to Kennedyland, and I began to think how I was so blessed. I can remember a time that I could not even imagine dating a man like Brandon. I thought this day would never happen to me. I was this feisty, and beautiful scared woman with flaws and insecurities that I only tried to cover up. I realized when Jesus began to heal me He started to uncover everything that I was trying to hide. I sat there looking around at the crowd filled with family, friends and church members who wanted to be a part of my wedding in some kind of way. I thought of Mrs. Johnson who taught Sunday School for the youth; she donated her time in helping getting the church dinner hall organized for this wonderful dinner/rehearsal along with my wedding planner, Amber.

The tablecloths were turquoise, with luxurious crystal vases filled with forty-two white roses on each table. Chocolate and turquoise china plates were displayed beautifully on each table. The stage was filled with crystal vases and white roses too; it was a lovely sight.

"Well, I know I can be longwinded so I will pass the microphone to my future wife London," Brandon said, while walking to our table.

I stood up and walked slowly to the front of the table while the crowd clapped again. I realized that the presence of God was resting over me. I looked out at all the familiar faces and I knew that no matter what I had gone through, I had finally made it to the place where God had led me.

"Hello, everyone," I said, noticing that my voice was trembling.

The crowd was beautiful; everyone was dressed well. I looked out over the room and I was reminded that tonight was the night that God had planned from the start, even with all the lonely nights and wrong relationships that had crossed my path. But God knew I would be here right now, at this very moment, preparing myself for life with my soon-to-be husband.

"You, know I just have to thank Jesus, He has taught me so much, even in the moments were I did not always make the right decisions."

The crowd laughed.

"I used to be that scared, insecure woman that was afraid of love, and of being alone," I said, knowing that I was not the only one who went through a season of not being sure of yourself and not understanding God's plan.

"I would hide behind my powerful personality and my smile, my career, and oh yeah, my hotness," I said, with a giggle.

The crowd laughed.

"It took me falling hard and learning how to ask for forgiveness, and learning how to forgive others just like how God forgave me! I had to let go of doing things my way and learn how to trust God! When I was able to do that, it was only then that God was able to lead me to love God's way! God had to allow my relationship with my future husband to be a reflection of the relationship between God and the church. The church is the bride and God is the groom and He will come for us to join Him in an everlasting ceremony

- forever! So I am excited about what the Lord has given me, love between me and the Lord first, and now with this amazing man! Thank you everyone!"

I looked out and saw my beautiful Mom and sisters and future mother-in-law crying. Amber came and took the microphone while I sat back down beside Brandon.

"Wow, that testimony really had me in tears. It's really good to know that God has not forgotten about us in the love area of our lives! Well, this night is not over. The waiters are going to come by each table to serve our dinner. While that is going on, we will have the families come up and speak, starting with Mr. Kennedy."

I was so excited! I had not talked to Dad in a while. I had been so busy with this wedding planning. It felt good to see my Dad doing well and looking good with his health and strength. My Dad stood on the stage in a black dress shirt and black slacks; he was looking good.

"Hey, everyone! I am just so blessed to be able to watch my daughter fall in love with Jesus and trust that God was going to work everything out for her good," said Mr. Robert Kennedy.

He was the man who taught me love, because he loved me like I was his own. My Dad told childhood stories about how I loved to have my way when I was a kid. Everyone started to clap and laugh.

"Well, London would go to school and tell all the kids, 'My name is London Kia Kennedy, and don't forget it!' Now, that's what you call demanding! Well, it is so good to see her use that gift with her jobs only and not on her loved ones! Everyone laughed again while Dad was closing his speech.

"I just want to say, I love you, London, and may God bless you both! Brandon, I am thankful that you are a strong man of God and a good man! I have truly gained a son!"

I was in tears, because seeing my father share the story about me being bossy and demanding when I was a kid was hilarious. But, also hearing my father say how he was thankful for having a daughter who trusted in the Lord meant a lot to me.

My Mom shared her story, and my sisters and brothers-in-law shared their love and joy about the new love that God had brought into my life.

The night was no longer young. We all ate and laughed and cried. It was truly a time of love and joy that I had never felt before! Yes, I have been happy before, but in this season of my life, God was truly blessing me. Every promise he had spoken in my life was now unfolding before my eyes. I was broken for years. When I let go of my way, God healed me and began to teach me how to love!

At the end of the night, after all the festivities ended, Amber told all the wedding party that we had a meeting next week, the day before the wedding, just to go over how everyone was supposed to march in. It became real to me that I was finally ready to share my life with this man named Brandon Gains! I would drop off my name that I loved so much; no more Ms. Kennedy. I hugged Brandon.

"London Kia Gains, man, it's happening baby!" Brandon said, while squeezing me so hard.

My beautiful Mom came over to us.

"Brandon, you look so handsome and London, baby, you look so beautiful sweetheart," she said.

I looked up and my Mom and Dad and Brandon's parents all surrounded us. Brandon's Dad came and gave me a huge hug!

"Son, I am so proud of you both," Mr. Gains said to Brandon.

He turned around and looked me in my eyes and said, "I know that you were sent by God, because you are everything that I prayed for, I asked God to send my son a woman who would love my son for who he is, not his title or money; just for him, and that this woman would love God with all her heart! God sent you!" Mr. Gains said,while fighting to hold back the tears.

Brandon's Mom hugged us both.

"I am so happy that you both listened to God!"

Brandon looked at me and I looked at him. We both were just so in love with this moment of celebration and the reality that we were finally getting married! Brandon and I talked to family and friends before we all had to leave. Brandon walked his parents to the car and said his goodbyes until the wedding. I talked to my sisters and they both hugged me and told me that God was faithful to His Word, and He never forgot me. After saying goodbye to everyone, I waited on Bran. He walked up to me, picked me up and began to swing me around.

I laughed and laughed like I was a little girl. My joy was overwhelming and I knew that God had been faithful over His promise in my life.

"Bran I thank you for your godly love for me," I said, while Bran placed me in the front seat of my car.

"Well, London thank you for just being everything God made you to be!" he said, and then smiled.

"Well baby, goodnight and I will see you again for another rehearsal and then we will both be husband and wife," I smiled and gave him the sweetest kiss on the cheek.

"Hey, that's the type of kiss I get? No kiss on the lips?"

"No Bran...goodnight. Oh yeah, you look so handsome tonight!"

"Well, you look so beautiful. When I saw you tonight my heart fluttered," Brandon said, as his eyes danced in his head.

"Really, Bran? Aww, that is so cute. I love you Bran. Goodnight. I'll call you soon.

I drove off while watching him hop into his Infiniti.

I returned to a lot of voice messages on my house phone message service. I had to relax before I listened to any of those messages and let the hot shower wash away all my stress.

God, thank you for this chance to fall in love, and this time it is real love. I don't have to try and be anyone but myself. I also know that Bran has his weakness, he is always trying to help others at the sake of going to the edge of the mountain to save someone. Brandon never really understands that he is not Superman; he is just a man. He tries to be Superman, and he manages to do the impossible with God's help. I love him and I know now that he loves me, but God gave him this heart to love everyone to the point where he is willing to try to make everything better.

I put on my red satin pjs and jumped into my soft bed. I closed my eyes and I was so tired that I went right to sleep.

The clouds only allowed the sun to peek through the sky, while hiding the beautiful beams of light. Today I had a business meeting. I was done with planning the wedding; all I needed to do was show up. I was leaving the cluttered streets of downtown of this wonderful city. I had met with a business owner who wanted to bring in more clients and service to their spa and salon. I was able to make this business deal work! I got the account; it may not be a million dollar account but it was income. I knew that I was going to work on this account after my honeymoon. The owner wanted to start on the ideas and plans in late May so that gave me time to relax while learning and loving my husband. It worked out fine as I was still blessed with a deposit up front. I was just so happy and blessed to have started my own business and was excited to see my business take off!

I stopped by my Mom and Dad for lunch. Lisa and Terry, Tony and Shon and the babies were all at my Mom's. Brandon was spending time with his family, but we all planned to meet up for dinner tonight. My Dad was walking around in his golf outfit, and Tony and Shon were brave enough to go golfing with my Dad the competitive monster.

"Hey, Dad! How are you feeling?"

"London baby, I am doing great, I cannot wait until this wedding!" Dad said, while cooking a pot of spaghetti.

Mom came in the kitchen to look over Dad's shoulder to make sure he was cooking the food her way; we all knew how Mom could be.

"Baby, I got this; the food will be ready in about five minutes," Dad said.

"Robert, don't burn the bottom of the spaghetti!" Mom yelled.

"Baby, get out of this kitchen and let me cook," Dad, said while pushing Mom out of the kitchen. My Mom laughed. My parents may fuss sometimes but they both have a way of balancing their lives out.

"London, don't worry, you and Brandon will find a way to laugh even when you might want to kill him," Terry said, while placing the baby in my arms.

"Feed him for me while I run upstairs to get my cell phone." Terry looked at me with a smile.

"Ok, but you better hurry up," I said, while rocking back and forth with this sweet bundle of love in my arms. Shon Jr was about three months old now and he was handsome; he had curly hair and light brown, soft coco skin. He had brown eyes, just like Bran's. I gave him his bottle while I looked at his face. I watched him suck the bottle as if he had not been fed in days, but by the looks of this fellow you knew he had not missed any meals.

My Dad made everyone plates of spaghetti with an awesome green salad with diced cucumbers, carrots and spinach; and red onions and cheese. He made a vinaigrette salad dressing as well.

Terry came downstairs smiling from ear to ear.

"See, he loves you already; ain't that right my little cutie baby?" Terry said, while taking him from my arms. Little baby Shon was already asleep.

"Did you burp him?" Terry asked.

My face had a blank stare. "Well, no he was sucking his bottle, and then he went right to sleep," I said.

Terry lifted her baby boy over her shoulder and he was still curled up asleep, while she softly patted his back, and a burp came rolling out. I laughed a little because just the sight of Terry and her bundle of joy was just heartwarming.

"See, he needed to be burped. My auntie will learn," Terry said, while she carried baby Shon Jr to the guest room were the baby beds were.

"Lisa, were is Meagan?" I asked, watching Lisa cut the French bread into small slices and lay them on a bread platter.

"Her Daddy is rocking her to sleep," Lisa said.

I then thought about my dream of this baby, she was so beautiful…

"Hey, London what are you thinking about? You look like you are daydreaming again!" Lisa said with a giggle.

"Oh, nothing, was just thinking about this dream I had of this baby girl," I said. Lisa turned around while she set the plate of bread on the table.

"Well maybe God is showing you your future baby," Lisa said.

I laughed a little when she said that, but I believed that God was preparing my heart for a baby!

My Dad, Robert, called us to sit down at the dinner table. I looked at my family; everyone was together, laughing and waiting for my beautiful wedding day! Dad said grace and we all began to all eat my Dad's favorite dish, spaghetti.

My Mom was smiling from ear to ear, sneaking peeks at my Dad.

"Hey Mom, what is going on between you and Dad?" I asked, smiling from ear to ear.

I knew that Mom and Dad had a secret. Lisa and Terry began to beg Mom and Dad to spill the beans but they kept smiling as if we were not going to get them to budge.

"Well, London have you talked to Brandon today?" Mom asked.

I knew it; Mom and Dad had a secret about Brandon!

"No, I have not talked to him yet. Why Mom?"

"Tell me what the big news is!"

"Well, Brandon has a super surprise for you!" Dad said. He could not hold it in. "Robert, you were not supposed to say anything," Mom said, while looking at her husband. I was now so excited I wanted to call my handsome Brandon.

"Ok Mom trust me - I won't say anything," I said, smiling ear to ear.

My Mom just gave me a look of disbelief.

"London Kia, you're not supposed to know that there is a surprise for you, ok?" Mom said, stressing that I'd better not ruin it.

There was a knock at the door. I could tell Bran was the one at the door but remembered he was supposed to come tonight for dinner.

"Tony, get the door, please," I said, ready to see my man's face.

Tony opened the door and Brandon, his Mom and Dad walked in. My mom greeted Brandon's parents and Brandon. I ran to Brandon and he gave me the biggest bear hug.

"Ok, Mrs. Kennedy, she knows!" Brandon yelled and started to laugh.

"Ok, but it was Robert who told her that she had a surprise."

Mom snitched on Dad. Everyone was laughing in the Kennedy house. God was surely bringing back joy, laughter, and happiness.

"Wait, let me defend my Dad; he did not tell me what the surprise was. He just told me that there is something very special for me," I shouted.

Bran wrapped his loving arms around me and gave me the biggest hug and he said, "Ok, let's go!"

"Bran, go where???"

"London, girl trust me and let's go."

Brandon and I left the house and I jumped into his Infiniti's soft black leather front seat. We drove off while the sun was shining through the clouds. It was still cold; the weather had not changed yet, although we were so close to spring.

"Ok, Bran….please tell me honey where are we going."

Brandon just smiled while I wiggled in my seat like a kid. I noticed that the city was more like a country suburb and we were just fifteen minutes outside of the big city. There were beautiful big brick homes with large porches and lovely neighborhood parks. I was so excited; I finally realized that he was taking me to see the house that he showed in the video at my bachelorette party. Brandon stopped the car at a house that was no longer in my price range, shall I say, The house was breathtaking.

"So what do you think, London?" I was speechless.

"Baby, this is so beautiful!" I said, while slowly getting out of the car to take a better look at our home.

"But I already knew about the house. Why were you acting like it was something different?" I asked.

"Well, put the key in and open the door and see for yourself."

I opened the door and my heart melted with excitement. I was speechless. It was like walking in a house that should have been on The Most Rich and Famous! The house was furnished and decorated, including vases and very expensive artwork on the walls, and granite countertops in the kitchen in the bathrooms. This house had every contemporary flair to it.

"London, tell me, what do you think?" Brandon was looking at me with a satisfied smile.

I was speechless, and there were only two things that could leave me speechless - food and winning a business deal. But Brandon had already won me over with his loving heart now with his gracious giving!

"Brandon, this is not a house; this is a mansion!" I said.

The entryways were oversized, and the foyer was spacious. I could not leave out the game room, theater, and walk-in closets throughout the house.

"Now this was the surprise; a decorated home plus you'd never seen the inside of the home in person. I already wanted our home decorated so after our honeymoon we would not have to worry about the details!"

"Well, Bran, thank you so much! We have a new home together to start our lives!" I ran into his arms and just cried and lay my head on his shoulder.

"My Mom and Dad, is calling. Hold on baby, let me take this call."

"Dad she loves it!" Bandon said, while he talked to his Mom and Dad. I was so happy. I never knew that my Brandon would go above and beyond to buy a home for us like this. I didn't think Brandon really cared about big homes or fancy stairways. But he knows that I just have a passion for nice homes and the fine details that are added to make them lovely. I went upstairs and looked at our master bedroom. The bed was absolutely wonderful. Scriptures were displayed in fancy artwork on the back wall in our bedroom.

"I prayed for a husband, and not just a good man but a godly man. Now God has brought him in my life. I know that I should pray that God will teach us how to keep this love alive. I also wanted to continue loving my husband with my whole heart. What happens when he gets on my nerves and I just want to leave but can't because we said I do, for the good and the bad? I lay in the bed and rolled around on the sheets. Brandon was down stairs on his cell, laughing with his Parents. Thank you Lord for this new start! I just wanted to relax so I closed my eyes. I felt this warm feeling of rest that came over me. I was in a dream world. I saw her again; this beautiful baby but then she was taking small baby steps towards me and then she reached for me and said, "Mommy!"

I woke up. I was looking right into Bran's brown eyes.

"Hey, did not mean to wake you."

Brandon was sitting on the side of the bed where I lay. I grabbed and hugged Bran. "I keep dreaming of this baby girl. I think God is showing me that we will have a baby girl!" I said, smiling.

"Ok, wait, calm down, that may be true or it could just be a dream because my baby that Mandy was carrying died."

When Brandon said that, my heart sank and I did not want to talk about babies anymore. My wall was up and I told my heart yeah, Bran, I must have dreamed about you and Mandy's baby. He curled up on the bed with me. Brandon wrapped his arms around me as if he was protecting me. I smiled a little but I told my heart no more thoughts of babies. Brandon looked in my eyes and he looked as if he knew I was hurt. I bet he was wondering, What now?

"London, when we have our babies then and only then we will worry about the next step."

He paused… and then began to talk before I could get a word in.

"But until then let's focus on the now!" Brandon smiled. I guess Brandon did not want to put his hope in something that was not here yet. I agree, it was too much thinking way ahead. I knew Brandon wanted to have a baby, but I knew he probably needed to heal from losing his baby boy with Mandy. I did not even realize that Mandy and Brandon had a funeral for their baby; now that was sad. I had been so caught up with my own pain during that time, I did not even think about Brandon's feelings and what he was going through. I was so angry with the idea of Mandy having Brandon's first baby that I preferred to entertain the thought that it was good that Mandy was no longer having my future husband's baby. So when the time comes for us to have a baby I hope that Brandon would be excited!

"Look, lets get back. It's getting late. How long was I asleep?" I asked.

"Well, sweetheart, for about an hour," Brandon said, while we both got up and headed for the car.

"Brandon, thank you for turning my dreams into a reality," I said, with joy in my tone.

"London Kia Kennedy, I love you, and as long as I have breath in my body, I will always try to serve you and give you what you desire!"

"Bran that is so sweet; how could this be? I mean dreams really do come true," I said, rubbing his shoulder while he was driving.

"Yeah, only when you give your heart to the Lord. Oh, yeah I have been asked by Pastor Roman to be the Youth Pastor for the church."

I can't believe that my Brandon will now be the Youth Pastor!!

"What!!! Wow! Brandon, God has really blessed us!"

I leaned in and gave him a big kiss on the cheek.

Brandon took me back to Mom's house; we pulled up in the driveway.

"Man, my parents are gone," Brandon said, while gazing at the car lot.

I noticed my sisters and their sweet babies are all gone home; it was now nightfall. "It looks like Terry and Lisa are gone home too. Well, are you coming in, Brandon?" I asked.

"I need to go to the gym and meet my mentees tonight for some basketball," Brandon said. I looked down at my tan Gucci flats with gold buckles on top.

"Hey London, baby, look, I will plan a nice day with just me and you. We can go to a play and then dinner or you can come with me right now to cheer for me!" Brandon said while touching my hand softly.

"Bran, it's ok, I will go home and relax," I said, really hoping that Bran could not pick up that something was wrong. I was always complaining or crying about something. I just wanted so badly to spend more time with him. I did not want the night to end. It was becoming hard to say goodbye to Bran each time we parted from each other. So I decided to give him a good night kiss on his sweet lips. We have been kissing each other on the cheeks, just because the closer the wedding date came, the temptation became stronger. So, we thought it was best to spend less time alone and no kissing on the mouth. But, my feelings were crossing the line; I could not stop myself. I guess I did not want to.

Electricity went up and down my spine as his soft lips touched mine. It was getting to hot in here, and we needed to get away from each other before someone wanted to take off their clothes. I knew Brandon was right; we needed to part from each other like the Red Sea.

"Baby, we have been trying not to kiss each other on the lips," Brandon said. Brandon eyes were wide and gleaming. I leaned in and kissed him some more on his lips and neck, this felt so good I knew I had crossed over to sinning.

Brandon grabbed both of my hands, and pulled his face back from mine. This time I felt embarrassed.

Brandon did not say anything; he just stared at me as if I had two heads. I was so heated because I was letting my emotions take the lead. How could I have done this? I could not speak either; tears just ran down my face because Brandon the minister, the soon-to-be Pastor, the man of God, was now speechless.

"London, what is wrong with you?" he asked softly.

I could not find the right words; my mind went blank.

"I am sorry, just a lot of emotions and I am sorry."

Brandon's facial expression finally got unstuck from that look of 'What the heck did she just do?'

"Look, London it is ok… we are just human, that is why we have to keep God in the center. That is why I don't hang out at your house like I used to. I may be a man of God, but I am still a man."

I was still embarrassed. I held my head down.

"London, baby, stop looking down to the ground. Don't do that; stop punishing yourself," Brandon said, while his light brown eyes expressed love and compassion for me.

"I am so sorry, Bran…and thank you for not being so mad." Brandon hugged me.

"Well look, get in your car and call me when you make it home."

"I will."

"London, I love you and hey, it was very flattering that you tried to attack me," Brandon said, while letting out a laugh so hard that my parents' neighbor who was walking his dog was startled.

"Brandon, hey this is between me and you!" I yelled from my car.

"Goodnight London! This will be a great story to tell everyone once we get married!!" Brandon said, while driving off and laughing. I had mixed feelings about what I did.

I wanted to keep on kissing him over and over. I am glad that he loves me and respected me to stop me. Brandon had integrity for himself and for me. Brandon really wanted to make sure God was in this relationship. I jumped in my car and began to scan for some encouraging tunes. I did not want to hear anything with sexually explicit lyrics. I changed the radio fast and heard one of my favorite Christian songs come on. The city skyline from my view was beautiful, the tall buildings were so high, they looked like there were touching the clouds. I made it home and took my shower and slipped into my blue silk boxers and a blue tank top. I pulled my curly hair back into a high bun. I felt relaxed and still somewhat embarrassed, that I kissed Bran down. I decide to call my Mom to talk to her about what happened.

"Mom, hey, how is Dad doing?"

Mom was yelling at Dan the dog because he was barking.

"Look…I don't know why this dog is barking at every car that passes this house. I am telling your Dad that this dog is getting old."

Dan the dog was not getting old; he was already really old, I thought to myself. "Ok, London, tell me, did you love the inside of the house?"

"Mom, I am truly blessed, God has blessed me double, that house is beautiful, and I cannot believe I own it."

"Well London, baby when you trust in God, really know that God will take care of everything only if we let him!" Mom said.

"Ok, Mom I did something bad…." I had to blurt it out, before I changed my mind.

"Well, what's wrong honey?" Mom replied.

"Ok I got carried away with Bran; I started kissing him, like way too long, too much…on his neck, he had to stop me."

"For real…London you know better." Mom started to sound like she was going to lecture me, but suddenly she paused right in the middle of her conversation. "London,…. I am sorry," she said with the most humble voice.

"London, look, me and your Dad had those moments before we got married," Mom said.

"Really Mom…but you just said that I should know better," I said.

"Well, that is what I thought, until the images and memories came back to mind. That was God's way of letting me know that I was human too and I made mistakes before my wedding day."

I was so glad that my Mom was honest and shared that information with me because I was feeling so down about it that the question came in my mind - was I ready for marriage?

"Mom, you just don't understand how much this means to me. I am glad you shared," I said.

"Well, you just need to make sure you pray and fast just to make sure you get out of any sexual feelings that don't need to be there before your wedding day." Momma was right, I did not need to entertain those feelings; I knew I needed to spend some alone time with God.

"Thank you Mom, I needed to hear that. I will spend some alone time with God." "Well sweetheart, I am so happy that you called me to talk about these things. It shows that you love God and you want to please him," Mom said.

"London, just know that it is natural for couples to experience those moments where their flesh will try and cross the line." Mom sounded so sure of herself now that she had been going to her Christian therapist.

"Thanks a lot, Mom. Kiss Daddy and you guys have a good night."

I checked my social media and my email before bed. Life was great! Bran called me.

"London, hey you… how are you?" he asked, sounding as if he was singing a song.

"Bran, everything is great. I talked to Mom and she gave me some real great advice about those feelings.

"What! You told your Mom?" Brandon sounded shocked.

"Yes, I did. That's my mom; I'm supposed to be able to talk to her."

"Well, what did she say?" Bran said.

"Basically she just said it was normal for couples to fight those feelings. Mom also said that if we both have those feelings at times we should just spend more alone time with God or even fast."

Brandon was really quiet. "I think that is good information," Brandon said, while coughing.

"You're not getting sick are you?" I asked.

"No, I am eating pecan pie and a little piece of pecan went down the wrong way," Brandon said, while clearing his throat.

"What?" I said. "You got pie?" I said, as if I wanted a piece.

"Yes, London…you should have come to the game. Mandy gave everyone a slice of pie after the game." Brandon said, now this time he was smacking in my ear. "Really, man, I should have come to the game so I could have gotten a slice of pie too."

We both began to laugh. I cannot believe that even after I crossed the line he did not judge me.

"Thank you, Brandon for not judging me." I said.

I was grateful that God had blessed me to have a man that loved me from the inside out! Brandon and I talked for a while about sharing our values and how we hope that we both won't cry at the wedding. I know that Bran would cry first. Then I said goodnight and got off the phone with my Bran, and got ready for bed because tomorrow was Friday, the last rehearsal, and that next day would be my wedding day!

The day was cloudy and I was at the grocery store picking up some fresh peaches, apples and grapes. I loved this marketplace because you could find the best organic fruits and vegetables. They also had great seasonings like cumin, rosemary etc., which were imported. There were fresh cakes and breads in the bakery.

I would have gotten my wedding cake from here if it was up to me; I would have saved a lot of money. I had my curly hair pulled back in a nice slick ponytail. My slim-fitted pink couture jogging suit matched my pink studded crystal baseball hat. I was dressed perfectly because there was a chill in the air, with the smell of rain. I went on the row where the frozen foods were and I looked up and ran right into Sherry, my ex-coworker.

"Wow, it's been a while since we have seen each other," Sherry said.

"Yes, so how is the baby and everyone?"

"Well London, girl, my baby boy is due in May and I have gained so much weight. I am ready to have this baby," Sherry said, while rubbing her large belly.

"But you still look great, Sherry."

I think I lied. Lord please forgive me. Sherry had gained more weight than my sisters did during their pregnancy. I mean, so much weight that she was almost unrecognizable.

"Well, tell me what is going on London?" Sherry asked while she began to eat the sticky glazed donut that was in her hand.

"Well, Sherry… Brandon and I are getting married!!! I said, while holding up my hand with my engagement ring on.

"Yes, Brandon and I will be married on this Saturday, April the forth at 4pm!"

Sherry looked down at the floor. She did not seem to be happy for me.

"Sherry, are you ok?" I asked, while checking my beeping cell phone. I had been in this store for about an hour too long. Sherry finally opened her small mouth to speak.

"I just heard a lot of drama from people at the work place about Brandon and his crazy baby Momma and how this woman hired someone to try and kill you....and how Brandon let it happen because he was still with Mandy while you guys were together."

Sherry just kept on talking, it was like she was sent to give me bad news. I knew since no one at work, not even Sherry, really knew the truth, they probably were hearing bits and pieces of hearsay.

"Look Sherry, ok Bran and I dated for a couple of weeks and then we both went our separate ways and during that time he had something with Mandy. To make things clear, Brandon and I were not together then."

Sherry was looking confused.

"Ok...girl that sounds like drama in paradise."

Sherry was trying to paint this picture that my relationship was so bad. I didn't understand why Sherry would go there.

"Look, Sherry, it was not that much drama. God was there the whole way and that's why I am getting married tomorrow," I said, with frustration in my voice, because I could tell that Sherry had a problem with me.

Sherry was the one who quit on me, and she was the one who left a workload for me when I needed her most.

"I am just saying, London Kennedy… you preached to me about waiting on a godly man, not just a good man, and your man, first off he was supposed to be a minister and somehow…blah blah gets his long time friend pregnant and then ended up with you! Wait, I am not done!" She shouted.

Sherry was up in my face like she could not wait to tell me how she really felt. It was crazy. I was the one who got her the Job at POPC and gave her a position that she was not even qualified for. But, this same woman is in my face at the grocery store being messy! She knows the old me; I don't understand why she thought she could tell me something.

"You had the nerve to tell me that I need to put God first when you cheated on Brandon and that was the real reason that you and him split in the first place…. keep it real London Kia Kennedy!!!"

Sherry had her chubby arms folded and was shaking her head with so much anger. I realized she was jealous and hurt that her plans must did not turn out right. I paused and breathed in and out before I said anything. I knew that if

I did not calm down, I would have been in jail for fighting a pregnant woman. I also knew that was the devil trying to bring up my past to make me feel worthless.

"Sherry, everything you said about me cheating on Brandon was true." I had to tell the truth and shame the devil. But the look on Sherry's face was priceless. I did not know if she was shocked that I cheated or that I was now telling her the truth.

"Look, Sherry…I was in a season in my life were I wanted to do the right thing for God, but had no clue on how to do the right thing. It was through my failures that I understand the things I do now."

I wanted to make this plain and clear for Sherry to understand that I am just human, and just because I claim to be a Christian does not mean I am protected from mistakes, bad choices and feelings.

"God gave me and Brandon a second chance to live for God and to honor our relationship by putting God first."

Sherry was just standing there with her hands folded.

"Sherry, I am sorry if I gave you the impression that I was perfect, but Brandon and I both failed, but the crazy thing is we did not fail with each other, which is a great thing. If that would have happened, we could have messed up something divine with something carnal, but we learned a valuable lesson about ourselves before we got back together.

Sherry's facial expression changed.

"Wow, London, you go ahead; you always want to be the one that lands on her feet. You always reminded me of Catwoman."

I could not believe Sherry; she was bitter and negative.

"Well, you know what, forgive me if I painted that picture that I was perfect, but I thought for the most part we were friends."

Sherry look down at the store floor and began to shake her head.

"I am sorry, you were good to me, you were the best boss I had," she said. As she looked me in my eyes, I could tell that she was hurting. I thank God that Sherry caught me in a place in my life were I want to do the right thing for God.

"Look, Sherry, it's ok," I said, as I began to move my shopping cart to pay for my food.

"Wait, London, I am just going through some very bad things, things that you warned me about."

Sherry began to cry. "I just wish my life could have at least turned out the way I wanted it to be," Sherry said.

While crying, her voice was fading out. "Well, look just because you made a mistake it does not mean that God cannot turn your mess into a testimony!"

I gave her a hug.

"Jay-t he… well, left me and divorced me. He got married to some younger girl and he left me with the house and alimony, which really came in handy because I did not have a job. I tried to get a job but nobody wants to hire a pregnant woman." Sherry was going through a huge change and reality check. I tried to warn her, but she did not listen.

"Look, come to my women's group and share your story and let God heal you," I said.

"I will, you have really changed, the old you would have cursed me out and sent me on my way," Sherry said.

I smiled and imagined myself cursing her out.

"True, that was the old me, but forgiveness is better than getting even with people," I said, while releasing her from my bear hug.

I knew it was time for me to go, as I needed to go home and prepare some lunch before heading out to the rehearsal at the arts museum.

"London, just pray for me. I want to come to your wedding. Is that possible?"

"I am so sorry, Sherry; tables are seated by name and every invited guest had to RSVP. I did not know that we would have ran into each other, sorry."

Sherry was not even dressing with the name brand any more. I mean, nothing was wrong with clothing that were not designer names...I am just saying. Sherry was big on looking her best and was able to afford the best! But it seemed like Sherry realized that money couldn't buy love or happiness.

"That's ok, I am just preparing for this baby boy," she said, while rubbing her belly again, as if she was only worth being someone's Mom.

"Here is my card and call me if you need me," I said.

Sherry had changed so it was kind of hard for me to really feel sorry for her. I wanted to tell her off but I did not.

"Hey, thanks a lot for everything, London. Sorry for the outburst and the negative energy I am sending out into the universe," Sherry said.

"I am more of a spiritual person but I am not a Christian anymore, so I might come to your little group, but I might not."

Sherry said, while she looked at me as if she was disgusted with my presence. Maybe because I told her she could not come to my wedding, and every seat was accounted for, she got upset. When Sherry disappeared into the huge supermarket, I noticed that she dropped my business card that I gave her. Oh well, some people want to get out of a bad problem but they don't want anyone telling them how to get out.

I paid for my groceries and left the store. I got into my Mercedes and headed home. I made it home in a flash, unpacked my food and had a quick shower. Time was ticking and I had so many things to do, like meeting with my sisters and then getting dressed for this rehearsal - and then tomorrow was my big day!

I slipped on a black Kenneth Cole sweater dress and my black leather boots. I pulled out my MAC nude lipstick to bring out my natural colors. I cannot express how I really felt. It is like everything in my life was just exploding in a great way!

Amber was calling my cell and I was going to meet with my sisters at the Café Lapon, where they had the best salads, and deserts, and wonderful, mouthwatering baked chicken. The café was simply elegant. Crisp tablecloths on the tables, waiters with ties and tasty wine that make your tastebuds dance. I was able to return Amber's call while I was seated.

"Amber, hello yes."

"London you need to be here because everybody is here, including your sisters. Amber said.

"What! I am so sorry girl… I will be there." Amber had just informed me that I was late and everyone was there except me. How did this happen? Brandon did not even call me nor did my sisters inform me. I left out the restaurant without even getting the chance to order lunch.

I was hoping that this freeway would not have traffic. I was wrong; traffic was jammed on I 30. I reached into my favorite designer bag for my cell phone and called Amber.

"Amber, look, I am so sorry. I thought that rehearsal was supposed to start at 4pm today," I said, feeling so off-track.

Amber told me that the wedding ceremony is at 4pm tomorrow and today we supposed to meet at the arts museum at 12 noon. It was now twelve –thirty.

"Ok, Amber, I will be there in ten minutes. I am not too far away."

I got so distracted from Sherry; I hated being late. I called Brandon.

"Bran!!! Why did you not pick up the phone and call me?"

"London, bae… look, I was running late too; I assumed you were already here." Brandon said in his smooth voice. I guess I was looking for someone to blame for me being late.

"I just wished someone would have called me," I explained.

"London, are you coming?" Brandon asked with frustration in his voice.

"Yes, I am pulling up now." I jumped out the car and headed inside. Everyone was here; Mom, Dad, Mr. Gains and Mrs. Gains. My sisters were here, and Amber was running up to me.

"London, ok we are going to try and do this really quick," she said, while she was trying to catch her breath. Amber was dressed down in red jogging pants and matching red tennis shoes and baseball hat.

"Ok…sounds good to me."

Amber rushed to the crowd of ushers and bridesmaids and my flower girl to give them instructions on what to do.

My flower girl was so pretty; she was nine years old and her Dad was my favorite preacher, Pastor Ramon. Her name was Miranda and she was gifted to sing.

"My sisters are rolling their eyes at me," I said to Amber.

"Well, because you are almost an hour late for your own wedding rehearsal," Amber said, while directing the groomsmen how to walk down the aisle.

"Ok, everyone please take your places; we are about to start," Amber shouted. "Groom, Bride please go out to your starting place."

Bran and I left the huge room. We giggled while pushing each other on our way out the door.

"You made Amber sweat," Brandon said.

"What do you mean?" I asked.

Before Brandon could speak, a short red-haired woman in her late fifties told us to be quiet so we could hear our cue, which was our wedding song.

"Look, this is important. You guys need to pay attention so you will know when it is your turn to walk down that aisle. Now, Brandon, you will walk first, then your groomsmen and then they will walk with the bridesmaids together holding hands," the lady said. Brandon and I shook our head to let her know that we got it. The soft song began to play. Brandon looked at me and smiled while he marched into the large, beautiful room that was being decorated for our wedding ceremony. The room was large, so large you could whisper and still hear an echo. The art was displayed on the wall and they moved some things around and placed the beautiful sparkly chairs that will seat two hundred guests. Brandon finally made it to the front of the stage that was beautiful decorated with large vases of white tulips and a large canopy with four posts, each covered with white and red roses. The canopy cover was white. The stage was so beautiful. I felt like this was a scene out of a fairy tale. I waited, and right after the bridesmaids and groomsmen found their spots, the flower girl started to sprinkle rose petals that were red, pink and white. Then it was going to be my turn. The music changed, playing the song I had selected for me to walk down the aisle. The song was slow; the piano played softly in the background and then the words: "I knew it was you, because God showed me in my dreams. I knew it was you la la la ooh ooh yeah I knew it was you…."

Over and over the words touched the inner parts of my soul; this was the moment I had waited for. After the flower girl made it down to the stage, I walked down the long aisle and allowed the music to speak to my dancing heart. I felt so peaceful, but excited at the same time.

Once I made it at the fifth row of the seating, my Dad was waiting for me and he then walked with me until we reached Brandon. My Dad placed my hand in Brandon's hands.

"Ok, that's a wrap everyone!!!" Amber shouted breaking the aroma of love that had everyone captivated.

Amber came to me and said, "Your Pastor could not make it; he is at the hospital visiting church members. But he said he will be here for the wedding for sure!" "Oh thank you so much Amber, everything is beautiful," I said, looking around at how everything was being transformed into a beautiful place, like a garden in fairytale land.

"Well, London you deserve it! Now go home and I'll see you here at three tomorrow. London, don't get diva on me!" Amber said jokingly.

Amber went on to inform the wedding party of the three o'clock arrival time for tomorrow Mom was making her way to me with Mrs. Gains.

"London, baby you are going to be a wonderful beautiful bride," Mrs. Gains said. "Thank you Mrs. Gains."

I started to look around for Bran; he probably slipped away from the crowd.

"Mrs. Gains, where is your son?" I asked, still searching the room for him.

"Well, he is with his father, I think," Mary said, while scanning the large room. "Well, I am just so happy, Mrs. Gains, I know that today is my last day being single."

My Mom and Mrs. Gains looked at each other as if they were in on an inside joke. "Hey, what's so funny?" I asked, demanding for them to let me in on this joke. "Well daughter, if you think marriage is going to be all sweet and cute and happy, we got news for you." they said, while shaking their heads.

"He is my son, so I know how he is a super-neat freak, he gets mad if his underwear is not hanging up on those racks with the clips."

I looked at my Mom and then at Mrs. Gains and I said with surprise, "He likes his drawers hanging up?!?"

I burst in to laughter and the three of us laughed together.

I guess the men could tell that we were talking about them. Brandon, my Dad and Mr. Gains were headed our way. Brandon looked so handsome in dark-colored jeans and a gray shirt.

"Bae, what is so funny?"

I was trying to play it smooth, while my Mom and Mrs. Gains were shaking their heads trying to hold in laughter. But as soon as I said, "Brandon," my Mom and Mrs. Gains burst out again in laughter.

"Brandon, it sounds like your mother has been talking," Brandon's Dad said.

I could not speak as I had joined in laughing too.

"Well at least they are laughing and not crying," My Dad said.

"Honey, it's ok, We were just telling London to make sure she takes care of you once you guys move in together," Mrs. Mary said.

"Mom, I am sure you told her some things that are private," Brandon said with a grin.

"Nothing is a secret any more, you have a wife, boy…so she will find out all your bad habits."

"Don't feel bad Brandon, we understand how critical it is to not want people to know how you like your underwear stored," my Mom said laughing again.

"I knew it, Mom, you told them!" Brandon said, laughing so hard he had to hold his stomach.

"Bran, bae, I will make sure I will buy those hangers with the clips at each end so we can make that happen," I said jokingly

"You know, we have to go because Amber and her crew will need to have everything set up before 12 midnight tonight," Bran said while placing his hand on the lower part of my back.

"Well with all joking aside, we want to say that we love you both and cannot wait to be at the wedding tomorrow," Mr. Gains said, while placing his arm across our shoulders.

"Thanks Dad and Mom for loving us both," Bran said with tears welling in his eyes.

I had never seen him really cry. I knew he was really excited about our love journey.

"Well, Brandon, take care of my daughter, she is the last one to get married," my Dad said.

"People, we need you guys to exit so we can go ahead and set up for tomorrow," I yelled.

My sisters ran over and kissed Brandon and me on our cheeks.

"Tony and I have dinner prepared at the house and we invited some new friends and everyone is coming over. You all are invited."

"Well, Linda and Robert has invited us to dinner at a spot named Edelmans; we are going with them," Mark Gains said.

"Dad what do you know about that spot?" I asked.

"London, girl they have the best food and they play real music," my Mom said. "So you guys were not going to invite us, your kids?" Bran asked, while giving them this 'you should be ashamed' look.

"Brandon enjoy your last night of being single, and we love y'all. We've got to go!" my Dad said, while taking his bride by the hand and leading her to the parking lot.

My sister, Bran and I watched our parents walk out the door.

"So, we are waiting. Are you guys coming over?" Lisa asked.

"Tony, did you cook that chicken and rice dish?" Brandon asked, while smiling. "No, we had food catered, and invited some friends from work."

"I'm in," Bran said.

"Ok, we'll see you guys in about a hour," I said, "because I need to change and get really dressed up."

"You will have time; it is only five-thirty. The dinner starts at seven on the dot, London Kia…" Lisa said.

Terry was smiling.

"You guys better show up because this is the only time I get the chance to party without my Shon Jr.," Terry said.

"Yes, you got a babysitter!" Brandon said.

"Bran, it is hard to try and have a social life once you have kids, because Terry and I used to just get up and go out to dinner or a club; now we need to find babysitters," Shon said.

"I know, that is why I think I want to wait on babies," Bran said.

Everyone began to talk and walk to the parking lot. I did not say too much. I realized that Brandon and I were not on the same page when it came to kids. I thought we were. I mean, we had a long talk about kids three months ago. But, I guess he changed his mind. Ok.

"Well, London baby, we are going, right?" Brandon asked while I got in my car to head home.

"Yes, of course! We can't miss this great dinner party at Lisa and Tony's house, I mean they went all out by inviting friends, and having it catered," I said smiling, but the thought of a baby lingered in the back of my head.

Brandon was smiling widely.

"I cannot wait to see you there. I know you are going to be so pretty," Brandon said, while closing my car door.

"Thanks, Bran. See you there."

On my drive home I felt weighed down and confused about Brandon and me. I know that God had brought us together, but the question was, were we really ready? I got home and checked my home phone voicemail and Amber left me a message saying to make sure I arrive at the arts museum at 3pm. I love that Amber. She had only a short time to plan this wedding and she really did an excellent job!

I took a warm quick shower and found a black Vera Wang cocktail dress, which would be perfect for the party. I pulled all my hair up in a high ponytail to look more elegant and I went for more of a natural look with makeup. I was ready in a short time.

I jumped into my black shiny Mercedes and made my way to the party. I was so shocked that cars were lined up the entire block. My sister's house had at least over hundred people. Brandon was already there; I had saw his car parked in front. While I was on my way to the door, Mandy walked out with her big belly.

I know I said I forgave her and was ready to give her a chance, but a part of me was still uneasy with her. I smiled and gave her a hug.

"Mandy, what a nice surprise," I said.

For real, this was a big surprise to have her at my sister's party.

"Well, Tony is friends with my husband so that's how we got the invite," Mandy said.

I think she could tell that I was feeling awkward.

"Well, why are you out here in this night air?" I asked, while my cell began to ring. "Hold on one second. Yes, Brandon, I am outside talking to Mandy. I will be inside in just a moment. Love you too."

Brandon always brought a smile to my face.

"Wow, you are blushing," Mandy said.

"I always blush when he calls me or when we go out together," I said, reminiscing. It only reminded me how I used to get nervous when I would talk to Bran.

"Well, that is very unique to have that kind of love in a marriage, because everyone who is married does not always show love and affection like that."

"True, Mandy. Man, I don't think I would want to be married to a person that could not show me that they care," I said.

"Well, I came outside just to get some fresh air," Mandy smiled, and then her facial expression changed suddenly. Mandy grabbed her belly.

"What's wrong Mandy?" I asked, very concerned.

"I am hurting, please God help me!" Mandy said as she put both hands on the lower part of her belly. I got really nervous, and started looking around, for help. "Ok, look Mandy I am going to get your husband!"

I shouted as if she could not hear, but Mandy was so close I could feel her breathing.

"Please go, London get him!" Mandy yelled again.

I ran in the house that was filled with loud jazz music, and people laughing while drinking the cocktails that were lined up at the bar. I squeezed through the crowd that was in the living room only to run into another crowd of people in the den. I was so nervous that I forgot Mandy's husband name so I called out Brandon's name loudly.

Lisa came over to me and said, "Hey, you know that girl is here."

"Lisa, yes please find her husband. That girl is in labor!!!" I said.

Lisa's face was now red.

We saw Brandon, Tony and John. We both ran up to them while they were having a conversation about the football game.

"John, Mandy is in labor!" We both shouted at the same time.

John began to shout as well while he ran through the crowd looking for Mandy. "No, she is just seven months. It's too early!!"

John kept shouting that as we all ran towards the front door, but before we could get outside, a short Spanish lady coming running in saying, "Someone call the ambulance! A woman is laying on the front porch in labor!"

We ran right past the lady and John picked up Mandy from off the cold cement porch. We all stood outside as we watched Mandy breathe in and out and yelling, "This is so painful!"

I watched John place her in his gray Jaguar. Brandon walked over to the driver side to talk to John.

"John, be safe and try to get to the hospital as quickly as you can, but please be safe."

I was just shocked; I had never seen a woman in labor. Lisa and Terry both went into labor while I was at work or out of town, so to see Mandy in labor really freaked me out.

Brandon grabbed me and held me close.

"It will be ok London, just calm down," Bran said.

He could tell that I was scared for her. Brandon knew me. I looked up at him without saying a word and lay my head against his chest. I felt safe with him. Brandon always knew what to say to me every time when I had some type of doubt in my mind and I felt like maybe we were not on the same page.

God he always reminded me that Brandon could see past my words; he could feel almost what I was feeling. I can truly say that when two people love God, He will give each person the love and the ability to feel what the other person is feeling when they need them the most. Love is not a selfish act. Love is about being vulnerable, and giving your heart to the person who has the power to hurt your heart. I was learning that just because Bran does not always say the right things it did not mean he was wrong for me. Brandon was just a human that had flaws and made mistakes.

Everyone at the party came outside to see what all the commotion was about. Tony and Lisa directed everyone back to the party.

I was nervous because I thought that Mandy was going to lose this baby too. I could not believe the woman whom I used to dislike with a passion, the woman who gave birth to my Bran's first baby, was now someone I was scared for, or shall I say, cared for.

I could also tell that seeing Brandon watch Mandy go into labor with John's baby was probably awkward because last year Brandon was in John's place. Brandon was a proud father waiting to see his son born, but for him his baby died.

I looked up at Brandon and his eyes were as cold as ice. Brandon was staring as if he was somewhere else.

"Look London, I am going to go home and get some rest because we've got a big day ahead of us."

I nodded my head because this is what I was talking about; every time Mandy was going through something, Brandon would act weird. I know he loves me, but how can he separate his feelings from her? I now went from being caring to being angry. I wish in this very moment that I was not a Christian woman. I wish I could say every curse word that was popping up in my head. It was like the devil was in my left ear giving me each word to say and how I should say them, while God was in my right ear telling me to let it go and pray for Brandon. All I wanted to do was explode!

"Ok, fine! Go home, Brandon. Every time Mandy gets hurt she changes your mood! I don't understand that Bran… do you still want her?" I had blanked out, and I found myself screaming and shouting at my soon-to-be husband.

This time he did not try and quiet me down or say he was sorry. This time he looked me in my eyes and just stared at me for about a second. Brandon was not going to back down from this fight. I think I had pushed the wrong buttons. Part of the large crowd was still outside and when they heard and watched me get up in Brandon's face. They all stopped to watch the show that was going down. Tony and Lisa ran to us both.

"Hey!", She yelled. "London, you are out of line, and you need to go home now."

I could not believe Lisa said that in front of everyone. Lisa was my sister, how could she make me seem so horrible?

"Lisa, you can tell me that, but you are not walking in my shoes. Mandy has some kind of hold on Brandon. Every time it is Mandy this and Mandy that, only because she carried his baby first," I yelled."

The crowd gasped because some of my sister's guests were church members and they did not know about all of this drama. I had now exposed what was a private matter to everyone who was at the party. Brandon walked closer to me, so close I can feel his breath on me, and not in a good way.

"Brandon, what, you know I am telling you the truth; you favor Mandy over me because she carried a part of you," I said, but by this time, I was crying. I guess all along I had never got over the fact that Mandy was going to always have a special place in Brandon's heart and I was too selfish to share the small percent of love that he had for her. I wanted Brandon's whole heart.

"Yes, I don't like the idea of sharing your heart with Mandy."

Brandon was quiet and he had a frown on his face, standing in front of me with his arms folded. But like always, when he is really mad he stayed quiet for a long while before speaking.

"London, please stop, you are just having wedding jitters," Lisa said, trying to pull me away from Brandon and the crowd. But my anger was out of control, all of these insecurities had built up and now my jealousy had reached a level that I could not imagine.

"I am so sick and tired of Mandy having some kind of effect on you."

"Lisa, I am sorry that this happened, but I am done," Brandon said, as he stared at me with the meanest look that I had ever seen.

When Brandon began to walk towards his car, right before he could get in, I ran up behind him and jumped in front of him screaming,

"No…No…Brandon, you will face me and tell me what is it with you and Mandy." Brandon stopped, took a few steps back, and just stared at me again, saying nothing. Brandon just frowned. I felt angry and hopeless. I was acting foolish. But I was acting on how I felt, I was tired of being the good woman and watching my man take up for Mandy and watch him mourn over Mandy's baby without including me.

"Brandon, why did you not tell me about the funeral that you and Mandy had for the baby!!!" I yelled again. "I can tell you guys why," I said, while so exhausted from screaming,

I was about to trip on the sidewalk and a random guy helped me by grabbing me to keep me from falling.

"Because, it didn't matter, it was not me that was carrying Brandon's precious baby boy that died!!!" I said shouting again. During all of this shouting I glanced out at the crowd and they were shaking their heads in embarrassment.

My sisters were angry. I had ruined the party. My sin had got the best of me and my anger was now out of control. I could not stop; I was on a roll.

"STOP!!!!! STOP!!!!!" Brandon screamed to the top of his lungs.

Everyone knew that it was time to leave. When they heard Brandon scream, they were shocked. They were so used to this man of God staying positive and uplifting. They could not stand to see him angry, and so angry that he looked like the Hulk. You would have thought that scared me, but now I was now ready for anything.

"Look, I am done with you!!! If you are so insecure about a woman who has clearly moved on, then we cannot move forward until you seek some professional help. I thought that this was a phase and you would get past this, but now to make a scene in front of church members and family all because of your feelings and what you think!!!! No, I cannot marry a woman that clearly needs healing. I am done!"

Brandon jumped in his car and left me standing outside with the rest of the crowd that refused to miss out on a good argument.

"Lisa," I said.

But Lisa and Terry and everyone else just looked at me, shook their heads and went inside.

"Look everyone, the party is over." Lisa said.

I jumped in my car. I was so mad because no one understood me. No one could relate to my feelings. Brandon was done! I had just messed up my chance at having a happy life with Brandon. I couldn't believe that my wedding was over. I had taken it too far. I got home and no one called me. Everyone was upset with me.

I lay down on my bed and just cried.

I finally got a call; Lisa was on the other end.

"What Lisa," I said, ready for her to come down on me.

"Look, London. Tony, had a talk with me, and he understood where you were coming from. Tony is talking with Brandon right now at our house. Brandon came back looking for you."

I felt so dead inside because I thought I had lost Brandon forever. So when Lisa said that Brandon came back looking for me, I was shocked. I was so sure that it was over.

"London, you are human, but you cannot bring up issues in front of other people," Lisa said. Lisa was right. I could learn a lot from my younger sister; I had never seen Lisa and Tony fight. And Terry and Shon were always happy.

"You are so right, sister, I should have listened to you when you told me to be quiet. But, I just had to take it there!" I said. Lisa giggled a little.

"Look, I did not show you any compassion or anything."

"I guess I can be so judgmental at times." I let out a sigh, just because Lisa finally understood me.

"Lisa, you just don't understand how much that means to me to, to feel like someone gets me." I said, with tears running down my face.

"Brandon wants to talk to you London," Lisa said.

"Well, I don't know why you are telling me. If he wanted to talk to me then he should call me; he has a cell phone."

"London… be nice, he just wants to give you a heads up." Lisa said.

I could hear Tony and Brandon in the background laughing for whatever reason. "Well, what are they laughing at?" I asked, being nosy.

" They are laughing at Tony joking on how he should have recorded you and Brandon and then put you both on a social site for real," Lisa said jokingly.

"Ok, look you and Brandon need to fix this mess, and, oh yeah Mandy had a baby boy. I know you might want to know that," Lisa said.

"Yes, that is such a blessing."

"London please let her go. If you don't, you are going to lose Brandon," Lisa said. Then Terry took the phone to speak to me.

"Hey, sis I know we don't talk much and I kind of keep my two cents to myself but listen, you have a man that loves you. Trust that!"

Terry and Lisa were right. I needed to leave this Mandy girl and my jealousy alone. Lisa said, "London, Brandon just left to see you so he must be going to surprise you at your house if he has not called you already."

I rushed to throw away the three-day old pizza box away. I cleared my dishes so Brandon would not see that I was living like a little pig.

"Thanks Lisa for the heads up; gotta go before he gets here." I was now rushing to disconnect my phone call.

"Look London, be nice. You were right and wrong. My husband and I cannot be marriage counselors without getting paid," Lisa said, while laughing.

I lay on my sofa and relived the argument over and over in my head. I felt released but embarrassed at the same time. God did not want me to act like an out-of-control woman.

God wanted me to get my feelings in check and controlled. I now understand the reason why God had me to wait; he gave us time in our singleness so we could prepare to be better people, but some of us, like me, just used that time to complain about how long we had to wait. I finally heard a knock at the door. I look out my peephole and it was my Bran coming back either to tell me off, or explain.

I opened the door and as soon as he came in my living room he grabbed me and hugged me tight.

"Bran, hey is everything ok?" Brandon did not say anything he continued to hug me.

"Brandon please say something," I pleaded.

Brandon let me go and I watched as tears ran down his face. He cried out so hard that I could see his pain that he had kept in for a long time. Brandon fell to his knees still holding me around my waist while his face was buried in my belly. Brandon cried like a child. I had never seen him so vulnerable. I wrapped my hand around his head, rubbing the back of his head while his tears stained my shirt. Before I could say another word, my eyes filled with tears that rolled down my face like a rushing river. Brandon and I had kept pain hidden. We were polite when we should have said something or spoken up. Communication is more powerful than weapons in a war. If you don't have communication how can you strategize your plan?

Brandon and I both just kept on holding each other while we both cried. It felt like a release of letting go of unwanted thoughts, memories and regrets. Finally Brandon stood up and he looked me in my eyes. Brandon had tearstains on his face like a window after it rains.

"London, I am sorry for hurting you; don't talk just listen." Brandon said, while we both moved to the sofa and sat down he grabbed my hands and held them tight. "London, you kept feeling jealous, because of me. I made you feel that way because somehow I thought I owed Mandy something because I got her pregnant. I never once looked at her as a problem or her being wrong for getting me drunk and being sneaky enough to use my body while I was out of my mind. I kept on denying that Mandy had done something wrong, because if I done that to Mandy and gotten her drunk and had sex with her without her permission or while she was intoxicated I could have gone to jail," Brandon said while looking at me genuinely.

"I portrayed Mandy as the victim while she tormented you while showing off her baby bump when she was pregnant by me. I made you feel bad when you were hurting while loving me and watching another woman carry my child. When most women would have said Brandon I cannot do this relationship, you stayed. Although you were having problems, you tried. When you came to me to express what you were going through I just threw Mandy up in your face and told you to forgive. I was a jerk, and I did not cover you like I should have. That is why you felt jealous."

Brandon was telling the truth. When you date a Christian man, it does not mean that he will always get it right, but when Daddy Jesus steps in and says enough is enough, he will correct your man. That was why God kept telling me to stop. "London sweetheart, I did somehow punish you for the loss of my baby boy. I could not mourn him because I thought that I would have made you feel bad or some kind of way."

"Bran, I wanted you to let me in," I said.

I could not keep quiet for long.

"London wait, you were supposed to feel connected, not feel like you were on the outside of any relationship I may have with anyone. I am sorry baby!" Bran said, with a warm smile.

"I am sorry too, babe," I said, without saying anything more. I just wanted to enjoy this moment, this peace.

Chapter 18

LACE & LOVE

Who would have thought that Brandon and I would break our own rule. Bandon slept over! I jumped up and the sun beamed in on both of us. We fell asleep holding each other at my place. I did not remember how we could have just allowed this to happen. Thank God we both were fully clothed. Brandon and I knew better. This was a big no no, We broke the rule when he came over at midnight and we both were so emotional that we held each other on the sofa and just fell asleep.

My cell phone was ringing. it was my Mom. Brandon was still asleep. I eased up from up under his arm. I ran into the bathroom. I looked a mess. My eyeliner was smeared over my face. I looked like a raccoon.

"Mom, hi. Why are you calling me at nine in the morning?"

"Because we are worried about Bran," my Mom said.

I could not believe this. Now everyone will know that Brandon slept over!

"Well did you guys call his phone?" I whispered, hoping that I would not wake Brandon up, because he was going to freak out.

"Yes, we did and it is going to his voicemail," Mom said.

"Mom ok please don't jump to conclusions," I said, but before I could tell her she said, "Uh huh, he did spend the night at your house! We all said it!" Mom said. "Who is we?" I said, hoping she wouldn't say Brandon's Mom.

"Well Mary and her husband and your dad and I all went to Lisa's house last night for some food to take home. Your sister Lisa told us everything."

I was so shocked that Lisa snitched on us.

"Well Mom, Brandon and I… we love each other and we forgave each other."

"Well, good the wedding is still on!" Mom shouted.

I could tell Mom had faith in me; she knew I would not mess things up this time around because sometimes second chances are not easy to come by.

"Look, I know you and Brandon remained faithful to God, right?" she asked, hoping that with everything I went through I actually learned to wait on the Lord.

"Momma, yes. We did not plan to spend the night with each other. Brandon held me while we both told each other how we truly felt, and we both cried together, and we both asked each other for forgiveness," I said, while standing in the bathroom mirror, removing last night's make up from my face.

"Well God's presence showed up, Mom," I said. I was still feeling the Lord's presence at that moment.

"Baby, God has blessed you two, and he will continue to grow you both. Brandon and you had to be tested. Marriage is not always pretty, and sometimes you're not always going to feel like you are being treated fairly. But when you can go through the fire and still hold on to each other than that is the sign that you guys truly love each other," Mom said.

But before I could speak my Mom began to tell me how she and Dad enjoyed themselves at Edelman and how she falls in love with my Dad everyday. "Sweetheart, baby, that Brandon is a keeper, because your sisters told me how you acted a fool!" Mom said.

I knew she was now ready to tell me how she really felt.

"Mom, but I got so mad I let my emotions run."

"You know you got that loud mouth from me," Mom said.

I was so scared of that side of my Mom. If I look like her, then for sure I am going to need to see a therapist too, honestly.

"Yes, London, you need to express what you feel right then and there, or you will let it build up and build up and then you will explode."

My Mom was right; she made sense.

"I agree, Mom. How did you become so understanding, when you used to come undone with just a simple spill when we were kids?" I asked.

"Well baby, I did and said a lot of things that I wish I could change. But I took your advice and saw this wonderful therapist and I have learned how to communicate better," Mom said, sounding so happy and like a brand new woman. "I thought that God was healing me through prayer and fasting and going to church. But then I still exploded on Brandon," I said, not really understanding how I was not walking in clarity as I thought I should.

"Well for some of us we need a little more, like counseling. You faced a lot this year."

Mom was right.

"London, baby you faced losing a best friend whom you loved, then a new boyfriend and the challenges that came with that relationship, and ups and downs on your job, to walking away and starting something new, your own business.

London baby, it has been a roller coaster for you. Finding out that your real Dad died, and I cringed at the thought of that man breaking into your home trying to rape you. I can say that God has done a wonderful work in you."

She talked about me with such dignity, and most of all she was proud of me. I used to think that my Mom never could understand me. But now my Mom saw right through me.

"Thank you Mom, I love you so much," I said while heading to the kitchen to place my frozen waffles into the toaster.

"Well, look you better get ready and I will see you at the arts museum at three o'clock," Mom said, while disconnecting the call.

I placed my hot waffles on my plate. I knew once Brandon could smell food he was going to wake up. I was right. Brandon tossed for a while and he was finally up. I rushed to him while he sat up from the sofa. He looked around as if he was shocked that he was at my home.

"London! London! Sweetheart, why didn't you wake me up?" He asked, sounding nervous.

"I was shocked too, I just woke up about fifteen minutes ago. My Mom and your family know that you spent the night. Brandon's light brown complexion turned red.

"What, aww man, now we look guilty like people could have thought we slept together or something."

I brought him a nice plate of hot waffles with warm syrup drizzled over them. "Thanks, London," Bran said in a raspy voice.

Bran and I ate our waffles while making googly eyes at each other.

"London, thanks baby for this nice breakfast," Brandon said while we both sat next to each other.

Today was a perfect day for a wedding. The sun was shining like spring had finally showed up on my wedding day.

"I hope you liked my homemade waffles," I said with a sneaky smile.

"Yeah, right. Girl you know these waffles come from a box in the freezer," he said, while we both laughed.

"Look baby I've got to go. I have to meet with the guys for lunch and then head down to the arts museum so I can marry this beautiful woman. You don't mind, do you?" Bran said while he placed a soft kiss on my forehead. We both headed to the kitchen so we could put away or breakfast dishes.

"Bran don't worry about that plate just place it on the counter and I will wash them in a sec. I'm so glad we got the chance to really let go of the heaviness," I said, while walking close to my tall, broad shouldered well-built man. It was a plus that Bran was good looking, but I loved Bran for his love of God and for people.

Bran rushed and grabbed me. He held me so close I could hear his heartbeat. I laid my head against his chest, while his arms wrapped around my waist. I could still smell his cologne that lingered on his shirt from last night.

"Look, we have been tested, and this is God's way of telling us that no matter what we need each other to be honest, respectful, and open," Brandon said, while still holding me close.

"I agree, I do feel like what Pastor and his wife taught us went out the window," I said with a giggle.

"No , bae we did not throw everything away," Brandon said.

"London we prayed, no matter how bad things got, we kept the faith!"

Brandon's words went through my soul. It was a reflection of what God had been teaching us all along.

"Look, I'll see you at the altar. I love you forever." I turned around to face my soon-to-be husband with so much joy! I gave him a kiss on the cheek.

"Thanks bae, but now you want me to give you kisses on the cheek but in the beginning I got soft lip kisses," Bran joked.

"Get out!" I said loudly but I was teasing.

Brandon left and I wanted to spend some time alone with just God and me. I went upstairs to my walk-in closet to only stare at my beautiful wedding dress. The dress was white with sheer white lace in the back in the shape of a letter v. Crystals were placed all over the front of the dress. This dress made me look like a princess. It hugged the middle of my body and then it ballooned out. My dress was sealed and was in my dress bag, I packed my overnight Gucci bag, because the plan was to leave our wedding and spend the first night in our home together and then from there we would wake up the next morning and spend two lovely weeks in Hawaii! I felt like a princess that was planning her life with her prince and the King Jesus! I had already hired packers and movers that would move my belongings to my new home.

I took a shower and put on my favorite comfortable pink couture jogging suit and my pink Nikes. My hair was pulled into a high ponytail. I had no makeup on because the makeup artist was meeting the bridal party for makeup and hair at the museum. It was about noon and I was doing excellent on time; I was not running late. I put my Gucci night bag in the limousine that was waiting for me, and I did not forget my wedding dress bag. I was now on my way to the wedding. I started to feel butterflies and I was getting a little bit nervous, but I was ready for this moment right now!

I knew I was sharing this limo with my sisters and the flower girl so we stopped by Pastor Jeff Ramon's home and picked up his beautiful daughter Miranda. Pastor and his lovely wife Cindy came out to the limo.

"Hey, London we are so happy for you," she said, while placing Miranda's bag in the car.

"Thank you First lady for praying for Brandon and me during our ups and downs. First Lady reached in the limo, grabbed my hands, and smiled.

"London, just remember that your marriage will be tested, but as long as you hold on to God, you will pass the test."

Mrs. Cindy Ramon was gentle and meek. I smiled and was so thankful to have my Pastor and his wife as mentors to Bran and me.

"We will see you guys soon." The limo drove off. I relaxed back in my seat, while Miranda placed her headphones on. I could not describe how I was feeling. I felt as if I was on a roller coaster ride. My emotions were all over the place.

I got a call from my sister Terry.

"Hey beautiful, wanted to tell you that I love you and that I am so proud of you!" Terry is such a mild-natured woman who was so sweet and kind, you would never really see her upset.

"Thank you Terry, I needed to hear your voice," I said.

"Well, Lisa and I will see you at the arts museum center. Love you!

"You guys are not getting a ride in the limo with the flower girl and Mom?"

"No. Lisa and I had to get the babies settled in with the nanny."

"Oh ok."

I was feeling so full and excited! The limo made it to my Mom's house just as she got outside with her things. I jumped out the limo because I had to hug my Mom right then and there.

"Mommy! It is finally happening!" I said, with tears in my eyes.

The cool breeze whipped through my Mom's hair. My Mom wore a long yellow dress that was comfy and beautiful. We both got in the limo and drove towards the art museum with no more stops.

The drive was smooth. I felt like someone special, maybe a celebrity or a politician. I thought to myself: I could get used to having someone else driving me around. The limo pulled up in front of the art museum and Miranda and Mom and I noticed all the beautiful ice sculptures of butterflies at the entrance of the Arts Museum Center. Amber came rushing over to greet us with her beautiful smile.

"I am so happy that you ladies are here on time! Ok, my assistant will show you guys to your room."

We all followed the dark-haired Caucasian woman on to the elevator and into a beautifully decorated room that was set up just for us. There was a comfortable sofa, and a vanity that was covered with curling irons, flat irons and hair spray. Beauty products surrounded us. The make-up artist was setting up her table and the Caucasian lady who showed us to our room began to tell us what was next.

"Ok ladies, I will be assisting you three with whatever you need. My name is Danielle; you can hang your bags in this closet," she said, while taking our things and finding a spot for our bags.

"Ladies, there are three chairs; please choose a chair and your hair stylist will assist you in just a second."

We sat and relaxed.

"London, girl, I feel like I am some kind of celebrity," Mom said jokingly.

"Mom, I was just thinking that," I said.

Mom slumped down in her chair so she could relax more.

"They have everything so organized," Mom said.

"Yes, I love the way they set up this room into a suite for us."

Miranda's stylist was now approaching her chair. The tall and slender African American woman was in her early twenties.

"Hello, Bride, my name is Justine and I will be styling your flower girl Miranda."

"Great! Nice to meet you! Please just make sure you give her soft, long lasting curls."

Miranda's hair was long and natural she had the biggest smile on her face.

"Ok your other stylist will be here, and after your hair is done then you will put on you beautiful dress. I will come back up to your room to make sure things are moving on time."

Danielle was very professional and organized. Danielle left the room.

The hair stylist finally came in the room to work on our hair. Amber came into the room with the most amazing smile.

"Well we are doing great with timing. Brandon and your brother-in-law are now in their dressing room and your sisters, the bridesmaids, are in their dressing room too so we have about an hour before we start this wedding. You ladies are looking great!"

Amber left the room.

My hair stylist flatironed my hair and then began to put big curls in so when she was done my hair could just flow with nice soft curls. My Mom's hair was pulled in to an elegant updo; she was beautiful. I just thought about all those random guys who never wanted to give me a real chance, and who just wanted to use me. Brandon saw me from the inside out. We both felt this connection even before we connected. I knew that Brandon was my husband, but it took him three years to consider me.

My makeup artist was now ready to do my face. She had already finished Mom's and Miranda's and they were both stunning.

"Well, Miranda, you look so beautiful!" My Mom said.

"Thanks Mrs Kennedy," Miranda said to my Mom.

It was something about the way Miranda said 'Mrs. Kennedy.' I was dropping off my last name. I did not believe in keeping my father's name. It was time to become Mrs. Gains, I thought.

In the room there was a big window with a gorgeous view of downtown Dallas. I felt like the happiest woman in the world.

"Ladies we are all done here. You ladies are beautiful; I hope you love your look." We were beautiful! It was now time for us to get dressed. Danielle was now walking in the room.

"Ok, I see you ladies; you look fantastic!" She said, while clapping her hands. Danielle was short and fair-skinned with dark brown hair. She was dressed in all black, just like all of Amber's assistants.

"So now I will start with the bride; London would you like to take a bathroom break before we help you with your dress?"

Danielle said. I got up from my seat and headed towards the bathroom. I softy spoke to Danielle

" Yes, I will go ahead and take that bathroom break."

When I came out of the restroom, I looked at my Mom. She was all dressed and ready, and pretty! She was wearing a black long fitted formal gown with crystals that covered the dress with a sweetheart neckline. My Mom's hair and make up were flawless.

"Mom, you are breathtaking," I said. My Mom walked towards me with a small box that was wrapped in fancy gold gift-wrapping paper.

"Here's something old; your father and I are giving you my sweetheart ring. This is the ring I got from your Dad when we first met. He said that this ring was only going to be substituted for the wedding ring that he had not gotten me yet," Mom said as she laughed.

"Your Dad was always wanting to help or to give to me."

"Thank you Mom," I said.

When I looked up my sisters were dressed in black long form-fitting dresses just like Mom's but without the crystals. Terry's and Lisa's hair were in high buns; they were absolutely beautiful! They came and hugged me and admired the ring that Mom gave me.

"Now Mom, why did she get the ring?" Lisa asked.

"Because she is the oldest," Mom said.

"Ok, I want to give you something else," Mom said.

She pulled out another fancy box. I was so shocked.

"Mom, this is too much. You guys are going to make me cry, and I don't want to cry because I'm going to mess up my makeup."

I opened the box while my two sisters was standing around me ready to see what I had gotten. They were diamond heart-shaped earrings.

"Mom, thank you so much!"

I was so thankful. Mom and Dad made me feel like a beautiful princess! Danielle was back in the room to give orders.

"Ladies, I need the flower girl, the mother of the bride, and the bridesmaids."

"Love you," Lisa whispered while leaving to get in her position for the wedding.

I had to fight back my tears; I was super-happy. Brandon would be waiting for me at the altar in fifteen minutes. My Mom and Miranda left to take their place. "Well…London lets help you get this gown on," Danielle said, while pulling the dress over my head. She placed my veil over my face and said,,"Now you are ready!"

This was my moment; everyone was in place. I heard the music start and I could hear the Minister Shoranda speaking about Brandon and me about how God brought us together.

God wrote my love story. I walked down to the hall with Danielle; she had her walkie talkie and she was told that the groom was now at the altar. My heart started beating fast and I wanted to cry, and then I heard the song that was chosen to play while I walked down the aisle. "I knew it was you, because God---- showed me you in my dreams. I knew it was you la la la ooh ooh yeah I knew it was you….." Over and over.

I got closer to the door waiting on my beautiful flower girl to drop the flower petals, and then I walked down the petal-covered aisle . My father stood up to walk me down the aisle to meet the groom. The room was filled with about two-hundred people; everyone had come to see London and Brandon join their lives together. I was now facing my handsome Brandon. My Pastor Ramon came closer. My sisters were standing in place. I gave my bouquet to my mother and the Pastor began to say that God had brought two God-chasing individuals together to chase the love of God together, to walk in God's perfect plan for their lives.

"Do you, Brandon Gains, take London Kia Kennedy to be your lawful wife, and promise to love her and honor her for the rest of her life?"

Brandon was handsome; he was wearing a tuxedo and he had a white tulip pinned on the right side of his suit jacket.

Brandon looked into my eyes and said, "Yes, I promise."

Then the Pastor asked me the same thing. I said, "I do." I felt like I was not really there; it felt like everything was a dream, as if this was not happening. But God had made my dreams come true. The Pastor looked at the both of us.

"Brandon & London Gains, I pronounce you husband and wife. You may kiss the bride."

The crowd began to yell as if we were at a football game. Brandon leaned in and pulled me close and gave me the sweetest kiss. I was now Mrs. Gains! We took each other by the hand and began to walk down the aisle and everyone began to throw red and yellow flowers at us. We both jumped over the beautifully decorated brown broom that was waiting at the last row of chairs. I was married! Brandon took me away from the crowd as we both vanished off into one of the rooms. Brandon was staring in my eyes while I had this smile on my face because I felt so happy. "London Kia Gains!" Brandon repeated, he leaned in and gave me the most, deepest kiss ever.

"I love you so much, I loved you before you were mine," I said.

"I love you so much too!" He said.

We both hugged each other again.

"Look, I am going to change into another dress that is comfortable and I will meet you at the reception. "Sounds great sweetheart," Brandon said, while placing a soft kiss on my neck. "I will see you soon."

I went in my room and changed into a form-fitting short dress that was a soft creamy color with crystals. A lace ribbon was wrapped around my waist.

I went to the reception room. The centerpiece was beautiful. The tulips were lovely in each vase all turquoise and chocolate colors, went well with the fine china. The ice sculptures were beautiful. I had the best wedding planner. My sisters came over to greet me. "London, you are so beautiful. We cried when we saw you and Brandon say your I do's," Lisa said.

Terry gave me a hug.

"Shon and I were just talking about how this reminded us of our wedding."

My father gave me the biggest hug.

"I prayed for this moment. God has been good to you London Kia Gains," my father said.

"Thanks Dad," I said, while hugging my father.

I knew that after tonight I would be entering a whole new life; no more sleeping in my bed alone, or just washing my clothes whenever. I knew that life as a single woman was now over. I looked out at my family and friends who were dancing and eating. The room was filled with sculptures and flowers and the waiters served the crowd with excellence. It was now time for me to sit by my king at the special table that was designed for us. He was already eating. I sat down next to Brandon.

"Oh, you couldn't wait for me?" I asked while Brandon enjoyed smothered chicken with mushroom gravy and whipped mashed potatoes and asparagus seasoned with Parmesan. The waiter came over with my food. It was excellent. "See, you now have your food in front of you, Mrs. Gains," Brandon joked.

"Hey, look at our parents out on the dance floor slow-dancing." Brandon gestured towards the dance floor.

I saw how blessed Brandon and I were to have parents that were great examples of love. Brandon's parents came over to our table.

"We are happy for the both of you. Brandon, son, I am so proud that you chose a good woman," Mr. Gains said to Brandon.

"Thanks, Dad."

Brandon's Mom gave me a kiss on my cheek, and I was thankful.

"I now have a new daughter-in-law," she said, as she walked back to the dance floor.

Once we both ate it was time for me to dance with my husband for the first time as husband and wife. Everyone cleared the floor and the soft tunes flowed as we swayed back and forth. Everything in my body felt complete. I was no longer haunted by the thoughts of Mandy. I was now starting my life with this handsome man whom I loved so much. Bran took his hand and placed it on the lower part of my back, while he whispered, "I love you," in my ear. The music was still playing. I wrapped both of my arms around his neck and laid my head on his chest.

This was the safest place; right in his arms. My family and church family, and friends were all enjoying themselves. When the song ended we had allowed everyone to enjoy this moment too. The Dj played the soft oldies and couples hit the floor. My sisters and their husbands were out there too. Love was all around the room.

My father got the attention of everyone so he could do my first toast.

"To the bride and groom, may God bless you both and you guys be fruitful and multiply!"

Next, my Mom had said her toast, and then all of my family started giving toasts!

"Well, let's go baby. I want us to leave the reception early, "he said.

We told Amber that we were leaving. The photographer wanted to take pictures of us leaving and getting into our limo.

Everyone followed us outside. Brandon picked me up and walked towards the limo. The stars were shining brightly and everyone was shouting and blowing party whistles. "Just Married" hung on the back of the limo. I moved over in the back of the limousine and looked out at all the guests as they waved. Brandon was holding me while we drove off. I was headed to my new home and my new life with my new husband, Brandon Gains!

Thank you Lord for writing my love story!

www.ingramcontent.com/pod-product-compliance
Lightning Source LLC
Chambersburg PA
CBHW071742110726

47908CB00006B/1672